W9-AGD-000

GAYLORD

LIBRARY OF CONGRESS CATALOGING-IN-PUBLICATION DATA

Warren, Tiffany L.
  The favorite son / by Tiffany L. Warren. — Large print edition.
    pages cm. — (Thorndike Press large print African-American)
  ISBN 978-1-4104-7983-9 (hardcover) — ISBN 1-4104-7983-8 (hardcover)
  1. African Americans—Fiction. 2. Musicians—Fiction. 3. Brothers—Fiction.
  4. Large type books. I. Title.
  PS3623.A866F38 2015
  813'.6—dc23   2015005205

Published in 2015 by arrangement with Dafina Books, an imprint of
Kensington Publishing Corp.

Printed in Mexico
1 2 3 4 5 6 7 19 18 17 16 15

Whew! It seems like it took me forever to write this story. I first got the idea of writing on the brothers' sibling rivalry after reading the Bible story of Jacob and Esau. I hope you enjoy and are blessed by the outcome.

I always have to thank God for these stories, the writing ability, the opportunity and for readers! My husband, Brent, always has to endure nights of fast food or spaghetti four days in a row while I finish. I appreciate him leaving me alone while the art unfolds. I have the most self-sufficient children a writer mom could wish for. Shoot, they take care of me. I love and thank them all.

My editor, Mercedes Fernandez, is theeeee absolute best! Sara Camilli is the bomb shiggedy as well (I wonder if she will know what bomb shiggedy is). So happy to be with Dafina!

This past year has been such an adventure for me! Turned forty, so I finally feel like I'm coming into my own. I have some great friends that are along for the ride and I feel blessed to have them. My ride or dies, Shawana, Robin, Tiffany, Afrika, Kymmie, Brandi, and Leah. One day, we are going on a girls' trip! It's past time! Thanks to the lunch bunch crew — Misty, Margie Faye, Bernie, and Jay. Y'all hold me down! To my newfound work family, Helen, Nicole, Jordy, Marcie, Kendrick, and Dustin — y'all ROCK ☺!

My author friends are better than yours! I love the love and support that we show one another and I want to see you all have everything God has for you. ReShonda, Victoria, Rhonda, Sherri, Pat, Dwan, Michelle, Vanessa, Pat S., Lutishia, and Renee, thank you for blessing me with advice, encouragement and friendship!

To my readers, book clubs, promoters, Facebook family, Twitter family, and everyone who helps get the word out about my books — God bless you! I appreciate every share, repost and retweet. I couldn't do it without you.

Enough of this sappy stuff. Time to read!

Prologue

Camden was not going to forever hold his peace. His brother Blaine had committed the ultimate offense. But there was a tiny window, a sliver of an opportunity to speak; to scream loud enough to reach heaven.

Camden rushed through the foyer of the church with his best friend Amber at his heels. "But Cam, Dawn said yes. She said yes! Maybe you should just walk away."

"I left her alone with him," Camden said as he turned the corner leading to his father's office.

"She made a choice," Amber protested. "Don't make this any harder for her."

These words stopped Camden in his tracks. "What about me? Did anyone think about how hard this would be for me?"

Amber threw her arms around Camden's neck and pulled him into an embrace. He felt his insides shudder. The hug almost made him lose it when he was doing such a good job trying to hold it all together.

He untangled himself from Amber's squeeze. "I have to do this."

"Then let me go with you," Amber said.

Camden continued toward his father's office, where Pastor Wilson married couples who couldn't afford to have a real wedding, or those whose lust had left them in an undesirable predicament. Neither Camden nor Blaine was supposed to get married in the office. The two sons of the famed and illustrious Pastor B. C. Wilson of Dallas, Texas, were practically royalty — princes of the church. Their nuptials were destined to be star-studded affairs with hundreds of guests in attendance.

Ironically, Blaine was the one who bought into that hype. Camden resisted all of the perks of their father's position, including the girls and the cougars who stuffed panties and hotel room keys into his pocket at church conferences. He refused to make a mockery of everything holy.

Finally in front of Pastor Wilson's office door, Camden reached for the doorknob. Amber covered his hand with hers.

"You sure, Cam?"

Camden's nostrils flared a bit. He wished he'd told Amber to wait for him in the foyer. "I'm sure."

Camden threw the door open and felt his resolve and determination evaporate at the sight of Dawn and Blaine. The couple stood before Pastor Wilson, gazing into each other's eyes. His mother, Lady Wilson, stood next to Pastor Wilson, looking on quietly. Dawn held on to Blaine's right hand for dear life.

Camden couldn't stop staring at Dawn's midsection, which held the evidence of Blaine and Dawn's lust. There was no bulge in her stomach. Not yet, but Camden knew the baby was there.

Dawn's mouth opened slightly when she saw Camden. Then she looked away. Blaine didn't move a muscle.

"They're just about to recite their vows, Camden," Pastor Wilson said. There was no emotion in his tone. No joy for the son getting married. No sympathy for the other.

"I'm sorry, Cam," Dawn whispered.

"Do you love him?" Camden asked.

Dawn pursed her lips together tightly. Camden knew that face. She made that face when she was holding back a flood of tears.

"Of course she loves him," Pastor Wilson said. "They're getting married and having my first grandchild."

Camden waved his father's reply away with his hand. "Do. You. Love. Him?"

9

After a long and pregnant pause, Dawn nodded. "It doesn't matter, Camden. I do."

There was no conviction in her voice. To Camden, it sounded like she was still trying to convince herself that this marriage was necessary. It wasn't.

"Son, just go," Camden's mother said.

Camden was at a loss. Learning about the pregnancy and their shotgun wedding had thrown him off balance, as had the sight of Dawn looking incredibly pitiful. Amber lightly tugged on his jacket.

He looked down at Amber. At six foot four inches, he towered over her, but in that moment, he was the one who felt small.

Amber mouthed the words, "Let's go."

Camden nodded and allowed Amber to pull him toward the door.

"Congratulations," Amber said. "Even though you cheated me out of my chance to be a maid of honor."

Dawn gave Amber a tiny smile. "But you're the baby's godmother. You can throw a baby shower."

"That will have to do, I guess," Amber said.

Pastor Wilson sighed loudly. "Are we ready to continue?"

"What about you, Camden?" Blaine asked, breaking his silence. "You gonna be the baby's godfather?"

Camden was almost out of the office when Blaine asked his question. He paused for a moment, thought of an answer to that question, but decided that he wouldn't say it in the walls of the church.

Camden stormed out of the office and out of the church. Amber couldn't match his long strides, but she ran behind him anyway, struggling to catch her breath.

In the church parking lot, Amber caught up to Camden as he got into his car. He glared at her through the window before rolling it down.

"You knew that it was Blaine from the start. Why didn't you tell me?"

"I couldn't. I honestly hoped that somehow you two would end up together anyway, in spite of Blaine and your father's plans. Pastor Wilson told them they had to get married or the group would be ruined, and so would the church," Amber said.

"All my father cares about now is the group! Isn't that funny? He never even wanted us to sing, and now the group means more than everything. It means more than me."

A single tear coursed down Amber's face. "You know that's not true, Cam. Pastor Wilson loves you."

Camden started the car. "Good-bye, Amber. I am never coming back here. The next time I set foot in this church will be someone's funeral, I swear on everything."

"So you're gonna leave the group? We need you."

Camden looked at his father's church and couldn't see himself walking through the doors again. On the other side of those doors the only girl he'd ever loved was marrying his brother.

"You don't need me. As long as you've got Blaine, you'll be fine. He's the face of the group. I just play the keyboard."

"But you're the heart. You brought us together. So G.I.F.T.E.D is your group."

Camden sighed and gave Amber a weak smile. He would miss her, and Akil, but he couldn't look at Dawn or Blaine without wanting to punch a hole in the wall. Or in his twin brother's face.

"I've got to go. Call me, okay?"

Camden sped out of the parking lot with no intention of ever coming back to Graceway Worship Center. And no matter what anyone said, he wasn't running. Camden knew his presence would make things hard for Dawn, so he would give them miles and miles of space.

Camden was closer to Dawn than anyone.

He knew what she wasn't saying — it was all over her face when she'd stared at him. Maybe she loved Blaine, and the child they'd conceived, but Dawn loved Camden still. But she hadn't spoken up. She'd held her peace.

And so would Camden.

PART I

CHAPTER 1

One year ago . . .

If Camden could have a supernatural gift, it would be the power to disappear at will. In fact, he'd spent the entirety of his twenty-five years trying to fade into the background. Especially when his twin brother Blaine was cooking up a scheme that would undoubtedly earn them a lecture from their father, Pastor Wilson.

But at six feet four inches and with skin the color of night, Camden couldn't be inconspicuous. It was always obvious when he walked into a room, and even more so when the equally tall Blaine joined him. Blaine's contrasting café au lait skin tone and hazel eyes had gotten the twin brothers dubbed with the nickname Ebony and Ivory by the girls at their church. Camden hated the nickname, but Blaine loved it and everything else that would draw attention to himself.

17

Blaine paced the choir room with his arms flailing. "All you have to do is play your song during praise and worship. It's ready. We're ready. You're just scared."

Camden didn't doubt that they were prepared for this. Their singing group, So G.I.F.T.E.D, had been singing "Born to Worship," a song Camden wrote, for about a year.

"I'm not afraid," Camden said. "But if we do it, Dad is going to trip."

Blaine grinned. "He won't trip if we do what we're supposed to do and get the congregation prepared to receive the Word."

The rest of the group, Dawn and twins Amber and Akil, burst into the choir room, all wearing looks of excitement on their faces. They had been singing together since their senior year of high school and had perfected their sound in the Texas Gospel Alliance youth choir. The two sets of twins and Dawn, the inseparable five, always sang together.

Amber, Akil, and Dawn were wearing royal blue and black to match Camden and Blaine — the church's colors. Akil, who at five feet eight inches looked small next to Camden and Blaine, wore a royal blue dress shirt and skinny black pants that added to his smallness. The petite and curvaceous

18

Dawn chose an ankle-length black skirt and royal blue jacket, a look that was sure to be approved by the church mothers. Her hair, held back with a plastic headband, brushed her shoulders in a sweet, blunt cut that made her look like a schoolgirl.

In contrast, Amber looked like she wanted the nurses to come and throw a sheet over her. She wore a knee-length blue pencil skirt that was plenty long, but snug enough to let everyone know that she'd been working hard at the gym. Her form-fitting sweater wasn't exactly low cut, but somehow her cleavage managed to swell over the collar. To enrage the church mothers even further, she had a big curly Afro with a flower in the side and full makeup complete with false eyelashes and red lipstick.

"I see you got them yams out," Blaine said to Amber as he motioned to her heaving breasts.

She punched him on the arm and then laid a hand on her bosom. "Whatever. My produce is ripe, honey. It is here for the picking."

"There is room at the cross for both of y'all," Dawn said.

"So are we going to do it?" Amber asked. "Are we singing it or what?"

"It's up to him," Blaine said as he motioned to Camden with his eyes. "Ask our *leader.*"

Camden didn't miss Blaine's apparent sarcasm, but he knew it wasn't for a valid reason. It wasn't Camden's fault that everyone deferred to his leadership. He was the songwriter, the musician, and the director of the group. Blaine could fill any of those roles if he wanted to, but he'd never tried. It was almost as if he was comfortable with Camden leading too, except when they disagreed.

"Everyone has a voice in this group. I'm not in control. God is," Camden said. "If y'all want to do it, I'm down."

Dawn and Amber sat down on opposite sides of Camden at the piano bench. They sang in harmony, Dawn on the soprano part and Amber the husky-voiced alto. "It's why I was born. It's why I'm here. I give Him all of my worship, and He draws near to me. His love is so precious. My purpose is clear. I was born to worship Him."

Camden played along with their singing and the men joined in on the tenor part. Camden felt tears come to his eyes. They did every time he played the song. The lyrics, the music, the arrangement were all personal to him.

Dawn grabbed a tissue from the box on

the piano and dabbed at Camden's eyes. "See, we need to do this song. I feel God's presence right now in here."

"I do too," Amber said. "God anointed you to write this song, Cam."

There was a knock on the choir room door before it opened, which made Camden wonder why the person even knocked at all. Of course, it was their father's assistant, Delores. Although she was just supposed to be Pastor Wilson's secretary, she took her role to mean that she was the emcee and coordinator of every service, especially the special ones like the revival they were having tonight. She was dressed impeccably, in a pink suit with a matching hat. The pink looked good next to her butter pecan skin and the auburn tendrils that hung from beneath her hat. No one could say that Delores wasn't fly, but her attitude took away from her good looks.

"Are you all leading praise and worship?" Delores asked. "Because that does happen at the top of the service, meaning the beginning. Ten minutes."

"We'll be there, Sister Delores," Camden said. "We're about to pray."

Delores held out her hands to Akil and Amber and bowed her head. "I will lead you."

All the way through Delores's prayer Blaine bit his bottom lip to keep from laughing. Camden shook his head and smiled.

"Amen and amen," Delores said when she was finished. "Now let's hustle."

Delores and her heels clicked out of the choir room. Everyone knew she expected them to follow her, but no one moved.

Blaine said, "She really needs somebody to break her off."

"Really, Blaine?" Amber said as she slapped his arm a second time.

Akil's shoulders shook with laughter. "I think you should do it, B. She probably been celibate for a long time, though. She might hurt you. Dig them heels right in and . . ."

"Stop it, y'all," Camden said. "We're about to go into worship. Get your mind on Jesus."

Blaine puffed his cheeks with air and blew it out slowly. "If all minds and hearts are clear, let's go, y'all."

Camden frowned as he followed the group down the long hallway between the choir room and the backstage of the church's pulpit. Camden was no super saint or deep spiritual wonder, but he didn't play when it came to leading the congregation in worship. No matter how annoying she was, Blaine and Akil's joke about Delores didn't sit well with Camden.

Camden said a quick prayer to ask God to remove his anger and to ask forgiveness. Lastly, he asked God to use them during the service.

So G.I.F.T.E.D rushed onto the stage and took their places behind microphones as Camden sat at the keyboard with the band. He turned to the bass and lead guitar players and nodded a greeting.

"We're going to do 'Born to Worship' after 'Glory to His Name.' Y'all good?"

Both musicians nodded. They knew the song as well as the group, because they all practiced together. Camden wasn't concerned about them. What did trouble him was the ever-present gaze of his father.

Pastor Wilson seemed to be enjoying the praise and worship so far. If they were going to go rogue and introduce new music into the service without his approval, it was a good idea to start out with the Byron Cage song they were doing. He was Pastor Wilson's favorite gospel artist.

As they transitioned into "Born to Worship," Blaine took the microphone from its stand and walked to the edge of the stage.

"We need your help on this next song

23

we're about to do," Blaine said to the congregation. "I know we sing a lot about purpose and destiny, but no matter what God has called you to do, He has first equipped and readied you for worship. From the womb, you were a worshipper. The first thing you did when you came out of yo' mama's belly was to cry out. So we need everybody to participate on this song. It's simple. Sing with us."

Camden glanced over at his father while he played. Pastor Wilson stood with his hands clasped behind his back. Physically, Camden was a carbon copy of his father. Pastor Wilson was over six feet tall, and his blackness shined under the pulpit lights. His black horn-rimmed glasses were perched on the bridge of his nose and motionless. While Camden couldn't see any anger in his expression, Pastor Wilson definitely didn't seem to be caught up in the spirit of worship.

The congregation, on the other hand, was on fire. With every key change, Blaine's rich vocals rang out over the sanctuary. Dawn hit every high note, Amber came with every gravelly ad lib, and Akil's deep tenor completed the harmony. If it was just a performance, it would be perfect, but because it was ministry, anyone who heard them

24

would say it was anointed.

Even if Pastor Wilson didn't approve of what they were doing, Camden knew he would save his anger for later. The congregation was ready for a revival Word, and Pastor Wilson would never leave them wanting.

After praise and worship was over, Camden got up from the keyboard to go and sit with the rest of the group for the sermon. Their father had a personal keyboardist who had played for him for years. They had an intricate collection of hand signals and vocal cues so that the music complemented the tone of Pastor Wilson's message. Since Pastor Wilson had never asked him to play while he preached, Camden never let on that he knew the signals as well — like an NFL quarterback taking plays from his coach.

Dawn had saved Camden a seat next to her and she smiled at him as he sat down. Lately, Dawn had been making sure that everyone knew they were an item, and Camden was okay with it. He'd never purposely kept their romance a secret, but he did know that once tongues started wagging about them, he'd only have a short time to marry her before his reputation started to suffer. At twenty-five, he wasn't sure if he was ready to commit to a lifetime.

When Dawn stared up at Camden, her long eyelashes glistening with a mixture of mascara and her tears from worship, it reminded Camden of the first time he met Dawn at Bible camp when they were thirteen years old. Back then, her chocolate brown face was chubby and she had a mouthful of braces and a big puffy ponytail that stood on top of her head.

"You Pastor Wilson's son?" were Dawn's first words to Camden as she stared up at him with a determined look on her face.

She'd caught him off guard with the question, plus he thought that everyone knew his father. It was their church's camp, after all.

"Yes. I'm Camden Wilson."

"Well, I hope you don't think we're gonna let your team win the Bible Bowl just 'cause you're the pastor's son."

"I don't think anything. I *know* my team is going to whip your team."

"We'll see about that."

Camden had been wrong. Dawn's Bible Bowl team beat his for the next three years straight until they decided to join forces and co-captain a team when they were sixteen. That was also when they'd started dating.

Everyone thought they were so cute and

had been planning their wedding since Dawn wore a puffy white gown to prom. Camden didn't object to it, because he loved Dawn, but she wanted marriage and children. He wanted to pursue a music career, and he didn't think he could do that with the demands of a family to take up all of his time.

After Pastor Wilson's rousing sermon, So G.I.F.T.E.D took to the microphones again and sang a reprise of "Born To Worship." So many people moved from their seats for prayer that the ministerial staff couldn't even handle them all.

Blaine made eye contact with Camden and motioned to the edge of the altar area. Camden's heart leapt into his throat when he saw the thin man in the electric blue suit. He was wearing big glasses that took up half his face, and his rings sparkled as he lifted his hands to heaven. He was Royce London, the highest-selling gospel artist of all time. He could make careers with just one recommendation.

Royce was from Atlanta and had visited their church in Dallas many times, but he'd never gotten up from his seat to participate in worship. Camden allowed himself to say a little prayer. If this was the time for So G.I.F.T.E.D to take off into the stratosphere, then so be it.

After service was over, Camden and the rest of the group made an escape to the choir room. They always did that after service so that they could decompress and not have to have conversations with everyone when they were physically and emotionally spent.

"I don't think Pastor Wilson will be angry," Dawn said as Camden randomly tapped piano keys. She sat down next to Camden on the piano bench and lightly stroked his fingers as he played.

"He shouldn't be," Amber said. "The congregation enjoyed the song."

Pastor Wilson walked into the choir room — he never did that. But this time he was escorting Royce London into the room. Camden's midsection tightened, but a huge smile broke out on Blaine's face. Camden was glad that his charismatic brother was there to do the talking. He was also glad to be seated because his knees would be knocking if he was standing up.

Pastor Wilson said, "Worship was incredible tonight, you all. I just love when you all walk in your giftedness."

Camden's eyebrows came together in a confused expression. Pastor Wilson *hated* when they did anything unscripted. This change of heart had to be because Royce London had taken notice.

"I want to introduce you all to Royce," Pastor Wilson said. "The two tall ones are my sons Blaine and Camden. Blaine is the lead singer of the group. And also, these young people, Amber, Akil, and Dawn have been members of this church since they were little. We just love them here."

Camden examined Royce's face closely. Something looked a little strange about his skin. It looked too smooth. Wait. Was he wearing makeup? Yes, he was. Camden could see a slight difference in the shade of his face and the shade of his neck. Also, some of the makeup had streaked onto Royce's shirt collar. Camden had heard of artists wearing makeup onstage, but to church for a revival?

Camden watched as Royce's gaze fell on Blaine. "I am pleased to meet you all. I felt the spirit move in a way I haven't felt since I was on tour with my group last year. Did you write that worship song?"

Blaine blinked twice before he answered. Camden wondered if he was going to try and take credit. "Uh, no. My brother Camden writes the songs."

Royce quickly turned his attention and gaze onto Camden. "Do you have any other

29

songs in your repertoire?"

"Um, yes. Yes, I do," Camden said. "Would you like to hear something else?"

Royce nodded, and Camden started playing the introduction to another one of his songs. This one started out with a solo by Amber that really displayed her rich vocal tones. She took a few steps toward Royce as she sang. He closed his eyes and pointed one finger toward heaven. On the chorus, everyone came in and sang perfectly. Royce clapped when they finished.

"That was wonderful," Royce said. "What is the name of your group?"

"So G.I.F.T.E.D." Amber was breathless as she said this, from the way she'd just extended her vocals after already singing all night.

"G.I.F.T.E.D stands for God is faithful, today and every day," Blaine said. "God's been faithful by giving us this tremendous gift, and we honor Him by giving it back to Him."

A faint smile graced Camden's face as he listened to Blaine explain with pride and relish the name Camden had given the group. Blaine hadn't even liked the name in the beginning. He'd wanted to call the group Flame and had even had some T-shirts made with a ball of fire on the front.

He'd been outvoted.

"Maybe we'll get to work together down the road. If you're in Atlanta, look me up," Royce said to Camden.

"We'd be honored," Camden replied.

Royce reached into his pocket and took out a business card. He extended it toward Camden, but as he stood up to take it from his hand, Pastor Wilson intercepted it. Camden swallowed and sat back down.

"We will reach out to you if we plan to branch out with the group," Pastor Wilson said. Camden wondered who he was talking about when he said "we."

Royce clasped his hands and nodded. "Please do. You are doing great things for the kingdom. Thank you for introducing me, Pastor Wilson. You preached an awesome word on this evening."

"I am happy you were in the house to see that move of God," Pastor Wilson said. "I believe God planned for you to be in the house tonight. Kingdom business indeed."

Pastor Wilson led Royce out of the choir room. Before he closed the door he looked back in and gave a nod of approval to Camden. It was a rare gesture that pleasantly surprised Camden.

"We about to blow up!" Akil said as soon as the door closed. He high-fived Blaine and hugged his twin sister. "Royce London is the truth, y'all. And he wants us on his next worship project."

"Yeah," Blaine said, "it almost sounded like he wanted to give us a record deal then and there."

Camden didn't necessarily agree with that, but he was glad they were all excited. Maybe now he wouldn't have to twist their arms to get them to practice.

"Does anyone think Pastor Wilson is going to fuss at us about singing that song?" Amber asked.

"Nah. He's all for anything that will put his ministry on the map," Blaine said, as his phone chirped in his pocket. He took it out, looked at the screen, and smiled.

"Hey, I gotta get with y'all later," Blaine said. "My constituents await."

Dawn rolled her eyes and said, "You are disgusting."

"But you love me, though," Blaine said with a laugh.

Camden chuckled. Just about every single woman in their church who was under fifty had *love* for Blaine. He could have a date every night of the week if he wanted, and a wife at the drop of a hat.

"Y'all want to go out and get something to eat?" Dawn asked.

Amber and Akil were obviously waiting for an invitation for food, because they grabbed their jackets and purses and headed for the door. Camden stayed seated at the piano bench.

"You not going, Cam?" Amber asked.

Camden shook his head. "I want to work on some music at home. If we're getting noticed by people like Royce, we have to tighten up."

"Do you want me to go with you?" Dawn asked.

"No, go on out to dinner, babe."

Dawn smiled at Camden and kissed him on the forehead as she picked up her jacket. "Okay. I'll call you when we get in."

"Okay."

When everyone was gone and the only sounds in the room were Camden's exhales and his faint tapping on the piano keys, he let the idea of success sink in and settle into his spirit. Getting a record deal or even putting a song on Royce's next record would absolutely mean *something,* but Camden wasn't sure exactly what that was.

Mostly, Camden thought, it would prove to Pastor Wilson that his music wasn't just something he did for fun or to keep from taking on more responsibility in the church. It was his calling.

Pastor Wilson did believe people were called to be musicians, just not *his* sons. He had a grand vision for Graceway Worship Center, and it didn't have anything to do with record deals. It had to do with one church and three locations. Three campuses, led by three Wilson men.

Pastor Wilson had it written on his vision board. He'd named it. He'd claimed it.

Blaine accepted it as his manifest destiny, but Camden wasn't feeling it at all. Camden had done everything but run from the idea.

Camden thought once more about that head nod from his father on his way out of the choir room. Something so small said so much. Maybe Camden didn't have to worry about being pressured about preaching anymore. Perhaps his father was going to change his mind. Maybe Royce London would rescue Camden from his father's vision.

CHAPTER 2

"I will never lie to you."

Blaine blinked a few times and batted his long eyelashes, as if he was holding back tears. Then he leaned across the front seat of his car and planted a kiss on Trina's lips. He pulled away and licked his lips slowly, tasting her bubble gum lip gloss. He savored the sweetness and smiled.

Blaine hoped that the heat generated from their kiss would make Trina forget the question she'd just asked. She wanted to know if he was seeing anybody else. Blaine thought, *What does it matter? I'm here with her.*

They were parked in the driveway of Trina's grandmother's house, but she didn't seem to be in a hurry to get out of his car. Her perfume filled Blaine's nostrils and made him a little dizzy, and added to the hunger caused by her flavored lip gloss.

Trina was one of Blaine's girlfriends. There were others. None of them was going to be his wife.

Blaine didn't even know if he wanted to get married. He didn't know anyone happily married — not even his parents. Plus, the smell, taste, and touch of a new woman excited him too much to get himself tied down to just one.

If the woman who was destined to be his wife showed up, Blaine would recognize her. On a scale of ten she'd be a thirty. She'd be educated, child-free, and drama-free. Everything about her would be real, from her hair and nails to every single body part. She'd know how to cook his favorite meal (chicken and dumplings). She'd be refined enough to be the future first lady of Graceway Worship Center because even though Camden was closer to Jesus, Blaine knew his father would leave it all to him.

And she'd be a straight-up freak.

Since Blaine hadn't met any women that met his qualifications to become his wife, he never made any promises to his girlfriends. He never commented on the future because he knew there wasn't one. When they declared their love, he gave them good lovin'. But Blaine never, ever lied.

He couldn't be held responsible for what they thought they heard.

"You did real good tonight, Blaine," Trina

said, changing the conversation away from their relationship to Blaine's relief. "I felt it all in my spirit."

Blaine nodded. "We did. We might even get a record deal."

"Really?" Trina's eyes lit up with excitement.

"Yep. Royce London wanted to meet us! Pray for us, okay?"

Trina dragged her acrylic nail across Blaine's chest, making him shiver. "You know I can sing, right? Maybe I can be in your group."

Blaine swallowed to hold in his laughter. Trina was taking great poetic license with the word "sing." Her wailing could marginally be described as yodeling, but definitely not singing.

"Camden does all of the auditions. He's really picky."

"He's your twin brother. Don't you have any pull with him?" Trina's glossy lips formed a pout.

Blaine leaned over to kiss Trina again and she pulled back, out of his reach. He sighed. He hoped they could change the subject away from her bad singing. Blaine didn't want to hurt her feelings, but he wasn't going to lie to her either.

"What's wrong?" he asked.

"You're ignoring me about being in your group. You don't want all this with you on the road?"

Trina unzipped her sweater halfway, giving him a glimpse of her cleavage and her pink lace bra. He definitely wanted her, but not as a part of So G.I.F.T.E.D.

"That's like bringing sand to the beach," Blaine said with a chuckle. "I mean . . . Well, you know what I mean."

Trina zipped her sweater back up and frowned. "I thought we had something, Blaine."

"We do."

"What?"

Here it was. The conversation that he hated having. The one he tried to bypass at all costs.

Blaine paused before answering. He took a deep breath and chose his words carefully. How to avoid lying and still get invited inside?

He said, "We're really good friends who have a lot of fun."

Trina sucked her teeth and glared at him. *Welp. There will be no fun tonight.*

"Ooh, I should've listened to Sister Regina. She told me you were no good," Trina said.

Blaine's nostrils flared as he exhaled

angrily. Regina, his mother's assistant, had cost him more than one piece of tail in the past six months. He should've never broken down and slept with her. She'd almost begged Blaine to take her to bed, and when he, in a weak moment, gave in, she decided that she was supposed to be his wife. Of course, that wasn't happening and Blaine had told her as much. Unfortunately, he had underestimated how vengeful some women could be, and Regina had been one of the worst.

"Regina is just angry that I've moved on, Trina. She wants what you have."

Trina frowned again. "I have nothing but a *good friend.*"

"You're hurting my feelings. You don't want to be my friend?" Blaine asked in a sweet voice as he gave her his signature puppy-dog eyes. If this didn't work, he could chalk it.

Then he saw it, a twitch at the left corner of her mouth. He could see it. She was on the verge of giving in, was almost grinning at him.

Blaine leaned in close again and this time Trina didn't back away. He blinked rapidly, flickering his eyelashes on her cheek. Butterfly kisses. Her lips parted and Blaine took that as an invitation. He smothered her mouth with his full lips and without forgiveness stroked her tongue with his.

After several minutes of this, Trina was breathless, but Blaine was full of energy. She placed one hand on his chest and softly pressed, pushing him away.

"Do you want . . ." Trina started and stopped.

"Do I want what?"

"Do you, um, want to come inside? My grandmother is asleep by now, and I have the whole first floor to myself."

Blaine wanted to shout his victory, but he maintained his composure. "Only if you want me to, baby."

"Baby . . . I do."

Blaine hesitated at her repeating his term of endearment. Had he gone too far with that? Did the stars in her eyes mean she'd forgotten that she was only a good friend? Well, he hadn't lied, at least, and it was too late now for him to change his mind. He was at the point of no return.

"Trina," Blaine said as they got out of the car. "Don't tell anyone about us, okay? My father wouldn't be happy about it, you know. It might not be good for the ministry."

Trina smiled, "As long as you don't tell anyone, silly, my lips are sealed."

"I got you."

Blaine wrapped his arm around Trina's waist as they stumbled into the house. He felt just a little bit bad because Trina maybe thought this meant more than what it did, but it would all work out for the good, though. Blaine would give Trina a great evening. He'd say all the right things and push all the right buttons, and at some point he'd move on to a new conquest without breaking any promises. Because he'd never made any.

CHAPTER 3

Three loud and rapid knocks on Camden's front door drew his attention away from his computer screen. He was working on a new song and burning the midnight oil doing so. He'd started over more times than he cared to count, and still, Camden felt something was missing. So the knocks on the door annoyed Camden more than anything, especially since he knew that only one person would show up at his door this late, rattling it on the hinges with his heavy pounding.

Camden pulled his robe on over his pajamas and almost got to the door before the knocks began again. At the end of the second knock and right before the third landed, Camden swung the door open and allowed his father to march through. Camden felt his annoyance grow a little bit closer to anger. It was too late for a surprise visit.

"I haven't interrupted anything, have I?" Pastor Wilson asked with a chuckle. "You don't have Dawn stashed away in a bedroom, do you?"

Camden didn't laugh at the joke. Not because he couldn't share a laugh with his father, but simply because it wasn't funny. Dawn was a virgin and was going to stay that way until they walked down the aisle if Camden had anything to do with it. He'd had his slip-ups over the years, but he wasn't going to take Dawn down that path.

"It's late, Dad."

"It's not that late. You're in your twenties. When I was your age, I wouldn't even be indoors at this time of night. You should live a little."

"Live a little," Camden repeated.

"Yes. And you ought to marry that girl. She's nice and thick, just like your mother was before we got married."

Camden could smell the bourbon on his father's breath. That scent always made him sick to his stomach. He'd been smelling it since he was a little boy and it always had the same effect.

"You want some coffee?" Camden asked.

Since his father would hopefully be heading home after he left Camden's apartment, Camden would rather he be more sober. His mother would appreciate it.

"No, no. Stephen is waiting for me in the

43

car. I won't be staying long."

It irritated Camden that Stephen had ferried his father over to his apartment. Stephen was Pastor Wilson's armor bearer, his right hand man. Sometimes Camden felt like Stephen was more a son to his father than he was. He wondered if Stephen was the one who fixed his father's drinks too. There was always a bottle of bourbon in his office at the church and one in his father's Benz, open bottle laws be damned.

"Okay, Dad."

"Are you going to ask me why I'm here?"

Camden shook his head and sat on his couch while Pastor Wilson remained standing. "You're going to tell me, I'm sure."

"What were you thinking choosing that song for worship tonight?" Pastor Wilson asked after clearing his throat and clasping his hands in front of him — his lecturing pose.

"I felt led by the Holy Spirit," Camden said.

"That's some bull, son. You felt led by your own ambitions. You saw Royce in the audience and thought you'd let him get a taste of some of that Dallas flavor."

Camden didn't respond. It was pointless anyway. Camden knew this was the beginning of one of his father's signature

44

bourbon-fueled rants. There was no point objecting.

"I have to say, I was a little bit proud of you. You're usually too scared to pull off something like that. Blaine probably put you up to it."

Camden's nostrils flared. He hated how his father always found a way to make Blaine's rebellious attitude seem like a strength and Camden's obedience seem like a weakness.

"It's my song. I decided," Camden said.

Pastor Wilson laughed. "Thank you for being honest. That show you put on tonight had less to do with the Holy Spirit than your mother's choreographed shout."

Pastor Wilson turned his back to Camden and put both hands behind his head as if pondering what to say next. Camden had seen this same performance so many times that he could anticipate the next move. The best (or worst, depending on who was on the receiving end) was yet to come.

"Graceway Worship Center is my church. Everything that happens in my church gets approved by me. I paid the cost to be the boss. Hear me?"

"Yes, sir," Camden mumbled.

Pastor Wilson picked up one of the books from Camden's coffee table. He'd given them to Camden as gifts. Effective ministry books. Books about growing churches. Books about being a great pastor.

"If you ever opened one of these books instead of using them as decorations, maybe you'd understand where I'm coming from. I let your mother get you those piano lessons. I should've had you at my side. You think I want to run this church my entire life? But who do I have coming behind me?"

Camden's eye twitched. This speech wasn't authentic. Camden had never expressed a desire to preach, and other than buying a book from time to time, Pastor Wilson hadn't encouraged it.

"You have Blaine."

Pastor Wilson narrowed his eyes at his son. "You're right. I do have Blaine. He needs some work, but I tell you one thing. He's loyal to this ministry. I know Blaine has my back."

Camden wanted to reply, "And I don't?" But he was afraid of the answer. He wasn't sure if he wanted to know his father's true feelings.

"From here on out, song selections are to be submitted to me at least forty-eight hours before service."

"What if the Holy Spirit dictates otherwise?"

Pastor Wilson stared at Camden with his head tilted and a look of incredulity on his face. "I *said* the music gets approved in advance. Do you understand?"

Camden swallowed hard. "I understand."

Pastor Wilson continued his tirade. "Whosoever thinks they're gonna come up in *my* church calling shots and making decisions has got it wrong. Whose church is it?"

Camden hated when his father asked this question. As a child, he'd gotten beaten with his father's leather belt for giving the wrong response. At the age of twelve, Camden knew that the church was supposed to belong to God. But not Graceway Worship Center. That church belonged to Pastor B. C. Wilson.

"It's your church, Dad."

"Don't you forget it."

Pastor Wilson walked to the door and grabbed the doorknob. Then he put a finger in the air and turned back to Camden.

"I'm not sure why Royce was so impressed with that song. You've written better ones, in my opinion."

Camden didn't know how to reply. Was that a compliment? An insult? He couldn't decide. Pastor Wilson didn't wait for an answer, though; he walked through the door and left the apartment.

In a burst of anger, Camden knocked all of the books on his coffee table onto the floor. His gift, his calling, his ministry wasn't enough for Pastor B. C. Wilson, not unless it benefitted him. And his church.

CHAPTER 4

It was the Sunday morning after revival, and there was still an energy in the church that Camden felt he could reach out and touch. He liked to think that So G.I.F.T.E.D had something to do with that. He *knew* they did.

On his way to the choir room, Camden popped into his mother's office. Lady Wilson, as she liked to be called by the congregation (Lady Rita to her friends), was wearing a royal blue and white suit that matched the blue and white china collection that adorned every free space in her office. The china was a way of paying homage to her sorority Zeta Phi Beta, as was her extensive collection of blue and white clothing.

"Good morning, Cam. You look exactly like your father this morning. Well, you do every day."

His mother's bright smile could always melt Camden's heart. He could never be angry around his mother, or sad, for that matter. She doted on both her sons, but Camden believed that he was her favorite.

"I might look like him, but Blaine is his real twin," Camden said as he stepped inside the office and closed the door.

Lady Rita laughed. "You're right. He reminded me so much of y'all daddy when he was singing that song the other night. Remember when your daddy used to sing before he preached? That's what made him so fine."

Camden scrunched his nose. "Mama, you fell in love with Dad when he was singing worship music? Somehow that just seems wrong."

"Humph. How do you think you got Dawn? And look at all the women chasing Blaine. One of them is gonna catch him when he least expects it."

"He's not hearing any of that caught stuff, Mama. He said he is never getting married."

"Oh, trust me. He will. But not before you and Dawn walk down the aisle."

Camden closed his eyes and smiled. He'd walked right into that trap. His mother already loved Dawn like a daughter and wondered why Camden kept dragging his feet.

"Okay, Mom. I hear you."

"All right, keep it up and that girl is gonna find someone else. I swear you Wilson men think you're God's gift to women."

"Dawn ain't going nowhere."

Lady Rita shook her head. "Just like your father. Are you all singing this morning?"

"No, it's the regular praise team, I think."

There was a light knock on the office door. Lady Rita said, "Come in."

Delores walked into the office. "Praise the Lord, Lady Wilson. I was just trying to find Camden, and it looks like I have. Pastor Wilson wants to see you and Blaine. Blaine's already in his office."

"Okay." Camden gave his mother a tight hug before leaving the office. "Thank you, Sister Delores."

Delores was on Camden's heels as he left his mother's office. The two women weren't friends, and they typically didn't exchange small talk or church gossip, but Camden wished she would've stayed behind. He hated that she was always a fly on the wall when his father wanted to speak with him inside the church. Delores knew more about church business than their mother.

When Camden walked into the office, Pastor Wilson leaned on the edge of his desk, seemingly in a good mood. He and Blaine were laughing about something. Apparently it was an inside joke, because the laughing stopped when they noticed Camden and Delores's arrival.

"Morning, Camden. Have a seat. Delores, thank you for finding him. Can you excuse us?"

Delores looked somewhat shocked as she turned on one heel and rushed out of Pastor Wilson's office. She wasn't used to being dismissed. Camden could hear her thighs swish together as she marched away. Her too-tight pencil skirt kept her from making any long strides, but it sure made for a good view — for a man who enjoyed big, round behinds. Camden averted his eyes but noticed that neither his father nor Blaine looked away. They both enjoyed the show.

Once they were alone, Pastor Wilson clapped his hands. "Effective today, So G.I.F.T.E.D is the official praise and worship team of this church."

"Sarah's not going to like that," Blaine said. "I don't know if I feel like dealing with her today."

"Maybe you didn't understand me," Pastor Wilson said. "Sarah and the current praise team are being replaced. Camden is going to be the new Minister of Music, since he doesn't like to preach. Blaine, you will lead the songs every Sunday."

Camden's jaw dropped. After his father's meltdown the other night, this was completely unexpected. And as much as he'd wanted the position, he didn't want it at Sarah's expense. She'd taught him quite a bit over the years. They were friends. This didn't feel right.

"Don't worry, I've got a job lined up for Sarah. A friend of mine is planting a church in Austin, and he needs a musician. The pay is good. Not quite what we're paying here, but she'll be fine."

"Does she know? You said effective today. What about the choir? You saying Brother Kelvin is gonna report to me? How's that gonna work?"

Camden didn't mean to sound like he was panicking, but he was. Brother Kelvin, the choir director, had been with his father since the beginning. He was an incredible choir director, and there was no way he was going to respect Camden's leadership. He'd watched Camden grow up.

"She's been told, and the rest of the praise team has been informed of the changes. They'll be singing with the choir today, and I'm going to give Sarah a wonderful send-off during service."

"And everyone is okay with it?" Camden asked.

"They'll do what I say, because this is my church," Pastor Wilson said. "And you're going to act like the man I raised you to be. This church is your legacy, Camden. Yours and Blaine's. Don't act like you didn't know. *They* know. They've only been holding your spots."

Blaine rose to his feet. "Well, what are we going to sing this morning, Minister of Music? I need to go warm up."

"Let's do 'What Can I Do' by Tye Tribbett."

Blaine smiled. "Oh yeah. Me, Dawn, and Amber have a sweet three-part harmony in the middle of that song. That's what's up."

"Tell them I'll be there in a minute, okay?"

Blaine nodded and gave Camden a fist pound. He started singing as he left Pastor Wilson's office.

"What is it?" Pastor Wilson asked Camden. There was annoyance in his tone.

Camden cleared his throat. "Dad, I was just wondering if you can pray over me. I know you made the decision and everything, but I just want . . . I want to feel like I have God's blessing in this, if that makes sense."

Pastor Wilson took a deep breath. "If that's what you need."

Pastor Wilson walked around to the other side of his desk and took out a bottle of anointed oil that had been prayed over by a group of pastors and bishops. It was Pastor Wilson's custom to pray for each one of his new ministry staff and to put a small amount of oil on their heads to symbolize the Holy Spirit.

Camden had no idea why his father was about to release *him* into ministry at his church without so much as a prayer.

Before Pastor Wilson prayed he said, "I'm asking you to take this position because I know you can do it. Your brother isn't ready for the responsibility, but you can handle it. One day, when I retire, you and Blaine are going to run this church. It's your inheritance."

Camden nodded silently. He hated when his father called the church an inheritance. How could someone inherit a thing that belonged to God?

Pastor Wilson touched Camden's head with the oil and prayed. "Lord, God, touch Your humble servant, Camden. Open up heaven and pour out a fresh anointing over this, Your son. Order his steps, guide his heart, activate spirit-led destiny. Grant Your favor, oh Lord. Cause him never to stumble. In the matchless and oh-so-holy name of Jesus we pray. . . ."

"Amen," Camden whispered.

As Camden rose to his feet, Pastor Wilson smiled at him. "Did I tell you that the seed offering on Friday night was the biggest one-service offering we've had in years? There was a shifting in the atmosphere, and I believe it is because you all followed the leading of the Lord and exalted Him in worship. I didn't make this decision just because you're my son. This is destiny unfolding."

Camden nodded and stared at his father for a moment. *Now* he was happy about Camden following the Holy Spirit, but the other night he'd read Camden the riot act. Pastor Wilson's words and manner of speaking were almost hypnotic. Camden didn't usually find himself caught up in his father's speeches — he'd seen too much of the *real* B. C. Wilson to give him the angelic status that the congregation did.

Camden's father had chosen him to lead instead of Blaine, and he wasn't going to let him down. Nor the congregation. Nor God . . . in the event that He was also a party to the decision.

Pastor Wilson dismissed Camden from his office so that he could prepare for service, and Camden went to join the rest of his group in the choir room. On the way, he ran into two of the previous praise team members — a married couple who had been at the church for years. Camden wanted to avert his eyes, but he didn't. He hadn't done anything wrong.

The husband said, "Congratulations, Brother Camden. I'm sure you're going to magnify His name."

"I'm sorry," Camden said. He hadn't meant to apologize, it just came out.

The wife, who was on the verge of tears, said, "Honey, your father is the angel of this house. We're trusting God with him for a supernatural transfer of wealth."

"A what?" Camden asked.

"He didn't tell you?" the husband asked. "He spoke with the praise team before he asked us to filter in with the choir. He said that when you were playing and your brother Blaine was singing, he saw it in the spirit, wealth changing hands. From the unrighteous to the righteous."

"And I know that was God, because just about everyone in the sanctuary laid a gift on the altar," the wife added.

Camden smiled at them both but said nothing. He didn't know how to respond to them. At least they weren't angry with him or Blaine. He hoped that everyone else felt the same way.

When Camden got to the choir room, Blaine was already in full rehearsal mode and on the piano playing the music for their worship song. They also had to do something upbeat to start the service off. Camden was glad that only So G.I.F.T.E.D was in the room; he didn't want to hear anything more about his father's supernatural explanation.

Dawn ran up to Camden and hugged him. "Congrats, babe."

Amber gave Camden a fist pound, their customary greeting, but when Camden's response was less than enthusiastic, she frowned. "What's wrong, Camdeezy? You know Sarah is cool right? She and your daddy weren't getting along anyway, so this is definitely a God move."

"Sarah had issues with my father?" Camden asked.

"Yep," Akil cosigned from across the room. "Supposedly, that's why we got to sing at the revival. Sarah was about to debut some new . . . uh . . . diverse singers, and your daddy wasn't feeling it."

"Come on, y'all, we got like fifteen minutes before service," Blaine said. "I ain't trying to look crazy on our first Sunday morning."

"We got this," Amber said.

Camden walked over to the piano and relieved Blaine from his spot. As he played the song and the group sang, Camden felt his spirits fall. Did his father *really* have confidence in his leadership or was he just showing Sarah who was boss?

It seemed like his father had told everyone a different story, and none of it was the truth. But no matter what his father's reasons, Camden had something to prove. To God, and not to B. C. Wilson.

CHAPTER 5

Blaine racked up the pool balls on the custom-made pool table in his father's entertainment room. He winked at Amber as she twirled her pool cue. He was about to put a hurting on her because she'd been talking smack since church.

"You sure you wanna do this?" Blaine asked. "I'll let you bow out now and save yourself from looking foolish."

"Whatever, Blaine. Rack them balls up so I can break 'em."

From his post on the wall, Akil burst into laughter. "That sounds painful."

"Right. Your sister is violent, man!" Blaine said.

"I know it. I put it on the prayer list, but she ain't had a breakthrough yet," Akil said, still laughing.

The entire group was there for Blaine's mother's monthly brunch. Lately, that mandatory meal was the only time Blaine visited his parents' home. He'd grown up in the mansion, knew every inch of the seven-bedroom, six-bathroom home intimately, but he was happy to be out on his own. Blaine and Camden had both shocked their father by putting their college degrees to work and getting jobs instead of living off them. Of course, their careers hadn't lasted very long. Pastor Wilson quickly put Blaine and Camden on the church payroll. He didn't want them to get too used to Corporate America.

Both Blaine and Camden still lived outside of the family home, though, and it was best, especially for Blaine. His mother didn't approve of his dating habits, and he didn't approve of her scrutiny.

Blaine narrowed his eyes at Camden and Dawn. She was snuggled up to Camden on the leather couch. Blaine didn't know how Camden could settle on just one woman with all the beautiful women they came into contact with. Their father's church had thousands of members, most of them women, and most of them lonely.

Plus, Dawn was *okay,* but she wasn't all that. She could lose a few, ten, fifteen pounds and she was entirely too needy. She stayed in Camden's face so much he could barely breathe, and she didn't seem to be ashamed of it at all. He preferred a girl like Amber who didn't chase any man. Well, a girl *like* Amber, but not her. She wasn't quite his type. That Afro on her head had to go.

Amber broke the balls on the pool table and called the solid colors. Blaine grinned as she knocked ball after ball into corner and side pockets without following any of the established house rules. It was okay, though. She was giving him a nice view of her cleavage every time she leaned over to hit the ball.

"Got them yams out," Blaine said as she hit another ball.

Amber chuckled and pushed her breasts up farther. "Always, hon. They got you mesmerized?"

"Nah. But I do think you're trying to use them to cheat," Blaine said. "New house rule. No low-cut blouses at the pool table."

"Or in the sanctuary," Akil added. "I'm gonna start throwing prayer cloths over you."

Amber scoffed. "Um . . . Camden. Mr. Minister of Music. Can you tell your underlings to leave me alone?"

Camden looked up from his private conversation with Dawn and smiled at Amber. "My underlings?"

"Yes. Praise team lead singer Blainesky and praise team doo-wop pop boy Akil. Your underlings. They answer to you, right?"

"Technically, I guess so. But that's just in name only. Nobody is my underling. We're doing God's work," Camden said.

Blaine didn't like where the conversation was going. He was the lead singer of So G.I.F.T.E.D not because Camden was in charge, but because he was a better singer and a better worship leader than Camden. This Minister of Music title did not put him in charge of anyone. Blaine hoped he wasn't getting a big head, because Amber was clearly confused.

Just as Blaine was about to raise objections, his father's assistant, Stephen, walked into the game room. Even though no one was doing anything out of pocket, they all fell silent. Stephen always felt like an undercover narcotics officer, just spying and waiting on something to report to Pastor Wilson.

"Lady Wilson wanted you all to know that brunch is ready."

Camden rose to his feet. "Thank you. We'll be right there."

We'll be right there? So now Camden was speaking for everyone regarding brunch too? Blaine laughed to himself and put up the pool table supplies.

Blaine purposely hung back while everyone except Amber left the game room. He sat on the edge of the pool table and folded his arms across his chest.

"What's wrong, Blainesky?" Amber asked.

He shook his head. "Nothing. I'll be up in a minute."

"You look angry, Blaine. You were okay until we started talking about Camden being the Minister of Music. You feeling some kind of way about that?"

"No. Why would I want that headache of a job? It's all good. I'm not angry."

Amber twisted her full lips to one side. "I don't believe you. Don't be mad at Cam, though. You know he probably is only doing this because your father asked."

"Not. Mad."

"Okay, then. I'm going to eat. Come walk in with me. Pretend that I'm your date," Amber said.

"You would want everyone to think we're together. Are there any honeys up there?"

"I don't know. Maybe Delores."

Blaine frowned. "I look like Pastor B. C. Wilson to you?"

"Actually, no! You look like your mama. And you know you are beyond messy with that comment."

Blaine smiled and jumped down from the table. He locked his arm in Amber's. "Maybe a little messy. Come on, sweet potatoes. I'm ready to eat now too."

"Good."

Everyone in Pastor Wilson's inner circle was seated at the table. His assistant Stephen, Delores, and Lady Wilson's evil assistant Regina were all present, along with the members of So G.I.F.T.E.D. Assistant Pastor Damon Brennan was there with his wife, both looking hungry as ever. Blaine thought Pastor Brennan would be buried one day with a chicken leg in his hand. There were only two available seats for Blaine and Amber, one next to Pastor Wilson and the other between Dawn and Akil. Blaine wanted to dash for the latter, but he wasn't going to play Amber out like that.

The seventy-five-degree sunny day was perfect for dining outdoors. Late April in Dallas was usually a beautiful time of year, and Blaine's mother loved having her outdoor parties before the weather got too hot.

"Thank you for finally joining us," Pastor Wilson said.

Blaine didn't reply. He wasn't trying to get embarrassed. He just took a seat while his father rose to pray over the food.

While everyone's head was bowed, Amber

leaned forward and winked at Blaine. He smiled. If he hadn't planned on hooking up with Trina later, he maybe would've tried to see what was up with her — even with that wild Afro.

Delores was seated directly across from Blaine at the table. Instead of having her eyes closed like everyone else, she frowned at Blaine and shook her head as Pastor Wilson continued his excessively long prayer. Blaine grinned at Delores. She lifted an eyebrow at him and grinned back.

When he was done, Pastor Wilson sat down and cleared his throat. "You all did a good job this morning," he said, "but it could be stronger. I didn't fire my whole praise team for nothing."

Blaine watched Camden clench his jaw and stare straight ahead. So the new Minister of Music wasn't going to say anything in defense of *his* group?

"We didn't get to prepare," Blaine said. "We'll slay them in the aisles next week."

"You should always be ready," Pastor Wilson said. "No excuses."

"No excuses," Blaine repeated back.

Regina smirked and looked directly at Blaine. He knew she was enjoying watching him get reprimanded by his father. Blaine didn't care. He still wasn't planning on dating her, which was what she really wanted.

"Well, I think they sounded good," their mother said. "I was proud to see my sons walking in God's anointing."

Pastor Wilson gave his wife an irritated glare. "I agree that they're anointed. That's why my sons are going to be co-laborers in the vineyard with me. We're going to start having weekly services in Dallas as well as in Oklahoma City. It'll be Graceway Worship Center, the church in two locations."

"Who's going to pastor the Oklahoma City church?" Regina asked.

"Initially, I will, but then, when he's ready, I'll pass it on to Blaine," Pastor Wilson explained.

Blaine looked around the table and took in everyone's facial expressions. The only one who didn't have some sort of shocked or disapproving look was Camden. Camden had a tiny smile on his face. Regina's look was especially amusing to Blaine. She looked like she'd just swallowed a mouthful of crushed glass. *Take that,* Blaine thought as her face cracked and frowned.

"Aren't you going to say something?" Pastor Wilson asked.

Blaine blinked a few times and nodded. "Yes, of course. I've always wanted to follow in your footsteps, Dad, but it just seems like a lot."

"It won't come all at once. I'm going to start using you more, giving you more responsibilities, putting you out there more. The praise team is just a start. Another part of the Wilson brand."

"Look at God," First Lady Wilson said. "I knew God had a plan when He gave me these sons. To God be the glory."

The Wilson brand. Blaine repeated the words over and over in his mind. He'd do it, whatever his father told him to do, because the thought of being the senior pastor of his very own congregation gave Blaine a rush. He imagined a queen at his side. Not the women he'd dealt with in the past, but royalty who would be on the covers of magazines with him.

It felt like a dream, but Blaine was sure Pastor B. C. Wilson would make it a reality. His father always got exactly what he wanted. He never failed.

CHAPTER 6

Blaine sat in the big leather chair in his father's study, still high off the announcement Pastor Wilson had made at brunch. When his father pulled him to the side and said he wanted to speak with him after brunch, Blaine assumed it would be a planning session of some sort. Since Camden wasn't there too, Blaine knew it was about his being a pastor.

"How are you feeling, son?" Pastor Wilson asked from the other side of the desk. He was sitting in an equally large leather chair.

"I'm excited," Blaine said. "I know I have a lot to learn, but just the fact that you chose me and not your assistant pastor speaks volumes about your confidence in me."

Pastor Wilson chuckled and stroked his goatee. "Damon is not senior pastor material. He doesn't have the balls for it. He can't even stand up to his wife. He's a follower, not a leader."

"Oh." Blaine didn't even know how to reply to that, or if he should. He'd known Pastor Brennan since he was a baby, and he'd never heard his father speak of him this way.

"You probably wonder why I have him in a leadership position at my church, if I hold him in such low esteem," Pastor Wilson said.

Blaine nodded slowly. "The thought did occur to me. He's been with you a long time."

"That's why he's in leadership. Damon would never betray me. He's been with me since before I started. Outside of your mother and Stephen, he's the only one I trust to always have my back. Actually, I might trust him more than I trust your mother."

Blaine's eyes widened as his father laughed. He couldn't possibly mean that, but he sure looked like he did, as hard as he was laughing.

"We've got a lot to work on, Blaine, before you can pastor a church."

Blaine nodded. "I know. I was thinking that maybe I should go to seminary or get a master's degree from a Bible college. I can do that while I sing with So G.I.F.T.E.D."

"Seminary is a good idea, but that's not

my primary concern with you."

Blaine swallowed hard and sat back, allowing the oversized chair to swallow him. He thought he knew what his father was going to say, and he didn't know if he was ready or willing to change that part of himself.

"The women, son. You're going to have to get that under control."

"I don't know what you mean, Dad."

Pastor Wilson threw his head back and laughed. "Well, at least you've got the deny, deny, deny part down. Never admit guilt when it comes to affairs of the heart."

"Right."

"You're going to have to find a wife. I see you and Amber have a good rapport. She's a little rough around the edges, but . . ."

"Wait, Dad. I'm not going to marry Amber or anyone right now. Marriage is the last thing I'm thinking about."

"Why? You're going to be a pastor. No one trusts a single pastor, Blaine. Women may flock to your church, but they wouldn't stay."

Blaine exhaled loudly. This was not what he expected when his father wanted to talk to him. He was looking for his father to pass the torch.

"Dad. Didn't you say it was going to be a

71

while before I even took over the new church? Let's cross the marriage bridge when we get to it."

"This is not a request, Blaine. If you want me to consider you for this church, you need to get an exclusive girlfriend and plan on marrying her within the year. Let me know right now if I need to find someone else for this vision."

Blaine bit his bottom lip and nodded slowly. His father was serious about this marriage thing. Problem was, Blaine couldn't see pretending that any of the women he was dealing with were anything close to marriage material.

"What about your mother's assistant, Regina? You've slept with her."

Blaine frowned. "No. Absolutely not her."

"Why not? She's good for the ministry. Your mother loves her, and we trust her."

Blaine shook his head. "She's been running around the church bad-mouthing me already. I'm not dealing with her evil self."

Pastor Wilson shook his head. "You've got to start thinking in terms of what is good for the church. Regina has great credentials. Her father and grandfather were pastors."

"Even if I wanted to date her, she wouldn't want me. She hates my guts."

"I'll have your mother talk to her. She'll

come around, especially if she thinks she's going to be a Wilson."

Blaine couldn't believe they were actually having this conversation. Regina. *Regina?* Blaine didn't want to go there. She wasn't even good in bed. She cried every time they did it, talking about she needed to repent.

"Dad, why don't you let me see if I can find someone else?"

Pastor Wilson's top lip quivered and he cracked his knuckles. Blaine knew he was frustrating his father, but he couldn't see himself with Regina, even if it was for show.

"Graceway is my church, Blaine. I'm not asking you. I'm telling you. I don't care what else you do or who else you do, but Regina is my choice for you right now. There is a strategy to this thing. I know what I'm doing."

"Dad. You married Mom and built your ministry with her, but you loved her."

Pastor Wilson stared straight ahead, but said nothing. The silence was saying too much for Blaine.

"Dad?"

"What?"

"You did love my mother, didn't you?"

Pastor Wilson cleared his throat. "I do love your mother. She gave me my sons. I couldn't have built this ministry without her."

Blaine wanted his father's declaration to be enough, but it wasn't. It sounded rehearsed, as if his father had been called on the carpet about the subject before. It sounded like a cover story. Blaine didn't want to have a scripted response about his wife. He wanted to brag on her and for everyone to brag on him for having her.

Pastor Wilson continued, "When you give your life to God and dedicate it to ministry, you make sacrifices. That is why it is perfectly fine for you to enjoy the blessings that are going to be poured out on your life."

And by blessings, Blaine knew his father was talking about finances.

"One day, you'll have everything I have and even more. But you have to trust me and follow my lead. I know how to do this thing."

Blaine nodded and believed. How could he not?

CHAPTER 7

Camden sat at the keyboard in his apartment and played the chords of a new worship song. He played to keep his mind off his father's announcement at brunch earlier. He tried to convince himself that he didn't care about his father choosing Blaine to pastor the Oklahoma City church, but it wasn't the truth. Camden *did* care about it, not because he wanted the position himself, but because he thought it was a horrible decision.

"Do you want some tea?" Dawn asked from the kitchen.

Camden looked up at Dawn standing in his kitchen in a knit blouse, a pair of sweats, with socks on and her hair pulled up into a ponytail. She looked sexy without even trying.

"What kind of tea?"

"Um . . ." Dawn picked up the box from the counter. "White peach and ginger."

"That tea is a man law violation. I don't even know how that got in my apartment."

Dawn giggled. "What? It's tea!"

"I'm a grown man. I need some tea that's made from like, tree bark, sticks, and rocks. You can keep those flowers."

"I'm sure that tea would be pretty nasty, Cam."

"But it'd be man tea."

Dawn laughed again. "Whatever you want, I'll give it to you. Man tea or something a little sweeter, maybe?"

Camden bit his bottom lip as Dawn unbuttoned a few of her blouse buttons and pushed her breasts up. He looked away and down at the keyboard. Lately, Dawn had been overt in her sexual advances. He wasn't a monk, and he definitely noticed, but he didn't understand why.

Dawn always said that she wanted to be a virgin on her wedding day, and Camden respected that. He wasn't a virgin — Dawn didn't know about the two women he'd been with in college, and she would never know if he could help it.

"Are you trying to seduce me?" Camden asked.

"Only if it's working."

"What happened to the wedding night pledge? You don't care about that anymore?"

76

Dawn crossed the living room and sat down on the piano bench next to Camden. He placed a hand on her back and rubbed little circles. Dawn seemed to relax.

She said, "If I thought the wedding was happening anytime soon, then maybe . . ."

"We're young! Why are you in such a big hurry?"

"Why aren't you? Are you waiting for someone better to come along?"

"No, I'm not. I love you."

"But . . ."

"A wife, a family — that all means responsibility. I'm not ready for you to lean on me for everything."

"Your father believes you are ready for responsibility. He made you the Minister of Music."

"But he's going to make Blaine a pastor."

"You don't want to be a pastor, and your dad definitely said that Blaine isn't ready yet."

Camden pressed his lips into a straight line. She was missing the point. No, he didn't want to be a pastor or preach, but his father had never asked him about that. He didn't know that Camden had no desire to be in the pulpit or run a church. He just chose Blaine for the top position, ready or not, without ever considering Camden. The same thing that he always did.

Camden should've known there was a reason he passed Blaine over for Minister of Music. As usual, he had something bigger and better planned for his favorite son.

"I think we should put a timeline on our relationship," Dawn said. "I don't want to be thirty having my first baby."

Camden winced at the words "timeline" and "baby." Why couldn't she understand that pressuring him would be the last thing that worked on him?

"I see nothing wrong with having our first child when we're thirty, well-off and home-owners. Hopefully we'll have a record deal too."

"It's not your body. Of course you don't care."

Camden didn't want to argue with Dawn. He loved her and wanted to provide a great life for her. Why wasn't that enough?

"So can we talk about it at the end of the year? I should know how a few things will pan out by then."

"So a timeline at the end of the year."

"We will discuss your demands at the end of the year."

"My demands? You make me seem like a terrorist."

"I feel terrorized right now, to be honest."

"So, a beautiful woman wants to love you, have your babies, and spend the rest of her life with you, and you feel terrorized?"

Camden nodded slowly and Dawn frowned. She stood up and started to pace the floor, wearing a footstep pattern in his carpet.

"This isn't fair, Camden," she said.

"Neither are timelines and ultimatums. You don't want to get me that way. I promise."

"You know everyone always talks about how Blaine is a womanizer. . . ."

"He is."

"But at least a woman knows what she's getting. He makes no promises."

"I haven't made any either. Not really."

"No, but you imply forever. It's subtle, but you dangle a carrot in front of me, tell me you want to marry me *one day.* And everyone would think I was a fool if I walked away."

"You want to walk away?"

"I don't, but I don't want to be stupid either, Camden."

Dawn's tear-streaked face touched Camden's heart. He got up from the keyboard and stood in front of her. He stroked her face, kissed her lips, and embraced her. He didn't want her to hurt, and the way her body shook as she cried told him that she was in pain. And he was the cause of that.

"By the end of the year, babe. I promise to make a decision on when we'll get married. I won't keep you hanging on forever."

By the end of the year. Camden repeated to himself. If he hadn't made some strides toward his musical future by then, maybe he was doing it all in vain. He might just use the IT degree and pursue a career that would allow him to marry Dawn and start a family. Maybe he would be okay with his position at the church and the fact that he might never do anything special musically.

And if he couldn't do that, if he couldn't live that life, he would let Dawn go. Maybe she'd find happiness with someone else.

CHAPTER 8

Blaine stood outside Regina's office door at the church, pondering what his father had said about her being the perfect choice as a first lady. He couldn't even imagine what it would be like to marry her. Not only was she boring in bed, she was boring in life too. But she was a hard worker — the perfect administrator. She would be great at running the behind-the-scenes business of a church.

Blaine lifted a hand to knock on the door, but he put it down again. Regina hated his guts. Even if he could wrap his mind around having a relationship with her that could result in marriage, she would refuse.

While Blaine was thinking, the door flew open. Regina's eyes widened when she saw him. Blaine couldn't help but smile at Regina. As evil as she always was, she was exceptionally pretty. Her skin tone was a smooth pecan brown and her heavily lashed eyes slanted slightly upward. She was on the thin side but had just enough curves to make a brother stop and stare. When they were dating before, Regina had worn her hair in a long, pin-straight style that she kept pinned in a low ponytail. Since then she'd cut it into a flirty bob that was full of bouncy curls.

"What do you want?" she asked. "Did you lose one of your hos on the way to the supply closet?"

Blaine smirked at the mention of the supply closet. It had been the place where he met Regina for a few trysts before she'd decided that he was the devil.

"No. I'm here to see you, actually. Well, you used to be one of my hos, so maybe . . ."

Regina growled and slammed the door to her office. Blaine chuckled and then got serious. This wasn't what he was supposed to be doing. He was supposed to be winning her over.

Blaine sighed and knocked on the door again. Regina threw the door open and glared. "What?"

"How have you been, Regina?" Blaine asked.

"How have I *been*? I'm blessed and highly favored. What about you? Do you know Jesus as your personal savior?"

"Very funny."

"It wasn't a joke, Blaine."

"Did you hear my father's announcement at brunch yesterday? I'm going to be a senior pastor soon."

Regina nodded. "I did. It made me wonder about your father's sanity. I was going to ask Lady Rita if she thought we needed to do an intervention."

"Anyway. I have a proposition for you if you can stop being evil long enough for me to say it."

"A proposition."

"Yes. I would like to call a truce. My father thinks that you would be perfect to help me run the Oklahoma City church."

"As your assistant?"

Blaine scratched the top of his head and batted his eyes. "No. As my first lady."

"And what do you think?"

Blaine shrugged. "I think he could be right. My father knows what he's talking about."

Regina's jaw dropped. There was a long, pregnant pause before she burst into laughter. "You have *got* to be kidding me! Cut the games, Blaine."

Blaine threw both hands in the air. "Forget this conversation ever happened. I'm good."

Blaine turned on one foot and walked

away. He wanted to kick himself for even coming to her. Now this would be a new piece of ammunition for Regina to use in her smear campaign against him.

"Blaine, wait," Regina said through her few remaining giggles. "Come back."

Blaine walked back up the hall. "Look, I am not all that thrilled about it either, Regina. It's not like I'm goo-goo ga-ga over you or anything."

"You mean ga-ga. You're not ga-ga over me."

"Huh?"

"Babies say goo-goo ga-ga."

Blaine stared at Regina, trying to figure out why she had to interrupt him for something so stupid. "Who cares what babies say? I'm trying to do what my dad wants me to do here. He says you're good for the ministry, and so I'm here. But if you ain't feeling it, I'm sure I can find lots of women who want to be first lady of a megachurch."

"A megachurch? You haven't even broken ground on the building yet and you're calling it a megachurch."

"Call me optimistic about my future, then," Blaine said. "I'm believing it, so it'll happen."

"I like that. I actually like what you just said."

"You act like you're surprised about that."

Regina chuckled. "I am surprised. I pretty much despise you."

Blaine's first thought was to agree with her and say, "Ditto." But he had actually started to buy into his father's idea. He could *see* Regina helping him build a huge congregation. He could envision himself enjoying the rewards of being a megachurch pastor. So G.I.F.T.E.D would sell millions of records with him in ministry. He'd be a pastor *and* a celebrity.

"I don't hate you," Blaine finally said. "I can see why you feel that way about me, but I don't hate you."

"But you don't like me very much either. I'm not stupid. I've heard the things you say about me around the church."

"Only in response to the things you say about me."

Blaine and Regina stared at one another. Neither of them was ready to give in, but neither was walking away from the other or the idea.

Blaine broke the silence. "It could work. You know you want me."

Regina rolled her eyes. "I agree with one part of that. It *could* work. Are we supposed to just announce that we're getting married, and go from there?"

"Whoa, whoa, whoa! Not so fast. My dad says we should start dating again, and then after a while we can get married. I think we should try to get to know one another."

"You mean like have a real relationship?"

If this was going to work, Blaine knew he'd have to be able to trust her. If they were enemies, there could be no trust.

"Yeah, at least a friendship."

"Oh, well you started this off by saying you had a proposition for me. I thought this was just a business transaction."

"It is both."

"So how much are you all going to pay me?"

Blaine blinked and shook his head. He hadn't thought about offering her money. He thought the prestige of being a first lady would be enough for her.

"I mean you're asking me to be one half of a loveless marriage for the sole purpose of working me like a dog to build your church. I believe a check is in order."

"Let me talk to my dad about it," Blaine said, having no idea how much would be offered for something like this.

Regina took Blaine's hand and squeezed. It didn't feel like a romantic gesture. It was more like how a kindergarten teacher would squeeze a little boy's hand if he said he had an accident.

"Don't worry, Blaine. I'll talk to your father. We'll figure out the particulars."

"You will?"

She nodded. "Pastor Wilson and I speak the same language."

"Um . . . okay then."

Regina smiled. "You can take me to Buttons on our first date. I like their Thursday night jazz."

"A lot of our members go there."

"That's the point, Blaine. It'll be a statement."

Regina's cell phone buzzed in her pocket and she took it out. "Yes, First Lady. Mmm-hmm. I sure will. . . . Okay.

"Your mother is so demanding," Regina said. "But that's okay. Someone else will have to deal with that soon, because I'll be too busy running my own assistant ragged. Maybe your brother's girlfriend, Dawn? She'd make a great assistant for your mom."

"I don't know. I guess."

Regina stood on her tiptoes and hugged Blaine. "Well, boyfriend, I'm looking forward to this. And don't worry. The secret is safe with me."

Blaine waited until Regina untangled herself from his arms. "Thank you. My dad is going to be happy about this."

"Forget about what your father will feel. Think about how you'll feel to be the pastor of a megachurch and have a congregation full of people putting you second only to God. It's incredibly sexy, Blaine."

Before he could respond, Regina was all over him again. This time she kissed him like a woman who knew him intimately. It stirred up every bit of his flesh. He pushed her away.

"Not in the church."

"Really? You never had that issue before."

"Never been up for a senior pastor job before. Not messing it up."

Regina grinned and wiped her lips, removing the excess lipstick. "You're right. Never let your good be evil spoken of. See you Thursday evening. I've got some work to do."

Regina closed the door to her office in Blaine's face as he stood there in a haze. This had happened too fast, almost as if he'd had nothing to do with it at all. It felt like the conversation was a formality.

Blaine would talk to his father about compensating Regina. He wasn't going to have them making deals behind *his* back. Regina was smart — too smart, but Blaine wasn't dumb. She would know from jump

that he was going to be in charge of the
Oklahoma City church — not his father.

CHAPTER 9

Camden looked at his watch and frowned. Blaine was forty-five minutes late for So G.I.F.T.E.D's standing Thursday night practice. He had a new song to teach the group and he wanted Blaine to lead it, but if they were going to sing it on Sunday he needed to show up.

Amber, Akil, and Dawn sat around the table in the music room, Akil picking a few strings on his bass guitar.

"Maybe Blainesky is out on a date with his new girlfriend," Amber said.

"Who? That girl Trina?" Dawn asked.

Akil shook his head. "Nope. She's to the curb. Her grandmother caught Blaine leaving their house late at night and told him he needs to marry Trina."

"Then who is the new chick? Anybody we know?" Dawn asked.

"Yep," Amber said. "But I need y'all to guess. This is top-secret intel."

90

Camden pulled his eyebrows together and frowned. "Why do we care who Blaine is dating?"

"Because this is juicy," Amber said. "Stop being a party pooper, Camden. Tap yo' little keys and look at your watch, and leave the fun to us."

"Spill it," Dawn said. "I want to know."

"Okay, I'll give y'all some clues. She's evil . . ."

"Delores," Akil said.

Amber shook her head and laughed. "Nah, she's too old. Plus, I think she's checking for Pastor's assistant."

"Stephen?" Akil asked. "If he can pull her, then I can pull her. Shoot, Delores is fine for an old lady."

"You're getting off topic," Dawn said. "Come on with the next clue."

Amber looked over at Camden before she spoke. He really didn't care to know which woman in the congregation Blaine was taking advantage of. Blaine's exploits were old news as far as Camden was concerned.

"Okay. Here's the second clue. It's a power move."

"A power move? What's he doing? An arranged marriage or something? Pastor Wakes across town does have a single daughter, but she's like nineteen," Akil said.

Amber covered her mouth with her hand and giggled. "You're partially right, Akil, but Pastor Wakes has nothing to do with it."

"Just tell us who it is. We're never going to guess," Dawn said.

"It's Regina," Amber said. "He's dating Lady Rita's assistant."

"What? He dated her before, and it didn't work out. What is he thinking?" Akil asked.

Camden was silent, mostly out of shock. He was fully aware of how things had transpired between Regina and Blaine. It hadn't just ended badly, it had been a nightmare. They'd both endured speeches from Pastor Wilson on discretion and sowing their royal oats in secret behind Regina's putting Blaine on blast to both their parents.

"Why would he be dating her again?" Camden asked. "They hate each other."

"Apparently, according to my source, it has to do with the church in Oklahoma City. Either Pastor wants them to get married or he wants everyone to know they're dating. Something about showing how much Blaine has matured."

Camden tried to contain his irritation at hearing this information. His father had not only chosen Blaine over him for the senior pastor job, but he was grooming him and playing matchmaker? It was beyond annoying, worse than Blaine's incessant tardiness.

"Enough about Blaine's mating habits. I have a new song for y'all. It's upbeat. We'll do it at the top of service and then move right into worship. Amber, you're leading it."

"Blaine usually leads on upbeat songs, right?" Dawn asked.

"Is he here?" Camden snapped. "Executive decision. Amber's leading."

Camden taught his new song "I Am Free," but felt the opposite of what the lyrics proclaimed. "What can separate me from His love? He made me more than a conqueror. I am persuaded now, I believe. In Jesus Christ, I am free."

But even if Camden wasn't feeling great about his father and Blaine's schemes, he couldn't help but cheer up at hearing Amber attack the lyrics of the song and wrap her velvety, rich vocals around the melody. Amber's voice was truly a gift from God.

As they worked on the vamp, Amber ignored Camden's ad libs and created her own. They were all caught up in the sheer joy of the song. Camden knew the congregation was going to be moved. Worship was going to be off the chain.

When they finished, there was a round of applause from the room's entrance. Camden turned to face their missing-in-action member, Blaine, as he leaned against the door clapping.

"That was good, y'all. We singing that on Sunday?" Blaine asked.

"We are," Camden replied.

"Cool. Dad is gonna love this one. I think we ought to put it on our record."

"Our record? We're doing a record?" Amber asked.

Blaine nodded. "Yep. Dad is working with a recording studio right now to get us a discounted rate. That's why I'm late, y'all. Sorry."

"Why didn't I know anything about this?" Camden asked, feeling his spiritual high evaporate as rage emerged.

"The recording studio contact is one of my homeboys. What are you mad about? We've always talked about doing this, now Dad is gonna fund the project. Isn't that what we've always wanted him to do?"

Camden knew his financial support came with a steep price. "In exchange for what, Blaine? What does Dad want in exchange?"

"He wants to be listed as executive producer. He's gonna put twenty thousand dollars into the project, Camden. He's going to launch So G.I.F.T.E.D! You ought to be shouting."

Amber, Akil, and Dawn were excited enough for everyone. They squealed, laughed, jumped up and down, and had a praise celebration.

"Look, Cam, I apologize for not telling you about this," Blaine said as he placed a hand on Camden's shoulder. "It all happened so fast that there was no time. But I meant no disrespect. I know what So G.I.F.T.E.D means to you. I would never make any decisions about the group without you. If you want to cancel everything, we can both go and tell Dad together."

Amber, Dawn, and Akil's praise break stopped instantly like a record scratching on a turntable. Everyone stared at Camden, waiting for his response to Blaine's *heartfelt* apology and offer. Of course, Camden could never disappoint everyone now. Blaine knew exactly how to back him into a corner.

"Nah, I'm happy about it. I want the world to hear these songs. What better way to make it happen than with Dad's money."

Blaine smiled and pulled Camden into an embrace. "Good! I knew you'd be excited about this too. We 'bout to blow up, brother!"

Camden gave Blaine a genuine hug back.

No matter what ill will and disrespect their father might have had for going behind his back, Blaine always wanted the group to be successful.

"Now you need to learn the song we're singing on Sunday, man!" Amber said. "I'm leading, so get your doo-wop pop background vocals together."

Blaine laughed out loud. "I will be background singer for you and your yams anytime."

"Uh-uh! You can't keep talking about my yams. You ain't about to have Regina trying to come for me. No, sir."

"How in the world do you know about that?" Blaine asked.

"So it's true?" Dawn asked. "I was so hoping that story wasn't true."

"Yes, it's true," Blaine said. "And I'm not explaining it to y'all. Let's just say we reconnected, and she's not that bad after all."

"As long as I don't have to be a part of the aftermath," Akil said. "You always putting me in the middle of stuff. I'm afraid of Regina."

The entire room went silent for a moment. Camden shook his head and looked at the floor with his lips pressed tightly together to hold in the laughter. He always told Akil to stop letting Blaine drag him into his chicanery and foolishness.

"All right, man. I promise," Blaine said. "I'll ask Cam to clean up the fallout this time."

The silence dissipated, and everyone roared with laughter. It made Camden think of all the fun times they'd had together as a group. Before anyone was given any titles or promises from Pastor Wilson. Camden wondered what else would change about them, and if it would be good for the music and the ministry, or if the changes would alter their destiny.

CHAPTER 10

"Do you know what tonight is?" Dawn asked Camden as they ate dinner at Gloria's, Dawn's favorite Mexican restaurant.

"It's Saturday, and we have church tomorrow," Camden replied. "I hope I made the right decision letting Amber lead that song. You know she can be temperamental sometimes. What if she gets to church tomorrow and decides she doesn't want to sing it?"

Camden struggled to hold his laughter in. He knew exactly what day it was. It was May fifth, the anniversary of their first real date. They were teenagers then, and they'd had Mexican food that day too. Back then, Gloria's wasn't in Camden's budget. They'd had tacos from Taco Casa and sweet tea that tasted like a whole bag of sugar was in each cup.

"Really, Camden?" Dawn asked.

"What?"

"How could you forget our anniversary?"

Dawn asked sadly.

Camden grabbed his forehead and gasped. "I am the worst boyfriend ever. I would not be surprised if you traded me in for someone else. There was a new guy at church last week. I saw him look at your behind. Wait. It is him, isn't it? You've already moved on, haven't you?"

Dawn threw her napkin across the table at Camden. "You're teasing me."

"Of course I remembered, Dawn! Don't we celebrate it every year? Why would I forget now?"

Dawn shrugged. "Because you've been so wrapped up in music lately that I feel invisible."

"No music tonight. It's all about you."

Dawn beamed. "Good!"

"So, tell me what you did all day. I tried to reach you this morning and afternoon, but your phone kept going to voice mail."

Dawn took a deep breath and then exhaled it slowly. She seemed nervous, which had Camden nervous.

"Are you okay?" Camden asked.

"Y-yes, I'm fine. I just hate that I missed your calls today."

Camden cocked his head to one side and frowned. "What are you not telling me, Dawn?"

"Oh, all right. Your mother and I went to a bridal show."

"What?"

Dawn blinked rapidly, as if Camden's reply was a blow to the chest. He heard how harsh his tone sounded, but he didn't care. If Dawn was trying to force him into marriage by teaming up with his mother, then that was a complete violation.

"Let me explain. Your mother invited me to the show, so I thought that you'd told her we were thinking of marriage soon. Of course I was happy about that. How could I not be happy about that?"

Camden's eyebrows nearly touched from the severity of his frown. "My mother invited you."

"She did. And when I got there, I asked her if it was your suggestion and she said no. She told me you didn't know, and I don't want you to be mad at me. Don't be mad at me."

Camden was silent for a long moment. "I'm not mad at you. Did you have a good time hanging out with my mom?"

"Yes. She said that she can't wait until I'm her daughter-in-law. And she introduced me to everyone as her son's fiancée."

"I don't know how I feel about that."

"No harm, right? I will be your fiancée

one day, so maybe she is just as hopeful as I am."

Camden took a sip of his sweet tea and swished it in his mouth before he swallowed it. His mother was almost as bad as Dawn with her requests for grandchildren.

"It's cool."

Camden reached into his pocket and took out the gift that he'd gotten for Dawn to celebrate their anniversary. He sat the small box down and slid it over to her.

"Is this what I think it is?"

Camden smiled. "No. Not exactly, but it's a token of my love for you."

Dawn opened the box and took out the sapphire birthstone earrings. "They're beautiful. Thank you."

"You're welcome."

Slowly, Dawn closed the box and looked up at Camden. "You seemed really mad about your dad and Blaine setting up that studio time."

"I was really upset. I don't like them doing stuff regarding the group behind my back, and I'm absolutely uncomfortable with my dad being interested in So G.I.F.T.E.D. There's always a hidden reason with him."

"Maybe he's just behind it because it's his sons and he wants y'all to blow up."

"That could be it. You know his favorite line . . ."

" 'If it don't make money, it don't make sense.' Maybe he wants y'all to start bringing money into the ministry."

"And us having a record deal would definitely do that. I just don't trust it. I wish we'd sold chicken dinners and gotten up the money to go in the studio ourselves."

Dawn laughed. "And who, pray tell, would be the ones cooking those chicken dinners?"

"Duh. You and Amber."

"We don't know how to fry chicken. At least I don't."

"Well, instead of going to bridal shows with my mom, you need to ask her how to cook. I expect my wife to cook."

"So cooking is mandatory?"

Camden threw his head back and laughed. "I'm a big guy, Dawn. I like to eat."

"Well, I don't see why a grown man can't cook his own dinner. Who's cooking for you now?"

"When I want fried chicken? My mama."

Dawn shook her head, her hair bouncing as she moved. "You know what, Camden? You are a mama's boy, I think."

"What does that even mean? It seems like an insult."

She shrugged. "Maybe it is. But from what

I can see, you are your mother's favorite person in the world. And you seem to feel the same way about her."

"I do love my mother."

"So you'd like to make her happy, then."

"This feels like a trap."

"It's not. Making me and your mama happy ought to be an incentive."

"Well, when you get some cooking lessons we can chat."

Now it was Dawn's turn to laugh. "Okay. I got you. Not a problem, big guy."

Camden believed Dawn. She would do whatever it took to become his bride. By the time he proposed, she'd be cooking dinners like she'd gone to Le Cordon Bleu chef school. Dawn wasn't going to let anything get in the way of her becoming Mrs. Camden Wilson.

She took the earrings out of the box and put them in her ears. She fluffed her hair and asked, "How do they look?"

"Stunning."

"Well then, come on and salsa dance with me. I want to work off the calories from this heavy meal. Can't let myself go before I get married."

"Or after!" Camden said as he stood and extended his hand to Dawn. "Don't worry. We'll stay fit together."

"But what if I have your babies and get all fat and squishy? Will you still love me then?"

"I will love you always, babe."

Dawn rose from the table and threw her arms around Camden's neck. She placed little kisses all over his face, and he kissed her forehead.

"Let's dance," Camden said. "If we keep this up, we may have some repenting to do tomorrow."

"I'm okay with repenting."

Camden shook his head and pulled Dawn out to the dance floor. He wanted Dawn just as much as she wanted him, but he took his ministry too seriously. He wasn't going to put it all on the line for something that was going to be rightfully his soon enough.

He would be patient, and Dawn would have to be also. No matter how much he loved her, she would always be number two. God was number one.

CHAPTER 11

Akil looked at his watch and frowned. It was one o'clock in the morning on Sunday and instead of having his own weekend fun, Akil was, yet again, playing wingman for Blaine.

He waited in the designated hotel parking spot for Blaine to come downstairs from his "date" with Trina. Akil wondered how Blaine was able to hold on to so many women at once. He never made them promises, but they all hoped to be his wife one day. Well, he didn't used to make promises. But now, with Regina, of all people, Blaine was making plans. Unfortunately, the plans didn't stop him from his escapades.

Every time Akil set foot inside the church, another woman gave Akil a note, a phone number, or a gift for Blaine. And he accepted them all. That's what wingmen were for.

Akil was okay, for the most part, with

Blaine's exploits. If the women were stupid enough to keep giving it up to him, then maybe they liked being played. The only time Akil had an issue with Blaine was when he looked too long and hard at his twin sister.

Blaine and Akil had been friends, it seemed like forever. Akil and Amber's parents were founding members of Graceway, so they had all played together when they were little. Even Amber. She'd climb trees, play army men, and swim in Joe Pool Lake right with the boys, until she started getting curves and Blaine's gaze began to rest too long on those curves. That was when their foursome became a trio.

Finally, Blaine came dashing out of the hotel, with his shirt barely buttoned and his belt in his hand. He was on his cell phone as he jumped into Akil's car.

"Hey, Regina," Blaine said as he closed the car door. "Yeah, I know it's late. I'm out with Akil. . . . Why didn't you let me know you were coming by?"

Akil covered his mouth and laughed as Blaine's frustration showed all over his face.

"Are you serious?" Blaine asked. "Man . . . okay."

Blaine handed the phone to Akil. "She wants to speak to you," he said.

Akil shook his head and put the phone to his ear. "Hello?"

"Hi, Akil. This is Regina. I just wanted to verify Blaine's alibi."

"What? You are tripping."

"Maybe so, but I know Blaine. Where are y'all?"

"Huh? Speak up, I can't hear you."

Akil looked at Blaine with wide eyes. Blaine made motions like he was shooting pool, and then he pantomimed eating.

"You hear me, Akil. Where have y'all been all evening?"

"Oh, we went to shoot some pool and we got something to eat."

"Mmm-hmmm. What did y'all eat?"

Akil glanced at Blaine. "W-what did we eat?"

Blaine held both hands up and clamped each index finger down on his thumbs, like he was holding a chicken wing.

"Girl, stop playing," Akil said. "Wings, of course. You need to stop interrogating my brother like that."

"Your brother needs to stop creeping. I'll see you tomorrow in church, if you can roll out of bed in the morning."

"I'll be at church. Probably beat you there."

Akil disconnected the call after Regina

had already hung up on him.

"How long y'all been back dating? A couple weeks? She's already checking up on you like that?" Akil asked as he started the car.

"I know, right? I'm starting to think my father was wrong about this. I'm sure there's another woman out here that can be the first lady of the church."

Akil laughed. "But not Trina."

"Heck naw. That girl can barely read."

"Wow. Well, I guess you don't see her for her intellect."

Blaine shook his head emphatically and ran one hand over his wavy hair. "Not at all. She's incredible, man. I can't break it off with her."

"You better. It sounds like Regina isn't going to just let you have her like that. She's about to put the smack down."

"That's what she thinks. But as long as I have my wingman, I'ma be straight."

"Yeah . . . about that . . ."

Blaine's eyes widened. "What's wrong?"

"Don't you think we're getting a little bit too old for this wingman stuff? I think it's time for you to cover your own tracks."

Blaine nodded slowly. "Well, I was going to ask you to come with me to the new church and be my assistant pastor. You'd be more than a wingman then."

"I don't want to preach, brother! That's your dream."

Akil shook his head and laughed. When they were little, all of the Graceway kids would play "church." Blaine was always the preacher, Amber led the choir, and Camden played the organ. Blaine would always be a miniature version of Pastor Wilson, with the whooping and everything. He had the routine down. But Akil had always been comfortable playing the background.

"Okay, so you don't want to preach. I get that. But you can be like Stephen is to my dad. You can be my right hand."

"That sounds like a synonym for wingman. I think I'll just stay in Dallas, be a part of So G.I.F.T.E.D and see where it goes."

Blaine looked at Akil as if he'd hit him. "Man, I can't do that Oklahoma City church thing without you."

"You'll have a wife. You'll be okay." Akil felt bad that Blaine looked so offended. "But it's a ways off, right? Maybe I'll change my mind by then. Maybe I'm just mad that it's the middle of the night and I'm not on my own date."

"You need me to hook you up with someone?" Blaine asked. "Trina's got a cousin.

She's fly."

"I'm good."

"You sure? 'Cause it's no problem. For real."

Akil laughed and shook his head. "You know, I just thought about something. Why don't you ask Camden to come with you to the Oklahoma City church? Then we can all stay together."

"Did Camden put you up to this?" Blaine asked.

Akil could tell Blaine's defenses were up for some reason, so he put both hands in the air in surrender. "Naw, man. I just thought it would be a good idea."

"When it comes to anything church related, it's not a good idea unless my dad says it's a good idea."

"So, make him think it's his idea, then. We all need to stay together. We're a crew. We run in packs," Akil said. "Well, one pack. We're a gang."

Blaine laughed. "You're right. I'll talk to him. But what about Amber? I don't think she'll move to Oklahoma City."

"She'll go if we all go."

"I really hope all of y'all come with me, because for real, I'm scared. I don't know how soon my dad plans on making it happen, but I don't know. Like, people be coming to their pastors with some real heavy stuff, man. What if I don't know what to tell them?"

Akil thought about his response for a moment. The answer that he wanted to give was gonna hit hard, and he didn't know if he wanted to hurt his friend. He was already feeling afraid, but Akil wanted to tell Blaine that if he was truly going to do this pastor thing, he needed to stop sinning and get his life together.

Instead he said, "Well, God didn't give you a spirit of fear, brother. We got you."

CHAPTER 12

Camden was enjoying Sunday service. Especially after So G.I.F.T.E.D brought their A-game. Blaine and Amber ended up sharing the lead on "I Am Free," and it was perfect. And once again Royce London was in the front row getting his praise on.

Pastor Wilson was in an extremely good mood too. He cut a little praise step while they were singing — something he *never* did. He still had a little pep in his step as he walked up to the podium to start preaching.

"Before I get into the Word today, church, I just want to share some of the wonderful things God is doing in *this* house! You could go to church anywhere in the city, but you chose to come here, and for that I appreciate you and this city appreciates you."

Blaine made eye contact with Camden. Blaine smirked and Camden knew exactly what it meant. Pastor Wilson was about to go into one of his infamous speeches.

They'd been hearing the speeches since they were little boys, and they weren't mesmerized by them. The congregation, on the other hand, was completely enthralled.

"Some of you have been with us since the beginning. You've seen my family grow up before your eyes. A few weeks ago, we installed Camden as Minister of Music, and in the very near future we're going to watch Blaine walk into his destiny as the pastor of our first satellite church in Oklahoma City. I wanted to keep this under my hat, but I feel that God wants you all to know. He wants everyone in *this* house to pray for the success of my son and this ministry."

Camden felt his jaw tighten. Blaine being elevated to the office of pastor was good news. Camden chided himself for feeling irritated at the announcement.

Pastor Wilson held one hand out to Blaine. "Son. Come forward, please."

Blaine's eyes widened and his jaw slackened. He seemed genuinely surprised, so Camden was sure he wasn't in on this. Yet he quickly rose to his feet and crossed the enormous stage to where his father stood behind his podium, or as Pastor Wilson called it, the sacred desk.

Pastor Wilson placed both his hands on Blaine's shoulders and pushed Blaine down until he was on one knee. Camden's eyebrows came together in a frown, and he remained glued to his seat while many of the congregation members — including Dawn — stood. Blaine bowed his head, and from where Camden sat, he appeared to be trembling.

Pastor Wilson took a huge sheet that had Hebrew markings on it and draped it over Blaine's shoulders. Then he took a large container of oil and poured it slowly over Blaine's head.

"Son, I am about to pray an Elijah prayer over you as I pass the ministry mantle. I hear in the spirit that God will perform awesome miracles through this ministry just as He did in the days of Elijah. In fact, the spirit revealed that even greater work will we do, because we will operate together. Elijah passed his mantle on at the end of his ministry, and I bestow the mantle at the height of mine."

Pastor Wilson started his prayer and the congregation joined in with him. Well, almost the entire congregation. Camden was too floored to pray. He'd had to beg for a prayer when he was being released into a ministry, but Blaine was having a full coronation.

When the bottle of oil was empty, Pastor

Wilson leaned over and rubbed the oil that hadn't dripped onto the cloth into Blaine's hair and scalp. Many of the women, including Regina, shouted and danced.

After Pastor Wilson was done with his prayer, he pulled Blaine up to his feet and hugged him.

"Walk in destiny, my son. We are going to take a season of prosperity from our congregation here in Dallas to Oklahoma City. People will look upon our congregations, and seeing them living the abundant life, they will ask, 'What can I do to be saved?' "

Camden felt his stomach churn at the blatant disrespect of the Bible. He *knew* that his father was twisting the story of Elijah and Elisha for his own purposes, but the church didn't care. They were in a frenzy.

After the excitement died down, Pastor Wilson went into his sermon. Camden did something he hadn't done since he was a little boy. He got up during service and walked out. He just couldn't listen to his father another second. Amber saw him get up and followed him.

"You okay, Cam?" Amber whispered as they stood in the narrow hallway between the pulpit area and the church offices.

"Why wouldn't I be okay?"

"I don't know. You just look like you're . . .

I don't know."

"I'm cool, Amber. Thank you for asking. I'm okay."

Amber stepped close to Camden and took his hand. "I understand. No matter what Pastor does, it doesn't change who you are. You know that, right?"

"I had to *beg* him to pray for me when I took over as Minister of Music. He acted like he didn't want to do it, really. And he's pouring oil over Blaine's head like he's anointing King David or somebody." Camden's whispers were full of fury.

Amber squeezed his hand tightly and stroked his arm with her free hand. "I know. I know. Just try to be happy for Blaine. You know he's always wanted this, and you love him. He's excited for you."

"I am happy for Blaine."

"Well, let's go back into service, and maybe try to look like you're happy for him."

Amber pulled Camden into a tight embrace and rubbed his back. As she kneaded his muscles, Camden felt his tension leave.

"Thank you," Camden said. "You always know what to say."

"Only to you, Camdizzle, and my brother. With everyone else, I'm pretty much clueless."

Camden and Amber both returned to their seats. Dawn gave Camden a curious look as he sat down next to her.

"Everything okay?" she whispered. "Where did you go?"

"Yes. Bathroom."

Camden surprised himself with that lie. He wasn't quite sure why he said that. Dawn knew that he and Amber were friends and it wasn't like Dawn would ever be jealous of her.

No. Camden thought, *It wasn't Amber at all. It was Dawn.*

Dawn was caught up in Pastor Wilson and Blaine's show just like everyone else. She was enraptured and shouting out Hallelujah while her man was hurting.

"Church, we are about to dismiss, but before we do, I want you to listen," Pastor Wilson said. "I want each of you to be able to lay hands on Blaine and give him the gift of your collective spiritual anointing. He will be in the vestibule immediately after service. Please note that I did not say monetary offerings. I want only prayers and impartations for our young Elisha. There will be plenty of time to contribute financially to the ministry. Come on, Camden, give us some shouting music. I feel another praise in my spirit."

Camden walked over to the piano with a tight-lipped expression on his face. He sat down and played some shouting music for his father. Pastor Wilson rarely carried on the way he was doing this morning. Clearly he was making a point about Blaine.

Camden continued to play the upbeat music while everyone streamed out of the sanctuary. He stayed at the piano after everyone was gone. He couldn't make himself go out in the church's foyer to give Blaine well wishes.

Camden jumped at the light touch on his shoulder. He looked up and saw his mother standing there with a sad smile on her face.

"Are you coming, honey? Your brother is looking for you."

"He's not looking for me."

Lady Rita sat down next to Camden on his piano bench. "Blaine needs you. He's not strong like you. He won't be able to do this without you."

"He's got Dad."

"And that's not the same as a brother. He looks up to you. Always has. Don't leave him alone in this."

"I won't."

Camden rose from the piano bench and followed his mother out to the foyer. He untightened his lips and got ready to show

a united front to the world. Because that
was the Wilson brand.

CHAPTER 13

Camden couldn't believe they were actually in the recording studio. After things had died down from Pastor Wilson's announcement concerning the new church and Blaine, it was back to the status quo. So G.I.F.T.E.D practiced new music, rearranged some old music, and then practiced some more. Finally, they were ready to record.

Their strategy was to do an upbeat praise song and a worship song, and to release them both as singles. If the singles did well, they'd release an entire album and go on tour with it. But first, they had to get the songs down.

Pastor Wilson joined them in the recording studio lounge. The plush carpet and expensive high-end furnishings hinted that they were at a quality establishment. Camden had recorded in spaces that were a lot less sophisticated — nothing more than a few microphones, some noise-canceling foam on the walls, a keyboard and a computer. This was absolutely a step up from all that. The best that Pastor Wilson's money could buy.

"How long is this studio session going to take?" Pastor Wilson asked. He sat on one of the couches with his arms folded tightly across his chest.

Camden smarted at the question, just as he was annoyed at his father's presence at the studio. Pastor Wilson knew absolutely nothing about recording, or even music, so he didn't need to be there, but since it was his money buying the studio time, no one was going to tell him to get out.

"We're prepared, so I'm thinking no more than three hours per song to lay down the lead and background vocals. It'll take longer to mix them down. We're looking at a full day."

They had blocked ten hours for studio time with an hour break for dinner. None of which Pastor Wilson had approved or was privy to.

"A full day at one hundred fifty an hour?"

Camden's nostrils flared as he tried to control his irritation. His father had made millions off his speaking engagements, devotionals, love offerings, etc. There was absolutely no reason for him to be penny-pinching on this. If he really cared about their musical talents he could've built them a recording studio. But no. The only thing he ever offered to pay for was seminary, which Camden and Blaine had both turned down.

Blaine said, "Dad, are you sure you and Stephen don't want to just come back when we're done?"

"You all don't want me here?" Pastor Wilson asked. He sounded genuinely hurt.

"It's not that. This will be very boring for you, and you're kind of stressing everybody out."

Pastor Wilson nodded slowly and rose to his feet. "I'm sure you all don't need me. You know what you're doing. Stop by the house with the final product. I want to hear what I paid for."

Pastor Wilson motioned toward the studio front door with his head, and Stephen rushed ahead of him to open the door. Stephen got on Camden's nerves. He seemed like he wanted to be one of Pastor Wilson's sons.

But Stephen had no idea what it was like to grow up in the house with Pastor Wilson. Camden wouldn't wish it on anyone. He hated having the memories.

"Ooh, I thought they would never leave!" Amber said. "He was irking me for real!"

Camden laughed out loud. "He was on my nerves too."

"Well, I don't mind my future father-in-law being here," Dawn said.

Everyone was silent, probably waiting for Camden's response. He lifted both eyebrows and smiled, but Akil, who sat next to Dawn on the other couch, picked up a couch pillow and hit her in the head with it.

"Ow, Akil!" Dawn shouted.

Everyone burst into laughter, and Dawn pouted. Camden rushed to her side and knocked Akil out of the way.

"Leave her alone. My mom took her looking at wedding dresses, so she can call them her future in-laws. I am not mad at that."

Amber chuckled. "Well, as long as you're not mad. . . ."

"Why would he be mad?" Dawn snapped. "We've been dating since we were in diapers."

"Y'all have," Blaine said. "I'm not sure I'm okay with that."

"So he should be more like you, then? He should date ninety-seven percent of the women in a megachurch?" Dawn asked.

"Not ninety-seven percent!" Amber said with a laugh.

"Maybe not that many, but er . . . uh . . . a little variety maybe," Blaine said.

"Okay, come on, y'all. Let's not lose focus," Camden said. "We've got a lot of work to do today. Akil, lead us in prayer."

Camden pulled Dawn up from the couch and they all joined hands. Blaine tried to take Dawn's other hand and she rolled her eyes.

"You about to go before the Lord with an attitude?" Blaine asked.

"You about to go before the Lord with that girl's lipstick on your collar?" Dawn snapped back.

Blaine reached for his collar, and Camden groaned. There wasn't even any lipstick there.

"For real? Junior Pastor Wilson, you gotta be more careful!" Amber said.

"You need to put out an APB for the comb that got lost in that horror movie on top of your head!" Blaine quipped. "You wish it was *your* lipstick on my collar."

Camden sighed again as his phone buzzed in his pocket. "I'm about to step out and take a phone call. Can y'all please have individual conversations with Jesus while I'm on the phone? The clock is ticking."

When Camden pulled the phone out of his pocket on the way out the room, he jumped when he saw Royce London's number in the caller ID. He quickly hit the talk button on the phone. He couldn't believe that he'd almost missed the call dealing with drama.

"Royce, how are you?" Camden said.

"I'm blessed, man. Did I catch you at a bad time?"

"I was about to start an all-day studio session with the group, but I have a minute."

"Okay, I'll be brief. I just wanted to share an opportunity for you and for your group. My record label just gave me my own label and they want me to bring on some new talent. I think you all have a fresh sound and I would love to meet with you about bringing you on board."

Camden nearly dropped the phone.

"Y-yes! I would love to meet with you. Just tell me when."

Royce laughed. "I was going to say today, but I want you to get your session in. How about lunch tomorrow?"

"Absolutely."

"Okay, meet me at two at the Oceanaire. My treat."

"Will do!"

Camden disconnected the call and shouted for joy. Everyone rushed out of the studio lounge.

"Are you okay?" Dawn asked.

"Yes. Yes! I am better than okay!"

Camden scooped Dawn up and spun her around. Then he set her down and scooped Amber up. She squealed.

"What is up?" Amber asked as he put her down.

Akil backed up when Camden looked in his direction. "Dude! You 'bout to spin me around too?"

"I just might! That was Royce London on the phone. He's offering us a record deal."

Blaine yelled, "That's what I'm talking about! Hey, we need to get in here and lay down these tracks."

"Yeah. He and I are having lunch tomorrow. I'd like to let him hear some great material."

"Let's do this, then," Amber said.

Akil said, "Can I pray now, then? Sounds like we're ready to roll."

This time, everyone willingly joined hands. Camden felt tears come to his eyes as Akil prayed for the success of their studio session and for the opportunities coming their way. Maybe it was God's will that Pastor Wilson didn't choose him to run his Oklahoma City church. All things — even the things that his father did to break his spirit — were working together for good.

CHAPTER 14

Camden cracked his knuckles nervously as he waited for Royce to disconnect his phone call. He, Royce, and Blaine were having lunch at the Oceanaire for their conversation about a record deal.

Camden had dressed carefully for the meeting. The warm May afternoon was too stifling for a blazer, so he wore a fitted button-down dress shirt without a tie and unbuttoned at the top, copying the style of men in Royce's Grammy-winning singing group, Spirited. Camden's muscular chest strained across the tight fabric and his arms struggled against the sleeves. He wondered how anyone could be comfortable in a shirt like that.

Blaine looked annoyed as he chewed furiously on a piece of bread. Camden kicked him under the table, and when Blaine looked at him, Camden smiled. Blaine got Camden's nonverbal "be nice" message, but all he managed was a grimace.

Camden had to admit that he was bothered by Royce's lack of table manners too, but he was known for that type of thing. Whenever Camden had heard stories about him from industry folk, they told similar tales. Royce was hard-core and talented, but he wasn't likable.

Finally Royce finished his call and put his phone down on the table. "So, let's get to it," he said. "I need songs for my new project."

"We've got songs," Blaine said. "Everything we do outside of praise and worship at church is original."

Royce nodded. "You *all* collaborate on the songs? The entire group?"

Camden cleared his throat. "For the most part, I write them. Amber helps me with arrangements."

"I do my own arrangements," Royce said.

"Of course you do," Camden said. "I was just . . ."

"You're who I need," Royce said to Camden. "I just need the songwriter in Atlanta. Not the entire group."

Blaine's grimace turned into a full-fledged frown. "You don't want us to sing on your record?"

"I have singers," Royce said with a mouthful of forty-dollar crab cake. "You're going to be doing a lot of work on So G.I.F.T.E.D while we get my worship project done."

"I thought this meeting was about putting So G.I.F.T.E.D on the map," Blaine said.

Royce swallowed his food and dabbed at the sides of his mouth with his napkin. "It is about both. Your deal and my project."

"So what are we gonna be doing while Camden is in Atlanta working on *your* project?" Blaine asked.

Royce laughed out loud. "If you really want to know, when I came to your church to hear you sing, your soprano singer was a little pitchy, and you aren't one hundred percent believable as a worship leader. I almost expected you to do a split or grind on the microphone stand. You give me a nineties R&B vibe, which is unfortunate, because your brother's worship songs are some of the best I've heard. The group needs work."

Camden wanted to pick Blaine's face up for him, because it had definitely fallen. It was probably somewhere on the floor near his feet. His jaw was unhinged with shock and his eyebrows were drawn together in a confused expression.

"If we need so much work, then why do you want to sign us?"

"I mean, you all have potential." Royce's voice softened. "You could be great with hard work and dedication, but the music is ready now."

"So are you saying that you just want *him* to come to Atlanta to work on your project?" Blaine asked.

"Is that a problem? Once I sign the group, I'll start setting up shows for you at conferences and expos. You'll be busy. You won't have time for Atlanta," Royce said.

Camden tried to hide his excitement at this turn of events. Of course he wanted to go to Atlanta without Blaine, without the shine-stealing twin. He would love to leave Blaine and his charisma in Dallas so that he could use his gift with no distractions.

"I will need to make arrangements for my ministry obligations here," Camden said. "But no, I don't think it will be a problem."

Blaine tilted his head to one side and stared at Camden with raised eyebrows. For a second, he looked just like their father. Everything about his expression said, *Really?*

"Good, because I'm really anxious to get started," Royce said.

"How long do you think you'll need me in Atlanta?" Camden asked.

"It could be a couple of months, but it'll

probably be closer to a year," Royce said.

"So who's going to play Camden's songs for us at all these shows you're gonna set up? Camden is a part of the group."

"I have a keyboard player for you all while Camden is away. He's top notch, and you'll love him."

Blaine took his napkin out of his lap, tossed it on the table, got up and walked away from the table. Camden sighed and shook his head. He guessed he should be happy that Pastor Wilson hadn't crashed the meeting as well.

"Your brother doesn't like this. Is that going to be an issue? We can forgo the record deal for the group for now if they are going to need you to be with them in order to perform," Royce said.

Camden paused before replying. There would be problems, but Blaine's anger would be the least of them. Everything in Camden's life would be affected by this — his relationship with Dawn, his position at church, and So G.I.F.T.E.D. But there was no way Camden was passing on this opportunity.

"No. No issues at all. I can handle my brother. Looking forward to working with you."

Royce said, "Just a piece of advice, Camden. Don't stress yourself about this decision. Everyone can't follow you everywhere. You don't need to feel guilty about a blessing. Just accept it and move on."

But Camden did feel a twinge of guilt, and not because Blaine had stormed out of the restaurant. He knew that if he did this, if he took this opportunity from Royce, that he'd be leaving Dawn in Dallas. There was no way he could take a girlfriend to live with him in another city, and he didn't feel it was time for marriage.

"I do accept it, Royce. I appreciate every blessing, man."

Camden sent up a little prayer of thanks and hoped that Dawn wouldn't view his blessing as a curse.

CHAPTER 15

"I'm telling y'all, Camden is tripping," Blaine said as he paced the floor in Akil's apartment.

Blaine had gathered the rest of So G.I.F.T.E.D at his apartment immediately after the lunch fiasco that he and Camden had with Royce. Several hours had gone by and he was still furious.

Amber and Dawn shared Blaine's royal blue velvet couch that was in the center of his living room. The couch was supposed to remind him of water, and the tan marble tile was his take on sand. His living room was his own personal beach, meant to calm him when he was feeling stressed. It wasn't working this evening.

"So what exactly did he do wrong? It just sounds like he accepted an offer from Royce, and it sounds like we now have a record deal," Amber said. "Isn't that why y'all were meeting with him?"

Blaine hopped down from a bar stool in his huge kitchen and walked into the living room to answer a defiant-looking Amber. Dawn's expression was the opposite of Amber's. She looked close to tears.

"Yes, but did you hear what I said? He's going to Atlanta to work on Royce's project while we work our behinds off singing at church conferences and stuff. Royce could've just brought us to Atlanta and put us on his project."

"I still don't see what the problem is. Camden doesn't sing with us, he only plays. I don't see why we need him to do a few songs," Amber said.

"This is where it starts, Amber," Blaine said.

Amber stood and walked toward the kitchen. "Mmm-hmm. Well, I'm sure if the tables were turned you would've done the same thing. Does anyone want some juice?"

"I-I'm happy for Camden," Dawn said. "If he can create an opportunity for us to go to Atlanta too, I know he will."

"You hope he will. But he might just get in Atlanta and find his wife. You didn't think about that, did you?"

Dawn's eyes widened as if she hadn't thought about that at all. "How long is he going to be gone again?"

"Royce said maybe a year. A whole year away from your fiancé. What do you think about that?"

"Don't do that, Blaine," Amber said. "Camden loves her, and we have a record deal. Is anyone hearing that? A record deal. We didn't have that before."

"Yeah, Blaine. Camden started this group. He wants us to be successful more than anybody," Akil said.

"Well, why didn't he say anything when Royce started clowning us, then? He called me a nineties R&B singer and he said that Dawn was pitchy! Camden just sat there grinning and looking thirsty. I don't even think the record deal is really going to happen. I think Royce just said that to get Camden for his stuff."

Blaine waited for his words to sink in. He watched Amber's smile fade and a tear trickle down Dawn's face. Akil's eyebrows nearly touched, his frown was so deep. Now the entire group looked like they understood why he was so angry. Camden was tripping no matter what they thought, and he was going to Atlanta and leaving them all behind.

"So he's gonna go? Leave the group for who knows how long?" Akil asked.

Blaine nodded. "Yes. Royce is sending us

a replacement keyboard player to do some shows with us."

"What does Pastor Wilson think?" Dawn asked. "He's going to be mad, right?"

"He is. I am too. He's playing us, y'all," Blaine said.

Amber walked back into the small living room and stood in front of Blaine with her arms folded across her chest. "Well, y'all can be mad at Camden if you want to. He is a good, no great songwriter. He deserves this. And Dawn . . . you were pitchy last Sunday."

"I was not!"

"You were," Akil said. "You went sharp a couple of times. On top of a few notes."

"Whatever," Dawn mumbled.

"That has nothing to do with anything!" Blaine said. "Y'all are missing the point. Camden's going to go to Atlanta, start writing for other artists, and then So G.I.F.T.E.D is gonna be through. Watch."

"If that happens, then it was God's will for it to happen. Shoot, you're going to be a pastor in a year or so. Whenever Pastor Wilson decides to *release* you. You're the lead singer, Blaine! You gonna preach and sing?" Amber said.

"I might! Pastors have singing careers all

the time. Ever heard of Pastor Marvin Sapp?"

"Yeah, of course. And Pastor Donnie Mc-Clurkin too. You can do it all, I guess, but Camden has to stay here and be the Minister of Music at your daddy's church?" Amber asked.

Her words hit home with Blaine. He wanted Camden to be successful, just not without him.

"So is this Cam-bashing session over?" Amber asked.

Blaine shook his head. He should've known that they'd have Camden's back, even when he was being treacherous. Amber took out her cell phone and started texting.

"Are you telling someone about Camden?" Blaine asked. "He might not want the news out yet."

Amber frowned at Blaine. "Um, no. I am telling Camden about our little powwow and seeing if he wants us to rehearse any music since we're all here together."

Blaine took a few steps forward and snatched her phone. She swatted at his head, but he ducked out of the way.

"Look, y'all. If Camden leaves, we can't throw away everything we've worked for so far. I know I'm not Camden, but I can lead too. We can't just throw it all away. Let's make a pact that we're going to stay a group, no matter what."

Amber and Dawn both looked at Akil, who nodded thoughtfully at Blaine's speech. He knew they weren't used to him giving speeches. That was usually Camden's job. Blaine didn't give speeches.

"I'm down," Amber said. "We have worked hard."

"That was a pretty stirring plea, sir," Akil said. "Maybe you are a preacher after all."

"He's gonna be pulling in those big offerings just like Pastor Wilson."

Blaine grinned. He *was* going to do well like his father. He was going to probably even surpass Pastor Wilson's popularity with his singing and his charm. He was going to sow church-growing seeds and reap bountiful blessings — including a wife who was worthy to be at his side.

CHAPTER 16

"Dad, I'm going to Atlanta."

Camden waited for his words to sink in. Pastor Wilson had been in his study, watching his sermon from the previous Sunday. It was a ritual that Pastor Wilson had. He watched the DVD and took notes on his performance, like an NFL coach might watch a game-day tape.

"Going to Atlanta for what? Use your words, Camden. Communicate like an adult."

Camden cleared his throat. He knew this wasn't going to be easy, but his father seemed to be in an especially snippy mood.

"I'm going to Atlanta to work on Royce London's new worship project. He wants me to write some songs for it."

"What about your ministry here?"

Camden had expected this question. It was valid. He'd just taken over as Minister of Music. Leaving his post now seemed like he was abandoning it.

"I prayed about it. I believe that working with Royce on his project and shadowing him as the Minister of Music at his church will better prepare me to run the music department here."

Pastor Wilson let out a loud and obnoxious laugh. "Oh! That's what you did? You prayed about it? Did you pray about what you'll do for money? You get your paycheck from my church."

"Royce is going to pay me as one of the musicians at his church and for every song I do on his record."

Camden didn't mention that they'd also be doing side gigs and that he had savings. He didn't feel the need to give his father all of the details. It wasn't necessary, and he would try to poke holes in all of his plans anyway.

"And how long are you planning to be gone?"

"Could be a year."

"So we're supposed to go without a Minister of Music for a year while you go and find yourself?"

"It's not about finding myself," Camden said, his anger rising. "This is a solid opportunity."

"Solid opportunity? Are you serious?

Don't you know gospel artists don't make any money! Why you think most of them are worship leaders, choir directors, and pastors? I gave you all the platform and opportunity you need for your music and you're throwing it in my face for that fruity Royce London."

Camden closed his eyes and tried to regulate his breathing. He was getting so angry that his breaths were quick and ragged.

Pastor Wilson shook his head slowly and continued. "You came to me and asked for a prayer to be released into ministry. God told me not to put you in that position, that's why I didn't want to pray for you. I let my emotions get the best of me, though, and I did it anyway."

"Wow," Camden said. "You told the praise team it had to do something with the supernatural transference of wealth. Wasn't that the word you gave?"

"That's for *them,* Camden, and you know it. Bottom line is, I built this church from nothing. No one should benefit from my sacrifices more than my family."

"But God told you not to give it to me."

"That is shocking, isn't it? I didn't listen to the voice of the Lord concerning a ministry position and look where it got me.

I fired one of the best Ministers of Music in the country because I was hoping that it would motivate you to walk in your destiny."

"You want me to walk in the destiny you've chosen for me. Sounds like God knows better. Sounds like He's got something better for me."

Pastor Wilson chuckled. "Well, what do you know? You might actually have some balls after all. Since you're asserting your manhood, I'm going to give you a choice. Stay here in your ministry position and I will put more money into this little gospel project. If you leave and go to Atlanta, I'm replacing you and you won't have a job here when you come back."

"Not much of a choice," Camden said.

"Talk to God about it. Maybe you'll do a better job listening to Him than I did."

"I already talked to God about it. I'm leaving."

"Good luck, then," Pastor Wilson said.

Camden shook his head. "Luck? We don't believe in luck, right? We're blessed."

"We're blessed when we stay in the will of God. You better hope what you're planning is in His will," Pastor Wilson said. He pressed play on his DVD and waved his hand at Camden, dismissing him.

Camden's top lip curled into a snarl as he

turned and left his father's study. He slammed the door so hard that it rattled on the hinges. Still, he could hear his father's laughter behind the door.

Camden's mother stood in the front parlor of their mansion, and she rushed to Camden as he headed for the front door.

"Honey," she said, "what's wrong? I heard the door slam. Is everything all right?"

"I'm moving to Atlanta, and I was hoping your husband would be happy for me."

She looked confused, and grabbed Camden's arm. "Atlanta? Why? We're building so much here. Your father needs you."

"I'm going to write music for Royce London! This could . . . You know what? I'm done trying to convince y'all. I'm a grown man."

Camden snatched his arm away and headed for the front door. His mother wailed as he turned the knob.

Camden paused. "Mama, it's only for a year. Please don't cry."

"Your father will never forgive you for leaving," she said between sobs. "If he doesn't want you to go, please don't go. Ask Royce if there's another way you can work on the project. You can go back and forth to Atlanta. Just be here on Sunday mornings."

Camden could commute from Dallas to

Atlanta. He could work on tracks, melodies, and lyrics in his apartment and send them to Royce. But the truth was, he didn't want to. Royce had asked him to relocate for the project, and contrary to what his father believed, Camden *did* talk to God about his choices.

"I have to do this," Camden said. "I believe that God wants me to do this, Mama. Isn't what God wants more important than what Dad wants?"

First Lady Rita hugged Camden and kissed his cheeks. "Honey, you're angry right now. Think this through. I just have a bad feeling about it."

"I've never been more positive about anything in my life. I'm doing this."

"You're right. You are a grown man. You've got to make your own choices."

Camden nodded and kissed his mother on the cheek. "Pray for me, okay? I'm doing this."

Camden's heart seized at the sight of his mother's tears, but they didn't change his decision. He would show his father — he'd show everyone — that his destiny wasn't tied to Graceway, or to his father's approval.

CHAPTER 17

Camden knew that it would be harder to tell Dawn about his move than anyone. Unfortunately, thanks to Blaine's diarrhea of the mouth, she along with the rest of the group already knew that he was leaving.

Dawn was very quiet as she and Camden stood side by side in his kitchen putting cookies on a cookie sheet to bake. They were going to have a group meeting later, and the cookies would be the snack.

"I just have one question," Dawn said as she placed one sheet of cookies into the oven.

"What's that?"

"Did you even think about taking me with you?"

Camden nodded. He had, in fact, thought about taking Dawn with him. But she had a good job, and she'd have to find work in Atlanta. She'd also have to find her own place. She had Amber as a roommate in

Dallas, to split the bills, but she wouldn't have that same assistance in Atlanta.

"Do you want to go?" Camden asked.

"Well, I don't want to be away from my man for a year."

"I'll visit lots, and you will visit me too. It's not like I'm moving overseas," Camden said. "Plus, you're going to be incredibly busy. I saw the shows Royce has you all scheduled for. That year is gonna fly by."

"So that's just it, huh? I get no input at all. I was hoping that at some point we'd start making decisions as a couple, but we're not there yet. Do you want to . . . I don't know . . . put this relationship on hold until you're done pursuing your music career?"

"What do you mean by on hold?" Camden's voice escalated a full octave. "You mean you want to see other people?"

"I mean I don't want to get left behind. If you leave . . . when you leave . . . I'll feel that way. Left behind."

Camden ran his open hand over his face and sighed. First his father was giving him ultimatums. And now Dawn? Why couldn't everyone just be happy about this? Why did he have to convince everyone that it was a good thing?

"You can do whatever you want, Dawn. Just know that it was your choice and not mine. Don't blame it on me."

She shook her head. "You're supposed to fight for us."

"You sound crazy," Camden said with frustration punctuating every syllable. "There's nothing to fight about. I'm taking a temporary job that can launch my career, and all you and everyone else can think of is how it impacts *you*. Well, what about me? What about what I want?"

"I thought you wanted me."

"I do," Camden said, bringing his tone back into the normal range.

"But not more than you want this opportunity with Royce."

Camden shuddered, his frustration returning. "They are two unrelated desires. I love you, and I want a music career. You're trying to make me choose. I shouldn't have to."

"Your mother said that you don't have to move to Atlanta to do this. She says you can write music from here, and that you just want to go. She says you're angry about Pastor choosing Blaine for the Oklahoma church and you're running away."

Those words rocked Camden to his core. The one person who always had his back, no matter what, his mother, was conspiring against him too?

"If you want to know why I'm doing something, you should ask me and not my mother," Camden said. "She doesn't know what she's talking about."

"I think she does, and you just don't want to admit it."

Camden's doorbell rang and he was happy for the reprieve. He tried to act as if he didn't see Dawn's tear-streaked face as he left the kitchen to open the door. Camden knew there *had* to be a tremendous move of God coming his way just because of the opposition from everyone he loved.

Camden opened the door to Amber and Akil. Amber was carrying a huge balloon bouquet full of balloons that said *Congratulations!* Camden grinned. Not everyone was against his decision.

"It smells like cookies in here!" Amber said. "Well, I brought cupcakes too. I got your faves, Camdeezy!"

Camden took the balloons and cupcakes from Amber and sat them down before scooping her up and hugging her.

"Thank you for being happy for me," Camden said.

Amber slapped his arm when she sat him down. "We all are."

"Not all," Akil said. "But we got your back, man."

"You don't want me to leave?" Camden asked.

"No, I'm all for it. I'm talking about your parents, Blaine . . ."

"And me!" Dawn said from the kitchen as she took another tray of cookies out of the oven. "Say it."

"I wasn't talking about you," Akil said.

Dawn took her apron off and stormed out of the kitchen and into Camden's bedroom. Camden sighed as she slammed the door.

"I guess everybody is gonna just have to be mad," Camden said.

Amber plopped down on Camden's sofa and stretched her legs out in front of her, taking up most of the cushions. "They'll get over it," she said. "Especially when the record that you and Royce put together sells millions of copies."

Camden moved Amber's legs and sat down on the sofa too. "I know! That's what I keep trying to say, and all my dad can think about is his church. He really doesn't want to tell the congregation, 'Oh, I fired Sarah and hired my son, but he's about to be gone for a year.' I didn't tell him to fire her."

"She was about to quit anyway," Akil said. "I heard she and Delores got into it really bad about something."

Camden frowned. "What beef could Sarah have had with Delores?"

Akil and Amber exchanged glances, and Camden just shook his head. The rumors about his father's womanizing were mostly only whispered by those in the inner circle. No one in the congregation knew what was being said behind the scenes.

"I don't want to know," Camden said. "One of y'all should tell my mother, though."

Amber put her lips into a tiny circle and blew out air in the sound of a whistle. "Puh-lease! I would never get in that there. Yo' daddy is off the chain, though. I think that's why Dawn is so worried. She sees the women all over you and Blainesky and she doesn't feel secure."

"The women are all over Blaine, not me," Camden said.

"They're all over you too," Akil said. "I have the notes to prove it. They think I'm your middle man too, like I am for Blaine. They want you, bro. You just aren't giving them any attention."

"I keep telling Dawn I love her. I don't know what else to do."

Amber cleared her throat. "Well . . . you could . . . marry her and take her with you."

Camden shook his head. "Not you too! As

soon as we get married, she's gonna be trying to pop out a baby. She told me the other day that she didn't want to be in her thirties having her first child. She's got baby fever."

"I was just making a suggestion, Camden. No one said you had to follow it," Amber said.

"Well, nobody asked you for your suggestions."

"Kick rocks, then! With flip-flops!" Amber said as she threw multiple couch pillows at Camden.

"Look, can y'all stop talking about Camden's love life for a second," Akil said. "I'm trying to see if I can slide up in this crib when you leave."

Camden raised his eyebrows. Akil's employment was sporadic, so he lived in between his parents' house and Blaine's man pad.

"Are you gonna be able to pay the rent?" Camden asked. "Because I would be cool with someone staying over here while I'm gone."

"Of course I can pay the rent. I am employed, you know. And it's not like this is a penthouse or anything."

It wasn't a penthouse, but Camden was proud of his multi-level town house located in Irving, Texas. It was right in the heart of the city and the neighborhood was great. One day when he bought a house, he'd probably move to one of the more elite suburbs, but his Irving crib was the perfect bachelor pad.

"Well, as long as you pay the rent, you can stay. I'll be in and out, though. I plan to visit at least once a month. Maybe twice."

"Just leave a sock on the door when you are . . . you know . . ." Blaine said.

Camden frowned. "Dawn and I aren't fornicating. Socks on the door won't be necessary."

"I don't see how you can do that," Akil said. "That's why I'm not dating anybody. I couldn't do that celibate thing."

"You could if you asked God to help you," Camden said. "That's the only way I can do it."

"And a year's supply of baby oil," Amber said. "Don't play, Camden. You are *not* a saint."

Camden threw the couch pillow back at Amber. "I'm not. That's why I need you to cover up your produce. You're about to have a nip slip."

Amber looked down at her heaving bosom and chuckled as she adjusted her peasant blouse to do a better job covering her assets.

"These babies are gonna get me a man someday," Amber said. "They can't do their job if they're not displayed properly."

Akil shook his head. "You need Jesus as your personal savior. When is this meeting supposed to start? Are we waiting on Blaine?"

Camden looked down at his watch. Blaine was forty-five minutes late. He took out his cell phone and called him.

Blaine answered on the first ring. "I know, I know. I just pulled up. I had to go get Regina, and you know she lives all the way in Fort Worth."

"Why are you bringing her? It's a group meeting about the promotional tour," Camden said.

"She's my manager and assistant for now. She's going to be coordinating my speaking engagements so that they don't clash with So G.I.F.T.E.D's appearances."

"Okay. I guess."

Camden disconnected the call and gave Amber and Akil a puzzled expression. "Did y'all know he was bringing Regina?"

Amber rolled her eyes. "I can't stand her. I don't know what y'all daddy was thinking when he authorized and mandated that hookup. She makes me itch."

The talk about Regina had to be put on

pause, though, because the doorbell rang, signaling their arrival. Camden let them in, and Regina walked through the door first, nose in the air and aloof expression on her face.

"Sorry we're late," Regina said. "We're in couples classes at the church, and it ran over."

Camden, Akil, and Amber all struggled to hold in their laughter, mostly because of the look on Blaine's face. He looked like someone who'd just stepped in a pile of dog poo and then discovered it on their foot. Just plain ole disgusted.

"I'll go get Dawn so we can start the meeting," Amber said.

Regina looked around. "Where should we sit?"

Blaine motioned toward the love seat. "You can sit here. I'll stand."

"Okay, whatever you want," Regina said. She pulled out a notebook and pen and smiled up at Camden.

"Thank you for allowing me to join in your meeting, Camden. I apologize that you didn't know in advance. I thought Blaine told you I was coming," Regina said with a friendly tone.

"It's not a problem. You guys are probably going to end up being one flesh soon, so it's all good."

Camden's chest burned from containing his laughter. Akil had given up the fight. He let out a fit of giggles.

"Y'all got jokes," Blaine said.

"I don't see what's funny. It's true. They can mock God's plan if they want to. But really, it's the other way around. When we make plans, God laughs," Regina said.

"You're right, Regina. We're just teasing Blaine," Camden said. "We wish y'all the best."

Dawn and Amber emerged from Camden's bedroom. Dawn's face was puffy and tear streaked, but she wore a smile.

"So, I'm glad everyone is here, because there are some exciting things going on with our group," Camden said. "The most exciting being the record deal."

"What kind of deal is it? Are we gonna be like those work-for-hire acts, where they pay us to sing on the album and that's it?" Amber asked. "Because if that's the case, I will pass."

Camden shook his head. "No. I took a look at the contract and you'll get points off the album."

"I want producer credit," Blaine said. "I'm the lead singer and pretty much the front man."

Camden nodded. "I'm sure that we can discuss that."

"Well, I want producer credit too," Amber said. "I'm doing all these vocal arrangements without compensation."

Camden scratched his head and jumped back in when he could. "So, right now we're not looking at doing a full-length record. We'll release both singles, get some radio play and do the shows. There is a big church conference in Houston this summer called the Superfest, and Royce was able to get us a fifteen-minute set there. He's also got us on the US Gospel Workshop schedule in Miami and the Ricky Johnson Gospel New Artist Showcase on the Gospel Entertainment Network."

"What do these shows pay?" Regina asked.

"Nothing. They're all about getting our name out there. All of the major players in gospel radio will be there, and they need to see us as the group to watch," Camden explained. "The money starts later, after we start getting invitations."

"Well, who's paying for our travel to Houston, Miami, and — where is the Gospel Entertainment Network show recorded?" Akil asked.

"It's going to be out of pocket. We can ask the record label to pay for it, but I don't want to start out in the hole and owing them money. I suggest we try to cover it ourselves."

"You're a big baller, I guess," Amber said. "I don't know how much travel I can afford."

"Do you think Pastor Wilson will pay for any of it?" Dawn asked.

Camden doubted very seriously that his father was going to foot the bill for anything related to the group now. But it didn't hurt to ask. Or rather, it didn't hurt to have Blaine ask.

"Blaine, I'll leave that to you," Camden said. "I'm not in Dad's good graces right now."

Blaine nodded. "I'll ask him, but then you'll owe me a favor. I'll decide how you'll pay me back."

"Whatever, man! I got you a record deal, so we're even," Camden replied.

"So we're going to be doing all these shows, and you're gonna be in Atlanta writing music?" Amber asked. "That's gonna be weird. Like . . . you're more than the keyboard player, Cam."

"You're right. It is going to be strange. I will be at the filming for the Gospel Entertainment Network, but Royce has a pretty intense schedule for his group. He wants me at all the practices because sometimes they come up with music in a jam session and he might want to build on it."

Camden ignored the skeptical looks that came from everyone except Amber. She was the only one who seemed to understand why he needed to leave.

"So, are we going to have a look?" Dawn asked. "We need to come up with a signature look for our group. I'm thinking a really updated look for Akil and Blaine. Some fitted suits, bow ties . . ."

"Not doing the whole bow tie thing," Blaine said.

"Yeah, I'm too thick for fitted suits," Akil said.

Amber laughed. "We need to get a stylist! Because I want people to look at us onstage and be like, 'I want to be them.' "

"I can help with that," Regina said. "I know a few stylists who have worked with some major gospel acts. They've reached out to style First Lady Wilson many times. I can hook that up."

"With Camden being gone, someone is going to have to run rehearsals too," Blaine said. "I want to step up and do that. I am making a commitment to be on time and at every rehearsal."

Camden raised his eyebrows and everyone

gave Blaine their own looks of surprise. He had never taken the lead with rehearsals or anything else. He always let Camden do the grunt work and he showed up and turned on when it was time to shine onstage.

"I'm going to make sure he does it," Regina said. "This is all part of his training to be a pastor."

"You're training him?" Amber asked.

"I'm helping. Pastor Wilson trusts me to get him together."

Regina laughed when she said this, but no one else joined in, not even Blaine. It wasn't like she was unwelcome, but Camden didn't know how he felt about Regina's involvement. It was like having one of his father's flunkies in the meeting.

"Well, I don't know about all that," Blaine said. "I'm just down for this group. We've been doing this too long to not make a real go at it. I don't need Regina for that."

"Let's do this thing, then!" Dawn said. "I'm excited. Y'all excited?"

For the first time since he announced that he was going to Atlanta, Camden felt that everything would be okay with the group he was leaving behind. Dawn's tears had dried up, Amber was planning costumes, and Blaine was on board. They'd hold it down until he returned. And that was all Camden needed to know — that everything would keep moving while he pursued his dream.

CHAPTER 18

Camden had never felt more nervous in his life. He was meeting with Royce's group, Spirited, for the first time. He had a feeling they were going to rake him over the coals. He thought he was ready . . . hoped he was ready.

Since he got to Atlanta, everything had moved so quickly that he could barely keep up. Camden thought he'd have to find an apartment, but Royce told him that he would be living in his six-thousand-square-foot house.

And what a house it was! There was an indoor recording studio and a bowling alley, and the outside looked just like a Caribbean resort, with multiple swimming pools, a hot tub, a water slide, and tennis courts. Camden had grown up in the lap of luxury, but he was still impressed. He wanted to take pictures of it all and send it to his father so that he could see the kind of money a *gospel* artist had made.

The meeting was a pool party, and Royce had an entire catering staff on-site, including a bartender. Since Royce was so busy giving orders to his staff, Camden didn't wait for instructions. He put on a pair of linen pants and a short-sleeved dress shirt — it was casual enough that he wouldn't be overdressed if folk were casual and formal enough that he wouldn't be underdressed if folk were formal. He was nervous all the same.

Camden went out on the back deck by the pool and sat down at one of the decorated tables. Before he was seated even an entire minute a waiter walked up with a tray of champagne.

"Would you like one?" he asked.

Camden shook his head. "No, thank you. I will have a lemonade or some sweet tea if y'all have it."

The waiter nodded and smiled. "Sweet tea coming up."

"Well, aren't you a country boy."

Camden turned his head to the voice, and was immediately starstruck. His manners had him immediately standing to his feet. It was Ivy Whitlowe, a Grammy-winning gospel star who had begun as Royce's protégée.

Ivy was stunningly beautiful. She could've been a model. She was tall, about five feet eight inches, with her heels making her close to six feet. She had long golden brown hair that hung in waves and eyes the color of honey. Camden had only ever seen her on television, and she was gorgeous there, but in person, she seemed otherworldly.

"You're Ivy Whitlowe. I'm pleased to meet you."

She chuckled. "Please sit! I'm happy to meet *you,* Camden Wilson. Royce can't stop talking about your music."

Camden held out a chair for her at the table and she accepted. "Handsome and chivalrous. These Atlanta birds are gonna scoop you right up."

"Oh, I have a girlfriend back in Dallas."

Ivy grinned. "Well, she's back in Dallas and you're here in Atlanta. She should've come with you. The women here are a different breed."

"Well, I'm the same here as I am in Dallas, so I don't think she has to worry." Camden smiled, but he did feel a bit concerned.

"She's got a great man, then," Ivy said.

The champagne waiter came back with Camden's sweet tea and offered Ivy a glass of champagne, which she readily accepted.

"You don't drink, Camden?" she asked. "You Holiness? Pentecostal? Do you think drinking is a sin?"

"Oh, I have a drink from time to time. I don't think it's a sin. My father's church is nondenominational."

"Good. I wouldn't want you judging me when we've got so much kingdom business to accomplish together."

"Are you going to be singing on Royce's new project?" Camden asked.

"I'll probably do a guest spot or two, but I'm talking about my new record. My record company is on my back about coming up with a hit, and none of what I have is making the cut. I'm looking for a fresh sound."

Camden nodded. "Have you thought of doing a duet with Royce? I've got a great song called 'Quiet Place' that would be great for your voice."

Ivy sipped her champagne and swallowed it before she replied. "What about you? Do you sing? I don't know about doing a duet with Royce. It'd end up being all about him."

"I do sing, but I'm not a performer. I like to stay behind the scenes."

"You're way too handsome to be behind the scenes. You need to be up singing or preaching or something. Do you preach too?"

Camden laughed. "No, I don't. I am — was — the Minister of Music at my father's church."

"Past tense, huh? Let me guess. He didn't want you to come out here."

"You're exactly right. How'd you know?"

Ivy smiled, and Camden swore her eyes sparkled. "My father is Bishop K. Phillip Carter of Heavenly Rest Church of God in Christ in Detroit. I was the choir director and opened up singing a solo for him every time he did a speaking engagement. Royce heard me sing at a conference and snatched me right up out of there."

"How old were you?" Camden asked.

"Twenty-three. My father acted a fool. He was ready to marry me off to one of his up-and-coming pastor friends and have me start popping out little singing grandbabies. God had other plans."

"Wow," Camden said. "Sounds a lot like me, except for popping out the grand-babies. I guess my girlfriend will be the one doing that."

"Who knows? You may end up like me. I got here and my entire life changed. I've never looked back."

"I think that's what everyone is afraid of."

Ivy shook her head. "They can't stop your destiny, no matter what."

Camden was glad that Ivy was the first person he met in Atlanta. She made him feel comfortable. They had a lot in common already, and he couldn't wait to hear her voice singing on some of his music.

"Looks like I was destined to be married to a pastor anyway. Dr. Norman Whitlowe. My daddy couldn't have been happier when we got together."

Camden smiled. "You're right. No one can stop your destiny, but you can't run from it either. I'm here now, so let's see what unfolds."

"Well, I'm glad you're here!"

Royce walked up to the table after giving some orders to the wait staff. The best way to describe his outfit was snug. He had on a pair of short jeans almost the length of capri pants and a tight button-down pink shirt with the sleeves rolled up. He was wearing a shiny tank underneath. It was gold, the same color as his leather boat shoes. He gave Ivy a big hug and kissed her cheeks.

"Girl, why didn't you tell me you were here?" Royce asked.

"I was just fine! Spending some time with Camden. He's a sweetheart."

Royce smiled at Camden. "You don't call

a grown man a sweetheart. He is a gifted musician!"

"She can call me anything she wants," Camden said.

"Gorgeous, isn't she," Royce said. "I keep telling her husband I'm gonna steal her from him one day."

Ivy shook her head and laughed. "You know you had first dibs, Royce. Don't even play."

Camden watched Ivy and Royce exchange glances, and he knew there was plenty not being said. Camden could imagine Ivy falling for Royce, who was all glitz and glam, when she was so young and eager to be a star.

Royce's wife, Kita, appeared on the patio, and Royce waved her over. She was so different from Royce, it was hard to believe that they were married. She had on a pastel blouse and skirt, very little makeup, and her hair was pulled up into a side ponytail. She was the opposite of glitz. It was as if Royce had sucked up everything shiny in his path and left Kita with everything dull.

Ivy jumped up and hugged Kita. "Hey, girl, everything looks nice!"

Kita laughed. "You know that was all Royce. I had nothing to do with this. I just show up like everybody else."

Kita sat down at the table with Ivy, Royce, and Camden. Other partiers had started to arrive and every one of them stopped by to say hello to Royce and Ivy first, like they were royalty.

One by one, Camden met everyone in Royce's group. There were about thirty of them, and once they all got there and the DJ turned the music up, Camden couldn't tell the difference between Spirited and a family reunion.

"We have fun," Royce said. "We're family, man."

"I see!" Camden replied.

For a second, it made Camden wish for the familiarity of his own group. This would be a lot easier with Amber by his side making jokes about her cleavage. Or with Blaine taking all the spotlight.

But Camden had stepped out. He was on his own. Destiny was ready to unfold . . . or not. He had to prepare his mind for this because Royce and now Ivy were looking for him to be something special. And he hoped that he wouldn't prove them wrong.

CHAPTER 19

Now that Camden was in Atlanta, Blaine had something to prove. He had to show everyone that he could lead the group in his absence. Because if he couldn't lead a singing group that had been together for years, how in the world could he lead a church?

They were at the first show that Royce had scheduled for them, the Superfest in Houston, Texas. There were a lot of other up-and-coming groups there, but none that Blaine had ever heard of. As far as Blaine could see there wasn't one headliner in the house. That was perfect. So G.I.F.T.E.D was going to be the act that everyone remembered.

The show was being held at an outdoor venue, and the weather felt like they were near one of the portals of hell, but onstage there were big fans blowing cold air. Backstage was another matter. Blaine felt like he was about to spontaneously combust in the hot, snug suit that Amber had picked out for him. He took the jacket off and slung it across his arm. He wouldn't be able to perform in that without passing out.

"Blaine, here is the water you asked for. Room temperature, right?"

Dawn handed Blaine the bottle of water and a couple of peppermints. That was what he always had before he sang. Regina was making sure the show went well, microphone checks, lighting checks and whatnot, but Dawn knew all the little details that came from singing with a person for years.

"Thank you. You ready?" Blaine asked.

She nodded. "Been resting my voice a little bit. Want to make sure I'm not pitchy when we sing."

Blaine tried to think of what Camden would do when one of them was feeling insecure about singing. He put one hand on Dawn's shoulder and smiled down at her.

"Just let the Holy Spirit move, Dawn. Your voice is anointed, so you don't have to worry about ministering. Just let God use you."

Dawn rewarded Blaine's wisdom with a big smile. "Thank you for that. Needed that. To God be the glory."

"Yes! He's worthy!"

Amber walked up to the two of them. Her

usually wild hair was slicked into a bun on top of her head, but her flower was still perched next to her ear. Their color scheme — royal blue, white, and black — had Amber and Blaine in royal blue with white and black accessories. Dawn and Akil were wearing white with blue and black accessories. Their look was eye-catching.

"They'll be ready for us in five minutes. We're gonna rock this, right?" Amber asked.

"And you know it!" Blaine said.

Amber whipped out her phone and started texting. "I'm telling Camden about our first real gig!"

"What did he say?" Dawn asked.

"He said he's praying for us, and do good!" Amber said.

Dawn nodded and her bright smile faded a little bit. Blaine assumed that things were not good between Dawn and Camden, but he didn't want to ask about it. Camden had been gone a month, and they hadn't skipped a beat with rehearsals and getting ready for the show, but sometimes Dawn looked sad. Like she did when Amber read the text message.

"Are you gonna put that suit jacket on?" Amber asked.

Blaine laughed. "It's the middle of June. You trying to kill me?"

"It looks good, Blaine," Dawn said. "Maybe if you wear it open."

"I'm not wearing it," Blaine said. "And we're still gonna slay the crowd. Watch."

Blaine was right. The jacket wasn't necessary at all. They opened with "I Am Free" and had half the crowd of one thousand or so shouting in the aisles. "Born to Worship" had the other half raising their hands and crying out to God.

After the show, several radio show hosts and managers made a beeline to Blaine to give him their information. Regina was on the spot. She took all of the information for them to look at later.

"So, we've made some really good connections," Regina said as they packed up their belongings from the backstage area.

"Good. Very good."

Blaine was barely paying attention to Regina because he was watching Akil out of the corner of his eye. There were two girls who had him hemmed up, and Akil was all smiles. Akil had his macking face on. Blaine wanted in on that action.

"So, can you check and make sure Amber and Dawn have everything?" Blaine asked Regina. "Dawn was in a bit of a daze. She's missing Camden, I think. She might need somebody to talk to."

Regina nodded with a concerned expression on her face. "Of course. I'll handle it. Thank you for wanting my help with that. It means a lot. I think we're becoming a team."

Blaine kissed her forehead. "Yeah, we are."

"Why don't I meet you back at the hotel? I'll take Dawn to get some dessert or something. We'll have girl talk."

"Okay. She'll appreciate it."

"Anytime! We're going to be sisters-in-law one day."

"Yep. You are."

Blaine wanted to kick up his heels and shout as he watched Regina rush away to find Dawn and Amber. He knew Amber had Dawn's back on whatever, but neither of them would turn Regina away — freeing him up for the evening.

Once Regina was safely out of sight, Blaine sauntered over to where Akil was still entertaining the girls. They were of the thick Houston variety: curves for days, tiny waists, and no girdles to contain their behinds that moved freely under their sundresses.

Blaine felt himself get excited at the possibilities. He'd been doing a good job for a couple of months on not indulging in his various girlfriends in Dallas. He'd been faithful to Regina at home. He had no choice because she watched him like a hawk.

But they were in Houston. This was a one-night-only type of thing. He could have fun with these girls and never see them again. Regina would never even know.

"Hello, ladies," Blaine said as he approached. "Did you enjoy the show?"

Akil said, "I was just telling them that we'd love some home cooking here in Houston."

Blaine nodded. Akil was a great wingman, whether he knew it or not. Home cooking meant a get-together at someone's house. No restaurants where they could be seen.

"My auntie made some rib tips, black eyed peas, collard greens, and macaroni and cheese. She'll fry up some chicken too, if I tell her y'all coming to visit. She watches your daddy's broadcast every Sunday morning," the butter-pecan-complexioned girl said.

Blaine grinned at her and tipped her chin upward as she giggled. Yes, she was perfect. "I sure do love rib tips and collard greens. You make hot water cornbread, pretty girl?"

"I sure do."

"Well, I think I worked up an appetite doing this show. So, point me in the direction of your auntie's house," Blaine said.

"What about Amber, Dawn . . ."

"It's cool," Blaine said. "Regina said they'd meet us back at the hotel. We're good."

Blaine and Akil followed the girls to their car in the parking lot.

"Y'all can follow us, okay?" Butter Pecan said.

Akil and Blaine rushed to their rental car and jumped in. Blaine was glad that they'd gotten separate cars. The girls would have a way back to the hotel.

"Man, I must say, I've trained you well," Blaine said to Akil as he started the car. "Those two are perfect."

Akil chuckled. "I really wasn't trying to score anybody for you. You've got Regina down here, man! What are you thinking?"

"Oh, she's on a mission. Helping her future sister-in-law deal with the loss of her man. She'll be busy for a while."

"I thought you were gonna give that up, though. Start being more like a pastor," Akil said.

"You judging me now?" Blaine asked. "I thought we were brothers."

"Yeah, we are. I'm just trying to look out for you. You've been doing good, going to ministry classes, leading the group like nobody thought you could."

"Nobody thought I could?"

"You know what I mean."

"I know. Camden is the one who has it all together. I'm just the wild card, right?"

Akil shook his head. "It's okay to give it up. It's okay to just have Regina, you know. You don't have to be like your father. You can be better."

Blaine swallowed hard and gripped the steering wheel. There was no one he admired more than his father, but he knew his father's flaws. Pastor Wilson had managed to be great in spite of them.

"Don't say anything bad about my father, Akil. You don't know how much he's sacrificed for this ministry."

Akil didn't say another word, and Blaine followed the girls to Butter Pecan's auntie's house. *You can be better.* The words echoed in Blaine's mind. Maybe he'd try to do just that. Be a pastor without blame, and serve the people of God with a clean heart.

But not today. He'd start tomorrow.

CHAPTER 20

Camden sat in Royce's recording studio and admired all of the state-of-the-art equipment. He wished he could have this kind of setup at home. He would do some phenomenal music with a studio in his townhome.

"I'm hearing great things about So G.I.F.T.E.D," Royce said. "They killed it at the Houston Praise and Worship conference. I'm getting phone calls left and right about how to book them."

Camden nodded. "I'm hearing the same. They are pumped right now for the opportunity, and as long as they're back at the church on Sunday morning, my father is cool."

"About that. They should start thinking about having a backup praise team. They'll be pulled away more frequently if things go the way we want them to. We will be releasing your single to radio next week."

" 'Born to Worship' is going to be on the

radio already?"

"They impressed a lot of radio power players in Houston. It's a done deal. I was worried that your brother wouldn't get it done without you on the keys, but he's impressive."

"Blaine knows how to work a crowd."

Royce nodded his agreement. "He does. And his vocals are powerful too. There's a YouTube video with their performance."

Camden frowned. "So my song is already being pirated."

Royce opened his mouth and laughed. "Gospel music is pirated more than it's purchased. You'll make your money, but it'll be from performances and radio play. Sales of the actual song are going to be low. If you do fifteen thousand on your independent singles, the record label will feel really positive about your record."

"First things first, right? Your project," Camden said. "That's why I'm here. I can work on our stuff in Dallas."

Royce played a few tracks that they had already recorded for his worship project, and Camden internalized Royce's unique sound. He would start there and add his own special flair to it.

"Do you already have anything in your repertoire that complements these songs?"

Royce asked.

"I actually want to write you some new material. Everything I already have was created for So G.I.F.T.E.D."

Royce said, "So, this might indeed take the year that I envisioned."

"It might. I want to hear your group perform. I need to hear the lead singers and get a feel for their voices."

"Well, you know Ivy sings with Spirited. You've met her."

Camden nodded. "Does your wife sing with the group too?"

"She used to. Now she prefers to stay here and take care of the home front."

Camden thought that was a little strange because Royce and Kita didn't have any children. They didn't even have a dog.

"Cool. I've definitely heard Ivy's vocals. Her range is ridiculous. I can write a lot of songs for her."

"Her voice is crazy," Royce agreed. "For many years, she was my muse. She would sing a few notes and it would spawn an entire record. She's gifted."

Camden didn't miss the passion in Royce's voice when he talked about Ivy, but he absolutely understood. As a songwriter, there were certain voices that inspired greatness in Camden's songwriting abilities. So far, Amber and Blaine did it for him, but he was ready to be inspired by others.

A tap on the studio's glass door caused Camden and Royce to turn around. Ivy stood there with a big smile on her face. She wore a snug red miniskirt and a tight T-shirt along with high heels. Royce waved her in and she opened the door.

"I didn't want to interrupt the geniuses at work," Ivy said as she entered the studio.

She hugged and kissed Royce on the cheek, slightly bending over to do so. Camden had to turn away from the view of her behind and thighs. Ivy also hugged Camden but didn't kiss him too.

She pulled up one of the chairs and sat down next to Royce. "So what are y'all doing?" she asked.

"We're listening to some of the stuff we've already done on the project. I want Camden to get a feel for what we're doing."

She nodded. "I hope you're not going to hog Camden while he's here. We could use him on my project too."

Royce poked out his bottom lip and lowered his eyebrows into a thinking pose. "We've only got, like, three songs done on your project."

"But doesn't the record label want a single from me?" Ivy asked.

"Not just from you. From us, and also from Camden's group that we just signed. We're going to be taking over gospel radio this summer and fall."

"So let Camden write me a single. I need something hot so I can get back out on the circuit."

Camden said, "I'll write you a song. Royce, I can do it on my own time. Your project won't suffer. I can multitask."

Royce smiled. "I don't own him, Ivy. Feel free. As long as he's available for my project, I'm good."

Ivy clapped her hands. "Great! I want a call and response worship song."

"Are you going to debut it at your church, First Lady?" Royce asked.

Camden chuckled at Ivy's reaction. She rolled her eyes and dismissed Royce with a wave of the hand.

"Of course. But stop calling me first lady," Ivy said.

"You don't like that?" Camden asked. "My mother loves being called first lady."

"I tried not to marry a pastor so that I'd never have to carry that title. It comes with too much judgment, so I hate it," Ivy said.

"Judgment? The congregation loves the first lady just like they love the pastor," Camden said.

He did not expect Ivy's response. She laughed so hard she started choking. Royce had to give her a tissue and a bottle of water to help with her choking.

"Why is that so hilarious?" Camden asked.

"It is funny because it's a big, fat lie. First of all, I am public enemy number one to half of the women in my church. The ones who think they should be married to my husband. Then the old mothers, don't let me get started on them. They harass me day in and day out because I haven't given my husband a son to carry on his legacy. They have taken to calling me 'Barren Woman' behind my back."

Even Camden had to laugh at her nickname. That *was* funny. He wondered if his mother had the same kinds of issues at their church. There was at least one woman after Pastor Wilson, so maybe she and Ivy did have some things in common.

"Okay, Ivy. I will be in prayer and supplication for you," Camden said. "Are you sure you don't want me to write a song about God preparing a table in the presence of your enemies?"

Now they all laughed out loud. Camden could imagine Ivy working the pulpit in a tight first lady suit, singing to all the groupies after her husband. He'd want to be in the front row for that.

"I like you, Camden Wilson," Ivy said. "I didn't think I would, you being a preacher's kid and all. But you are all right."

"Thank you, I think," Camden said. "I like you too, Ivy."

Royce gave Ivy a look that Camden couldn't comprehend, but it didn't look positive.

"Okay, now that we all like each other, let's do some music. I saw a new Rolls-Royce that I need in my collection."

Camden smiled. He wasn't used to thinking of his music in terms of dollars and cents. Perhaps that was because he hadn't made any dollars yet. Maybe Pastor Wilson's prophecy about a supernatural transference of wealth was all about Camden and So G.I.F.T.E.D.

Chapter 21

Blaine showed Pastor Wilson the YouTube video of So G.I.F.T.E.D's performance in Houston, in his study. Pastor Wilson watched it all the way through, nodded, and then watched it again.

"What do you think, Dad?"

"Y'all are good, but you already knew that. If you keep your nose clean, this could propel your ministry into the stratosphere."

"What do you mean keep my nose clean?"

"I got a report of you and Akil keeping company with some young women in Houston."

Blaine blinked and stared at his father. He and Akil were very careful with those girls in Houston.

"Did Regina tell you something? If she did . . ."

"It wasn't Regina, and you should be glad that it wasn't her. She has no idea about this indiscretion."

Blaine tilted his head to one side. "So you got someone spying on us?"

"Not spying at all. I just have people all over the country who care about me and this ministry. It's a close network, and they're at almost every major gospel event."

"Well, it wasn't really a big deal. Akil wanted to fellowship with some young ladies he met. . . ."

Pastor Wilson slammed his fist down on his desk. "Don't lie to me, Blaine. It's not necessary, and it's in your best interest to tell *me* the truth if you don't tell anyone else."

Blaine waited a few moments before he spoke. "We both fellowshipped with the girls."

"If you're going to insist on womanizing, at least be smart about it. Don't follow women anywhere. Get an address, use your GPS, and meet them there. Stay away from the daughters of other pastors. They talk."

Blaine was so in shock that he stared past his father and looked at the giant portrait of his grandfather, Pastor B. C. Wilson Senior, that hung on the wall in his father's study. Was his father actually telling him *how* to get women? And he was too intimate with his instructions, like he used them himself.

"Dad, I don't really feel comfortable with

this conversation. I'm trying to get used to Regina being my girl, and so I'm done skirt chasing. Houston was my last hurrah."

Pastor Wilson snickered, and that grew into a full-fledged laugh. When he was done laughing he said, "Okay, okay. But when you're done turning over a new leaf, remember what I said."

Blaine ignored that and said, "Dad, we're getting a lot of invitations to other churches. I think it would be a good way to build a network for the Oklahoma City church. I might even preach a little bit when we visit. Introduce them to future Pastor Blaine Wilson. What do you think?"

"Good strategy. Talk it over with Regina and see what she thinks. Also, give me your tour dates and invitations. I'm going to have guest gospel artists on those Sundays."

"We could pull some of the choir members and have Amber teach them some songs."

Pastor Wilson shook his head. "No. We always go higher and move forward. Remember that too."

Blaine's head was spinning with all of the ministry tidbits that he was supposed to remember. He was happy that the Oklahoma City church was still a ways off, because he had so much to learn. Some of it, he had no idea he didn't know.

He didn't know what Pastor Wilson saw when he looked at the YouTube video, but Blaine knew what *he* saw. He envisioned himself on top and walking in his destiny. He was glad that Camden was in Atlanta too, so no one could say that the "sensible and wise" twin was responsible for this.

When he got on the stage, Blaine became one with the music and the microphone. It wasn't even about the rest of the group. He didn't need them. But soon everyone would be clamoring for Pastor Blaine Wilson. They'd say his name in the same sentence as Pastor Marvin Sapp.

And then he wouldn't need any of his father's rules. He'd make his own.

CHAPTER 22

Ivy had invited Camden to dinner to talk about the direction of her music. She chose a French restaurant that was one of her favorites, called Babette's Café. As soon as he had his car valet parked and stepped inside, Camden immediately felt uncomfortable.

The restaurant was very intimate and romantic, with low lighting and tables for two. It was nearly empty, which was not surprising since it was a Wednesday night. Ivy waved to him from a table near the rear of the restaurant.

As Camden approached, he noticed that Ivy had taken great care with her makeup and hair. They were both flawless. He imagined what Dawn might think if she walked into the restaurant and saw them sitting across from each other. He was glad she was in Dallas and wouldn't have to answer that question.

Ivy didn't stand but she held her arms out for a hug. Camden obliged, and in the process caught a whiff of her very sexy perfume. Forget about Dawn. What would Ivy's husband think? Camden looked over both shoulders before he sat, almost afraid that he might end up at the business end of Ivy's husband's pistol.

"Don't you just love this place?" Ivy asked as Camden sat.

He nodded. "Yes. It's somewhere I'd take my girlfriend if I wanted to propose."

"It is very romantic, isn't it? I love it for the food, though."

A waiter came by with a bottle of wine and two glasses. "Your wine, madame."

The waiter poured a small amount in each glass. Camden followed Ivy's lead and took a small sip, swished it in his mouth, and swallowed it. He had no problem drinking wine, but he just kept wondering what someone might think if they happened upon the two of them. A single musician and a very married and very gorgeous first lady sharing a glass of wine.

Ivy nodded her approval to the waiter and he filled both glasses halfway and left the bottle on the table.

"Do you like halibut?" Ivy asked.

"I'm not sure. I've never had it."

"Well, you'll be trying it tonight. I took the liberty of ordering for us."

Camden was no farm boy, but he felt unsophisticated next to Ivy. He was nervous at this meeting even though it was about music — his favorite topic.

"So, you want to do a call and response? I have one that I've been working on."

"Sing it to me."

Camden laughed. "Right here?"

"Why not? It's not like we'll be interrupting anyone."

Camden took a sip of the water on the table and cleared his throat. "Okay. It's very simple. It goes, 'When God is in the midst of two or three, when God is in the midst of two or three, when God is in the midst of two or three, chains are broken, souls redeemed."

"Sing it again."

Camden sang the few lines once again, and Ivy harmonized on the last part. It was beautiful. Their voices blended perfectly.

"Why aren't you singing with your group? Did you already tell me why?" Ivy asked. "Your voice is beautiful."

"I'm not a performer. I'm a worshipper. Every now and then I chime in, but my brother is so much better at it than I am. I walk in my gift and he walks in his."

"Well, singing is a gift that you have too. I'd like you to sing this song with me if we do it for my record."

"Really? You want me on your record?"

"Yep. It'll be *featuring* Camden Wilson. What do you think?"

"I'm honored, of course. Thank you for asking me."

Ivy gave Camden a huge smile. "When am I going to get to meet the rest of your group? Are they coming to Atlanta?"

"Soon, I think, but Royce has them doing lots of shows to promote our single. He wants his record label to really believe in our project so that we'll have a budget."

"And you don't mind being away from your girlfriend all this time?" Ivy asked.

Camden lifted one eyebrow. "I do, but it's only temporary."

"I'm sure she misses you too."

"She does. We talk every night, though."

"That's so sweet. I always wonder how men can go long periods of time away from their women. Women aren't wired the way you are, so we don't need that physical contact as much as you do."

Camden was sure that Ivy had crossed the line now. She'd probably crossed it a few questions back, but she was so far past the line now that it was a nonexistent blur.

"I'm not sure what you mean."

"You know what I mean. You're a grown man."

"I'm a grown and Christian man."

"And that means that you don't have the same needs as any other man?" Ivy asked.

"It means that I go about fulfilling those needs in accordance with God's laws."

Ivy chuckled. "Okay, I'll give you that, man of God. But what about when you step outside God's laws? We all fall short of His glory."

Camden smiled. "If and when I do something displeasing to God, I don't make it dinner conversation with a married first lady."

"Have I offended you?"

"No. I was just wondering how we went from singing a worship song to discussing my potential backsliding."

Ivy pouted. "I *have* offended you."

"I'm very hard to offend, Ivy. I promise you haven't. But can we change the subject? It does make me a little uncomfortable."

"Understood. Let's talk about my project. I have to get as much time with you as I can while Royce has you in town. You're lucky that he's not on a work spree right now. You wouldn't get a moment's rest. He's tying up some loose ends, but once he gets ready to work it's nonstop."

"I welcome that."

"So let's try to record the song we just sang sometime next week. Do you have the entire thing? Vamp and all?"

Camden said, "It is a complete song."

"Great. At least I'll have one song down before Royce goes to hogging you."

"Sounds like a plan."

"So, let me ask you something. This is something I ask everyone in Royce's circle. What did you think of him when you first met him?"

"I . . . um . . ."

Ivy covered her mouth to hold her laughter in. Then she said, "Okay, let me tell you what I thought when I first met him. I first thought he was gay. Then I thought he was just strange."

"I didn't think he was gay," Camden said. "I definitely didn't get that vibe. But I noticed his makeup. And his blouse."

Tears rolled down Ivy's face as she laughed. "His blouses! Oh man. He is hilarious with those blouses. He says he's a trendsetter. I tell him it's a trend only if other people do it too."

"Yeah, he's all by himself with those blouses."

Ivy caught her breath and exhaled. "His

makeup is a necessity, though. He has very bad acne, or he used to. He's got scars all over his face. Since someone always has a camera in his face, he started wearing the makeup because he was self-conscious."

"I'm actually glad to hear that's the reason," Camden said. "It makes sense and isn't feminine at all."

"I thought you said you didn't think he was gay."

"I didn't, but that doesn't mean I didn't find that makeup womanly."

Ivy said, "Please don't tell him I asked you that question."

"As long as you don't tell him what I thought about his blouse."

"Deal."

Camden felt himself relax with Ivy, and he was glad that he'd finally made a friend in Atlanta besides Royce. Especially one who was the first lady of a megachurch. She could be very instrumental in helping to make his dreams come true. It didn't hurt that she was beautiful and funny. He almost regretted that she was married, but immediately chided himself. He *was* taken, even if he didn't have a ring on his finger. Camden just had to make sure that he and everyone else remembered that fact.

CHAPTER 23

Pastor Wilson never called special meetings of the church board unless there was some scandal that needed fixing or he had some special announcement that he wanted to share. Blaine hoped that it was the latter and not the former since he and Regina were in attendance. His father's lecture about his fun in Houston was still fresh, and he definitely didn't want the entire church board to know about it.

Blaine looked around the table. Every member of the church board was one hundred percent on his father's team. Delores, Stephen, Assistant Pastor Brennan, his mother, and several of the deacons. These meetings were almost a joke because there was never a vote that wasn't unanimous.

"Thank you all for taking time out of your busy schedules to meet with me. I don't typically call these meetings in the middle of the week unless I have something crucial to share with you. And this time is no different."

Pastor Wilson paused and looked at every person in the room. Blaine guessed he was giving them the opportunity to speak up before he went on a long tangent. Kind of like when a person goes to the bathroom before a movie starts. There'd be no interruptions once Pastor Wilson got going.

"I'm sure you have heard about the great feedback Blaine and the rest of our praise team has been getting on their new single, 'Born to Worship.' I believe that we should strike while the iron is hot and get Blaine launched into ministry at this Oklahoma City location."

"Do we have word on getting the loan approved for the building?" Pastor Brennan asked.

Pastor Wilson nodded. "We do. It's approved. And in the interim we are going to rent a convention center. We're going to do a huge marketing push over the last two weeks of July to let people know that Graceway is coming to Oklahoma City. Then, for the month of August, I will preach every Sunday at the Oklahoma City location. The first Sunday in September, Blaine will take over."

Blaine blinked rapidly and felt his chest

tighten. Was that anxiety? He'd spoken in church before and even preached for small occasions, but never on a Sunday morning. He thought he'd have more time than this to get used to the idea of being a pastor. It was already the middle of June. That didn't give him much time at all to get his life together.

Regina looked as if she wanted to burst from excitement, which irritated Blaine even further. She was just too thrilled at the thought of being called First Lady.

"What about the fact that Blaine isn't married?" Stephen asked. "Isn't that important? Part of the initial strategy was to have him married off first before he took to the pulpit."

Initial strategy? Blaine was furious that Stephen's thirsty self was in on any strategy at all. No one asked him, and he definitely didn't have a say on when, where, or who Blaine was going to marry.

"I'm not rushing into an arranged marriage just to fit your timeline or strategy," Blaine said.

Pastor Wilson frowned. "No one is rushing you, son. I'm sure Regina doesn't want to rush either. The marriage doesn't have to happen prior to your installation."

Stephen cleared his throat and shifted in

his seat.

"Do you have something to say, Stephen?" Blaine asked. "You seem to have something on your mind."

Stephen made eye contact with Pastor Wilson and then looked at Blaine. "No, I have nothing, Junior Pastor."

Regina and Pastor Brennan chuckled, while First Lady Rita closed her eyes tightly as if she was waiting for the aftermath.

"You can be dismissed from this meeting," Blaine said. "We don't need you here to make any decisions."

Stephen looked again at Pastor Wilson for confirmation. He shrugged. "You heard what he said, Stephen. You can wait outside for me in my car."

"But . . ."

"Blaine is going to be the senior pastor of the Oklahoma City church. You'll respect him as such. If he doesn't feel comfortable with you here, I respect his wishes. That goes for anyone else."

Stephen's face was red with embarrassment. He stood from his seat and rushed out of the room, but not before giving Blaine a glare that could kill everyone in the room if looks had that power.

Once the door shut behind Stephen, Pastor Wilson said, "Make sure you mend fences with Stephen. He's angry, but he needs to learn his place in the Oklahoma City hierarchy. In the new church, the only one who will trump your decisions is me."

"Yes sir," Blaine said.

"So, the wedding is on hold?" Regina asked.

"We're not even engaged yet," Blaine said. "It will continue to progress, but I don't want it to look like a shotgun wedding. People will be suspicious."

Regina looked at Pastor Wilson and said, "We may need to renegotiate some of the terms of our agreement, then. I would like to add a runaway groom clause."

Blaine cracked a smile. "Runaway groom? Maybe you need to make sure I don't run."

"Please, Blaine. Nobody has time for your shenanigans."

"This sounds like a personal conversation," Delores said. "What action items do we have as the board?"

"We need you to create bylaws and the same accounting structure that we have for our Dallas location. For the first few years, we'll funnel the Oklahoma church financials through the Dallas church. We'll pay all of the church expenses and Blaine's salary out of our accounts. We'll purchase a parsonage in the church's name for Blaine and Regina to live in."

Regina's eyes widened. "When can we go house shopping?"

"Delores will get with you on that, Regina," Pastor Wilson said. "Blaine has more tour dates this summer, though, so you may not have time to do this the way you want to. You may move into a furnished home."

First Lady Rita said, "And where does Camden fall in all of this? Will he be the Minister of Music at the Oklahoma City location?"

"I would like that," Blaine said. "That way So G.I.F.T.E.D can stay together."

Pastor Wilson's expression darkened. "Camden is no longer employed by this ministry. He chose this. He won't be at either church location. He can stay in Atlanta if he wants to."

"You will not shut my son out of this, B. C."

Pastor Wilson laughed out loud. "He shut himself out. I want what is best for the ministry. He wants to be a music star. We're on different pages. What does the Word say? How can two walk together unless they agree?"

"You're his father."

"And he's in my will. Moving right along."

First Lady Rita stood up and stormed out

of the conference room and slammed the door.

"That's two. Anyone else want to leave?" Pastor Wilson asked. "Damon, will you get me a glass of bourbon? They are stressing me out this evening."

Pastor Brennan scrambled from his seat to do what Pastor Wilson asked.

"Get Blaine one too," Pastor Wilson said. "He's gonna need it."

That sounded like a prophecy of doom and gloom. Blaine hoped this ministry wouldn't lead him to drink. Or his marriage to Regina. The thought of the rest of his life with her controlling and pestering self was more threatening than standing in the pulpit in front of thousands of people.

"Can you make that a double?" Blaine asked.

CHAPTER 24

It was the first Sunday Camden visited Ivy and her husband's church. They'd invited him into the musician's booth because while he was in Atlanta, he would serve as a backup keyboard player and worship leader. Even though he missed the musicians in Dallas, he was looking forward to this new crew — even if it was only temporary.

Camden hadn't forgotten that his father told him he couldn't come back to his position at Graceway, but he hoped that after So G.I.F.T.E.D topped the charts, he'd have a change of heart. The only thing that really mattered to his father was making his bank account grow, so if So G.I.F.T.E.D was successful, all would probably be water under the bridge.

Royce led the praise team, which was basically his group, Spirited, with a few others added. Camden had never seen praise and worship like this. The entire church participated. It was like a gospel concert.

By the time Dr. Whitlowe got up to preach, the congregation was good and amped. They Hallelujah'ed and amen'ed through the entire service.

Camden loved how Dr. Whitlowe did the church's offering. There was no guilt tripping the congregation, and no promises of a supernatural breakthrough. He told the church what they needed, and they gave. It was simple, and refreshing.

After service, Royce introduced Camden to Dr. Whitlowe.

"I really enjoyed service! You brought the Word, Dr. Whitlowe!" Camden said.

"Man, first of all, call me Norman. I feel like we're brothers. Your father has been such a mentor to me. And I take that as a compliment for real. Your father is one of the most talented preachers in the country."

Camden grinned without replying to that. It was hard for him to hear compliments about his father because he knew too much of what happened behind the scenes with him. But Pastor Wilson was well respected in ministry circles, so Camden listened without making comments.

Ivy walked up to the men and hugged Camden. It made Camden a little uncomfortable that she hugged him so tightly in front of her husband, but when she released the embrace Norman didn't seem to mind.

"Have brunch with us, Cam! We can let everybody hear the music we've been working on," Ivy said.

"You two have been in the studio already?" Royce asked.

"It was just a jam session," Camden said. "We haven't recorded anything yet."

"I'm trying to get a piece of Camden before you totally monopolize all his time." Royce laughed. "Because you know that's coming."

"I absolutely know that's coming, Royce. I know you!" Ivy said.

"Well, let's hear this music at brunch, then," Royce said. "I'm excited to hear what y'all came up with."

Ivy and her husband went to talk to some of their congregation members, leaving Royce and Camden in the pulpit area.

Royce said, "I see Ivy has sunk her hooks into you."

"She has? I thought we were just working on some music," Camden said.

"She's a charmer. She'll have you producing an entire record before you know it."

"Why aren't you producing her new music?"

Royce laughed. "Because Ivy doesn't want

to pay my producer rates. I love her, but it's all business on that front. I have paying customers and my own group."

"So you think she's just being nice to me for my music?"

"Maybe not, but I will definitely say that is a motivation. Ivy has plans to stay on top of the gospel industry. You're hot right now. 'Born to Worship' is in the top ten on Billboard Gospel, so get ready."

"I really want to get started on your project."

"Me too," Royce said. "But I have to be led of the Holy Spirit. I wait for God to reveal the direction of the music and then I go forward. I told you it might be a year or more. You in a hurry to get back?"

Camden thought about the way he'd left things at home and sighed. "No. I'm not in a hurry. Not at all."

At Norman and Ivy's brunch, there were several members of Spirited and some of the members of their church. The way Ivy fussed over the preparations, she reminded Camden of his mother, except Ivy cooked her own food instead of hiring a caterer.

Camden wandered into the kitchen while everyone mingled through the rest of the house. He leaned on the wall and watched Ivy stir a huge pot of grits. Her friend was flipping pancakes on a huge pancake skillet.

Ivy looked up and noticed Camden. She smiled and threw an apron at him from the counter.

"Wash your hands and help. Don't just stand there watching."

Since it seemed more like a command than a request, Camden did as he was told and washed his hands. Before he could refuse, Ivy had him cutting up fruit on a cutting board.

"I don't cook, you know," Camden said. "I just got finished telling my girlfriend that she needs to ask my mother to teach her to cook before I propose."

"She doesn't know how to cook? These young girls out here are not prepared to be wives but are always trying to get a ring," Ivy said.

"You're not that much older than us."

"Yeah, but it's almost like I was raised in a different millennium or something. I've been patting out biscuits since I was eight years old. Making chicken and dumplings from scratch since before I graduated from high school."

"Chicken and dumplings? That's my favorite."

"I'll have to cook you some, then."

Norman walked into the kitchen and burst

into laughter when he saw Camden wearing an apron. He reached over and stole a piece of bacon, earning him a slap from Ivy.

"I should've warned you not to get near the kitchen," Norman said. "You see how everyone else stayed far away?"

"Yeah, nobody had my back and looked out for me," Camden said. "I got caught in the cooking trap."

"A man who cooks is sexy, Camden," Ivy said. "Don't let my husband take that away from you. Your girlfriend would be proud."

Norman lifted his eyebrows. "Girlfriend back home in Dallas?"

"Yes. We've been together for a long time," Camden said.

"That's good. I'm all about young love. You know Ivy was my first love. Did she tell you the story of how we met?"

"No, she didn't."

"Well, this was before Royce was my worship leader. We invited him and his group to lead service one Sunday, and Ivy was there. She didn't even sing, but commandeered our church kitchen to make sure the entire group had something to eat between services. She fried chicken and made macaroni and cheese. I hadn't eaten that good since I left my mama's house."

Ivy laughed. "He wasn't even invited to

eat with us. He crashed our lunch."

"How does a pastor crash a meal being eaten in his church?" Norman asked. "You were supposed to make me a plate off the top and set it to the side."

"Humph!" Ivy said as she sprinkled cheese into her pot of grits. "Get out of here before you wind up in an apron too."

After a few final touches, Ivy started bringing platters of food into the dining room. She directed Camden on where to place the numerous trays and dishes.

When they were done she said, "Norman! Come bless the food!"

At the long dining room table, there was more eating going on than talking because the food was all that and more.

After devouring an entire plate of food, Camden said, "I was going to send my girl to my mom to get some cooking lessons, but I think she needs to come to you. My mom can definitely throw down in the kitchen, but I've never eaten like this in my life."

"Told you!" Norman said. "She'll have you looking like Professor Klump."

"I don't want that," Camden said. "Can somebody pass that bread pudding?"

Everyone at the table laughed as Camden continued to stuff his face to contentment.

As the meal died down, Ivy jumped up from her seat and clapped.

"I hope Camden didn't eat too much because I want you all to hear this song that we've been working on."

Ivy pulled Camden away from his plate and everyone, walking in a food-induced haze, followed them into Ivy's piano room.

"The name of this song is 'Two or Three,' and it is a worship song. After y'all get the words, you can sing with us."

"Camden is singing?" Royce asked.

He nodded. "She wanted to do this as a duet. I'm trying to get her to record it alone."

"That's nonsense. When you hear him singing with me, you'll want to record right away. Camden's voice is incredible."

Camden began to play the introduction to the song. When Ivy's vocals came in, loud and pure, Camden's voice was only there as an accessory to hers. By the time they got to the vamp, there wasn't a dry eye in the room.

"Wow," Norman said when they were done. "They weren't lying about you being anointed, man. I can see why Royce brought you here."

"I believe God sends me on musical reconnaissance missions, and he definitely

209

did that with Camden and his group. Did y'all hear that their single is number two on the Billboard Gospel chart right now? That is phenomenal for a brand-new group."

"I hadn't even heard that," Camden said. "Will you all excuse me while I go and make a phone call?"

"Yes, of course," Ivy said. "You can use my library."

Camden stepped inside the library and called Blaine.

"Did y'all hear? Number two!" Camden said.

"You know we heard, man! You're the one kicking it in Atlanta. We're here grinding our butts off doing these shows. We're watching the charts every day."

"I wish I was kicking it. I'm working too. Just did a song for Ivy Whitlowe."

Blaine smacked his lips like he was eating barbecue. "Ivy Whitlowe is a fine redbone. You hit?"

"Seriously?"

"I'm kidding. I know you're monogamous."

"And you aren't, Pastor Wilson?" Camden asked.

"Pray for me, Cam. This is hard, but I have to. Dad wants to launch the Oklahoma City church in August."

"August? Why so soon? Are you ready?"

"No, but I don't think I have a choice."

Camden was sure Blaine didn't have a choice. The Oklahoma City location was their father's vision. No one would be able to change his mind if he had decided.

"Is Dad still tripping about me being here?"

Blaine paused for a long time. Long enough for Camden to guess the answer.

"You know he'll come around at some point," Blaine finally said. "He just hates being defied. If he doesn't change his mind, you can come to my church."

My church. Camden didn't miss how Blaine had already stepped into that role.

"Right. Well, tell everybody I said hi."

"Or you could call and tell them yourself."

Ivy peeked into the library. "Everything okay in here?" she whispered.

Camden nodded. "I'll be out in a second."

Instead of leaving the library, Ivy closed the door behind her and held one finger up to his lips to shush him. Camden gave her a confused look, but she only smiled.

"Okay, Blaine. I'll call everybody. I gotta go."

Camden disconnected the call. Ivy was in his personal space. He was very uncomfortable with how close she was standing. Their bodies nearly touched.

"What's up?" Camden asked.

"Nothing," Ivy said in a throaty whisper. "I was just checking on you to see if you were okay."

"I am."

"I'm not."

Before Camden could stop her, Ivy had pressed her body against his and kissed his neck. Camden took two big steps back, and Ivy fell against the library shelf.

"Why'd you move?" Ivy asked.

Camden's face was furious. "Why would you do that? Your husband is downstairs."

"Shh!"

"Ivy, please don't ever put me in that position again," Camden said.

Ivy smiled mischievously. "What position do you want me to put you in?"

"You're joking. You think this is funny. I don't. You've disrespected me."

"You have got to be joking. I don't know a man alive who would feel disrespected when a beautiful woman comes on to him. Well, yes I do. But they're all gay."

Camden shook his head. "Then you don't know too many saved men."

Ivy pouted. "All right, all right. I guess I misread your signals. I thought the feelings were mutual. After our jam session, I believed you were as attracted to me as I am to you."

"You're attractive, but you belong to someone else. I honor that, and your husband."

"Unfortunately," Ivy said with an eye roll. "Let me sneak back downstairs. You can come down later. This can be our secret, okay?"

Camden shook his head as Ivy left him standing in the library, his neck still tingling from her uninvited kiss. Camden replayed his and Ivy's interactions, wondering what had made her think he was open to romancing another man's wife. Even if he didn't have Dawn back in Dallas, he wouldn't be open to that. Camden silently praised God that it wasn't Blaine in the same position. He couldn't say that Ivy's virtue would've been safe — in fact, it probably would've been forever tarnished.

That made him wonder how Blaine was going to survive running an entire church. Or how the church was going to survive him. Especially the beautiful and single women. They were in a world of trouble.

Camden considered the offer to be the Minister of Music in Oklahoma City. Maybe it wasn't such a bad idea for him to be at Blaine's side. Then Blaine could have someone he'd be able to trust, and Camden could protect the women's virtue.

CHAPTER 25

Blaine touched one hand to the veins bulging at his temple — a result of Regina's constant badgering. She'd caught wind of his and Akil's extracurricular activities in Houston and had proceeded with an interrogation. She was ten minutes in with no end in sight. Blaine wanted to kick her out of his apartment, but he was almost sure she'd fight him like a dude in the street.

"I'm not stupid, Blaine. I know you well. Don't forget that I used to date you. I know what you are capable of."

"How can I forget when you keep reminding me every five minutes?"

Regina stopped her pacing back and forth across his hardwood floors and put one hand on her hip. "Really? How about you keep reminding me? Every chance you get you are in some ho's face. I'm so sick of you."

"Well, you can step, then," Blaine said.

"My father thinks I need you, I don't."

"If it wasn't for your father and his deep pockets, I *would* step. You don't think you need me, but you're a complete mess. You'd never survive being a pastor."

Blaine knew that Regina wasn't going anywhere. Especially not since Pastor Wilson had told them that the Oklahoma City church was happening sooner than they thought.

"I will survive without you. With another beautiful and capable woman. She'll get to live in the parsonage and go on first lady shopping sprees. And hopefully she'll be a lot less annoying than you are."

Regina lifted her hand as if she wanted to slap Blaine and he burst into laughter.

"You don't really want to do that," Blaine said. "You're not that tough. Plus, it wouldn't be good for the ministry if the pastor went to jail on domestic violence charges."

"You won't hit me back."

"You come at me like a man, you get treated like a man."

Regina slowly lowered her hand. "Blaine, I'm not going to be married to someone who cheats on me. Your father told me you were trying to change."

"I am trying to change, but it's a process.

Here's some honesty. Yes, I did get with that girl in Houston. That's the truth. I didn't plan it. It just happened."

"It just happened."

"Yes, and I will try very hard not to make it happen again, but I can't promise you that."

"Just don't lie to me, Blaine."

He nodded. "Okay. I won't. But try to be my friend and be patient with me. I know I'm a whore. I like sex. A lot. And I like women. A lot."

Defeated, Regina sat down on the couch next to Blaine. "Will I ever be enough for you?"

"Yes, I think so. When we get married we can figure out how to spice things up in the bedroom. You can wear wigs and costumes so I can feel like I'm with a different woman every time."

"Why do we have to wait until we're married? It's not like you haven't already sampled the goods."

Blaine lifted his eyebrows in surprise. "You serious?"

"Yeah. You have a show in Miami soon. Those groupies there are on a whole other level. I want you to know what you have."

Blaine remembered Regina's mediocrity in the bedroom. He didn't know if she'd be able to bring it well enough to erase his need for other women.

"Last time we were together, you were pretty virginal. Am I gonna have to do all the work?"

"You *were* my first, Blaine. But not my last. I've learned some things since then."

"Is that so? Well, why don't you come over here and show Daddy what you learned?"

Regina pulled Blaine's face toward hers and kissed him deeply, and Blaine forgot all about their argument. Maybe Regina couldn't make Blaine give up all the other women forever, but in that moment, he was only thinking of her lips on his. And her hand in his lap, proving that she had indeed had a tutor.

"Maybe we shouldn't," Regina said after a long and drawn-out kiss.

"We're getting married, Gina. So, it's fine."

Her face lit up. "You called me Gina. You've never shortened my name before."

"Well, maybe I'm sick of talking."

Blaine pulled her into his lap with every intent to finish what she started.

CHAPTER 26

Camden watched the YouTube video over and over again and still couldn't believe his eyes. Ivy had been tagged by a roving reporter at a Praise and Worship workshop in Atlanta, and the interviewer had inquired about Camden. Camden didn't think he'd angered her when he'd rebuffed her advances. He'd done it kindly. But scorn dripped from her responses.

Camden noticed that the video had close to two hundred thousand views. That was more than the number of downloads they'd gotten for "Born to Worship" so far, and that was a hit record. People apparently wanted to hear gossip more than they wanted the gospel. Camden clicked play one more time.

Dr. Rae: So there's an interesting dynamic that's happening in gospel music right now. You're right at the cusp of it.

219

Ivy: I am. I feel so blessed to have had Royce London pull me out of obscurity like he did. I wouldn't be a part of this if it weren't for him. I am eternally grateful to his following the leading of the Lord.

Dr. Rae: Royce London is such an eccentric man of God.

Ivy: (laughs) That's a way to put it. Eccentric.

Dr. Rae: Well, how would you put it? He travels with an entourage of men with questionable sexuality.

Ivy: Royce is happily married, and I've only ever known him to honor his wife. He is not gay.

Dr. Rae: Yes, but the young men around him are not as honorable. What about his newest addition, Camden Wilson out of Dallas? We're hearing great things about him musically, but his personal life is also ambiguous. He's apparently engaged to a woman back in Dallas that he's known his whole life.

Ivy: You've done your research, huh? I don't like to gossip about people. I like to stick to ministry. Camden is very anointed in ministry.

Dr. Rae: But you don't know if he's a homosexual.

Ivy: I don't know if I like your line of

questioning. I thought we were going to talk about my upcoming project.

Dr. Rae: Tell me about your project.

Ivy: I just recorded a song written by Camden Wilson, and Royce is producing, of course.

Dr. Rae: So you're not going to answer the question.

Ivy: I can't say what that man does when he leaves my presence. I barely know him.

Dr. Rae: But you can speak definitively on Royce.

Ivy: Royce is my friend. Camden is a new associate. Can we talk about the project now?

Camden stopped the video. He didn't need to hear the rest of it again. He didn't want to listen to Ivy promote the music they'd been working so hard to produce, only to slay his character. Of course, no one could say that she initiated the conversation, but she definitely didn't do anything to refute the claims.

Camden's phone buzzed on the table next to his laptop. He had a text message from Amber. *You need to call Dawn. She's spazzing out. #emergency*

Camden was dreading that conversation. He didn't want to talk to her about this because it was stupid. He wasn't gay. End of story. The fact that she was spazzing out irritated him, though.

Camden sighed and dialed her number. Dawn picked up on the first ring.

"Cam. Have you *seen* this YouTube mess? I thought you said Ivy was a good person. I thought you said she was a friend."

Her words rushed out like the flow of water when the faucet is turned on at full blast.

"She didn't really say anything."

"Exactly. She just let them say all of those horrible things about you."

"I don't know what she could've done to stop them."

"She could've said it wasn't true!" Dawn yelled. "It's not true, right?"

Camden wanted to hurl the phone across the room. How could she even ask him that? She was the woman he was planning to marry and she was questioning his sexuality?

"You didn't just ask me that question, Dawn."

"I just want . . . I guess if it were true . . . that would explain why you don't want me."

Camden's breath caught in his throat. For a few moments he couldn't reply. He could just hold the phone and stare straight ahead.

"Camden, did I lose you?"

Finally, he responded. "No. I just. I can't talk to you right now."

"Wait! Wait. Don't hang up. I'm sorry! I'm confused about us, Camden. If we could only get engaged for real, and get married, then I wouldn't feel this way."

"Yeah, I feel really motivated to marry a woman who's known me for almost two decades and just asked me if I'm gay. I will call you later."

"I love you, Camden."

Camden didn't reply. He disconnected the call and slammed the phone down on the table. Maybe his father was right. Maybe he should've never come to Atlanta. Maybe he wasn't man enough to handle the responsibility.

There was a light knock on his door. Camden got up to answer it and it was Royce. He held up his smartphone with the screen capture of the YouTube video on the screen.

"I should've warned you about Ivy," Royce said. "But I thought she'd changed. No . . . let me take that back. I thought she was still enamored with me. I never thought she'd go after you."

"Well, she did, and now she's giving interviews and letting people think I'm gay."

Royce said, "If you're going to be in this industry, you have to get a thicker skin. Gospel artists get accused of being gay all the time. If I let that bother me, I wouldn't have the happy home that I have."

"Well, your wife doesn't believe the rumors. That helps."

"Your girlfriend does?"

Camden shrugged. "I don't know. She just asked me if I'm gay, so what do you think?"

Royce whistled through tightened lips. "I think you need a new girlfriend. It doesn't sound like she's built for the gospel industry."

"I don't know. I'm starting to feel that way. I can't believe she came at me like that."

"Well, you're not there, and she's probably worried. Why don't you do something to put her mind at ease? Bring her here for a visit. I'll pay for the flight."

"Thank you! I think we need the time together!"

Royce nodded. "All right. Get ready, because we've got a practice tonight. We have a big show at the House of Blues on Sunday. We'll be performing some of the tracks on Ivy's new record."

"Ivy's going to be here tonight?"

"Yeah. You gotta face her at some point.

Tell her she was wrong. She needs to hear that."

Royce's advice was welcome, but Camden didn't know if he'd be able to control his anger long enough to have a conversation with Ivy.

CHAPTER 27

When So G.I.F.T.E.D landed in Miami, Blaine got a whiff of the ocean air and felt exhilarated. He was, of course, excited about the concert, but he was more amped about the women he and Akil were going to see on South Beach.

The way he saw it, this was his last time to have any fun. Pastor Wilson had already started his marketing for Oklahoma City, and everything was on track to open the first Sunday in August. Even if Pastor Wilson was preaching the first four Sundays, Blaine needed to be above reproach. Which meant no women.

Their hotel was incredible. Pastor Wilson had sprung for an upgrade at the conference hotel, and they had two suites, one for the girls and one for the guys. Luckily, Blaine had convinced Regina to stay in Dallas and help her future father-in-law with marketing the new church and locating their home. Since they were having sex on a regular basis now, Regina felt a little more secure.

Fortunately for Blaine, Regina's instincts were completely off.

Everyone was excited about the hotel suites, except Dawn. She wasn't joyful about anything since that YouTube video about Camden hit the Internet.

"Y'all want to go to the beach?" Akil asked. "We don't sing until tomorrow afternoon, so we have plenty of time."

"What? We're getting invited out by the manwhores?" Amber asked. "Isn't that like taking sand to the beach?"

Blaine said, "It is. But I'm a changed man. I'm about to be a pastor. I can walk South Beach without ogling women. It's about the sand and the water."

Amber stared at Blaine and burst into laughter. "Shut up, boy! You might be able to sell that to your future bride, but I ain't buying it. What about you, Dawn?"

"I believe him. He's got to settle down at some point. Why not now?"

"Okay, clearly your judgment is a little cloudy lately. You're walking around in an I-think-my-man-is-gay haze."

"I'm not," Dawn said.

"And Camden ain't gay," Akil said.

Blaine didn't have any comment on the rumors about Camden. He honestly wasn't sure if the rumors were true or not. Camden had turned down so much quality booty over the years that it wasn't all that far-fetched to think maybe he was batting for the other team. It would be horrible if he was, and Blaine hoped and prayed that it wasn't true, but he wasn't going to be the one to reassure Dawn.

"It's okay," Dawn said. "I know it's not true, so I don't know what y'all are talking about. I do miss him, though. He doesn't call enough."

"He's working on a Royce London project," Amber said. "You know that he's got to be incredibly busy. I'm sure it has nothing to do with you."

"He did say he was going to fly me to Atlanta to spend some time with him when we get back from Miami."

"Awww . . . couple time. I love it. One day I'm gonna get a man," Amber said.

Amber pulled a swimsuit out of her bag and held it up. There was not a lot of material there. It actually looked like two handkerchiefs and some rubber bands.

Akil said, "I hope that has a cover-up."

"No, Gramps, it does not. My produce needs some bronzing. Where better than

South Beach? Y'all go get changed, and meet us back here in like twenty minutes. Then we can take over the beach."

Blaine and Akil left the girls and went into their own suite. They had a view of the beach through the big floor-to-ceiling windows.

"This is the bomb, for real. When we blow up all the way, we're gonna travel like this all the time, I bet," Akil said.

Blaine nodded in agreement. He couldn't believe that he was in a room like this without a woman. This was not a homeboys suite, it was a love nest.

"Are you really serious about giving up the women?" Akil asked.

"Shouldn't I be? I'm about to be a senior pastor in a few weeks."

Akil laughed out loud. "I ask because you hadn't experienced your epiphany in Houston. You had a good time with those country girls."

"I did," Blaine said. He bit his lip at the memory. "But I promised Regina that I was going to try to change. So, this weekend, I plan to look and not touch."

"You plan?"

"I never make promises, man. You know that."

Akil laughed. "Do you want me to try and

stop you if something goes down? I can run interference if you want."

"I'll give you a signal. If I want you to stop me, I'll say the word 'grace' in a sentence. If I don't think there's a danger or I don't want to stop, I won't say anything."

"Okay. The wingman is on the job."

Blaine nodded. "I'm gonna miss you, man. Come to Oklahoma with me."

"Maybe."

"That's all I'm getting?" Blaine asked.

"No promises, right?"

"Okay. Gotcha. Let's get changed so we can hit the beach while we've got some daylight left."

Blaine and Akil quickly got into their swimming trunks and water T-shirts. Blaine wanted to wear something that would transition from the beach to the bar. Hopefully he wouldn't run into too many other gospel artists there.

After they got dressed, Blaine and Akil went back to the girls' room. When Blaine saw Amber's swimsuit, his jaw dropped. Her produce was on display.

"Okay, I'm with Akil. You need to cover some of that up," Blaine said.

"I have a cover-up," Amber said.

She pulled on an almost sheer jacket that

didn't hide anything. Then she slipped on a pretty pair of flip-flops.

"Let's go," Amber said. "And y'all can stop looking at me like that. Ain't neither one of y'all my daddy."

Blaine shook his head at Amber as Dawn walked out of the bedroom. When Blaine saw Dawn's outfit, not only did his jaw drop again, his eyes bucked out of his head. Akil's too.

"Don't look at me like that. I'm already self-conscious," Dawn said.

Blaine couldn't remember ever seeing Dawn's curves on full display. In fact, he had always regarded her as kind of frumpy. Clearly, that impression was only because of the clothes she wore. Dawn was anything but frumpy.

She reminded Blaine of a video vixen or pinup girl in one of those hip-hop magazines. Her full and heavy breasts strained against the bikini top and her round bottom and curvy hips filled out the bikini bottom. There wasn't an ounce of fat on her either. Her waist was tiny and the curves were in all the right places.

Blaine cleared his throat. "Um, you need a cover-up too, Dawn. I can't look at you looking like that all day."

Dawn grinned. "Does that mean it looks good?"

"You're my brother's girl. I'm not saying if you look good or not. Put some more clothes on."

Dawn seemed to perk up as she put on a sarong that wrapped around the lower half of her body. Her top half remained uncovered, but it was enough to make Blaine's heart stop beating so fast.

They took the elevator downstairs and headed straight to the beach. The girls took off running toward the water and the guys hung back, taking in the sights.

There were beautiful women everywhere. It was a manwhore's playground. Blaine had no doubt that he was going to slip up at least once, and maybe more than once this weekend.

"You know someone told my dad about what we did in Houston," Blaine said to Akil.

"What? How did they know? I thought we were careful."

"We were. I think my dad has spies all over the place. He gave me some tips on how to creep and not get caught."

Akil frowned. "I need my pastor not to have creeping tips."

"Please! I need my *father* not to have

232

creeping tips. Especially when he's stepping out on my mama."

"Who you think he's hooking up with? You think the rumors about Delores are true?"

Blaine kicked some sand into the air and sighed. "Yeah. They're true."

"Would you ever tell your mother?"

"No! Camden might, if he had proof. But I wouldn't."

"You always seemed closer to your father anyway. I would hate to be caught in the middle of something like that."

Blaine did hate being caught between his parents. He would never betray his father about Delores, and it didn't matter if he did, because he was sure that his mother was fully aware of what was going on. Blaine wondered if Regina would be like that too, or if she would demand that he be one hundred percent faithful. The thought of it made Blaine's heart rate increase as if he was having a panic attack.

He had to admit, though, that Regina had definitely improved her bedroom skills since the first time they dated. He wondered how much practice she'd had and who with. She'd rocked his world a few times, which was pretty strange. It was usually Blaine who did the world rocking.

"I am closer to my father," Blaine said

after snapping out of his memory of Regina. "Camden is my mother's favorite. He's almost like her daughter."

"Ooh!" Akil said. "You wrong for that."

"I'm just saying. That Royce dude is absolutely suspect, and he's got Camden living up in his house. Like maybe Camden said something or did something that let Royce know he was on the other team."

"That's your twin, Blaine. Don't you think you'd know?" Akil asked. "Has he ever done anything that would make you think that he's gay?"

Blaine looked up at Dawn and Amber, who had shed their cover-ups and were frolicking in the water. His mouth watered at the sight of Dawn and he looked away.

"He's never slipped up with Dawn," Blaine said. "I didn't know she was holding like that. How could he *not* have tapped that, as badly as she wants it?"

Akil tilted his head to one side. "Yeah, she is banging. But maybe he just wants to protect her. You know she's a virgin, right?"

"If you ask me, she's past ripe."

Akil shook his head. "Man . . ."

"Nah, I would never do it. I just think that Camden is gonna lose her if he doesn't decide to make that official. As soon as she figures out that she doesn't have to wait for him, he might be in trouble."

"I think you're right about that. He better wife her soon."

At dusk, Blaine, Akil, Amber, and Dawn had grown tired of the beach and found a nice restaurant for dinner. They'd chosen it because of the expensive dining options and because Pastor Wilson had given Blaine a credit card to use for their food. They were going to live it up on his dime.

"I think I want the biggest steak on the menu," Akil said. "And a lobster tail. Gotta do seafood at the beach."

"I want one of those big pretty drinks with an umbrella in it," Amber said.

"You think you should?" Dawn asked. "What if someone sees you?"

Amber shrugged. "Jesus turned water to wine. Do you think he would actually be leading folk to drink if it was a sin?"

"Right, like our Lord and savior would be entrapping folk," Blaine said. "The Bible talks against drunkenness. One drink with an umbrella isn't going to send her to hell."

"So, is that what you're going to tell people over your pulpit?" Dawn asked. "That Oklahoma City congregation is about to be crunk!"

They all laughed, but Blaine considered

235

her words. "You know," he said, "I will probably tell them to follow the leading of the Holy Spirit. Not everyone can handle every vice. For some, alcohol will lead them to a pit, but for others, it's a pretty woman. I guess everyone has to know their own weaknesses and seek out their own soul's salvation."

Akil, Amber, and Dawn all gave Blaine blank stares. He started laughing. "Y'all act like I can't do this pastor thing. Like really? I've been ministering for years when we sing."

"It's just that what you said was really wise," Dawn said. "I didn't expect you to be wise."

"Thank you for the vote of confidence!" Blaine said.

"Boy bye!" Amber said. "We been knowing each other forever and she's just keeping it real, Blainesky. I'm glad you've got some skills, 'cause some of the people that are gonna walk through those church doors . . ."

"Right," Akil said. "They're going to need something real. I think you can do it, though."

Blaine said, "So, what do y'all think about leaving Dallas and coming to Oklahoma City too? I already asked Akil and he's on the fence. Maybe if everybody comes, he'll want to come too."

"I would have to ask Camden," Dawn said. "We may end up in Atlanta for all I know."

"That's true. Do you want to move to Atlanta?" Amber asked.

"I haven't really thought about it. I would miss Dallas."

The waitress came to the table to take their orders. She was a cutie for sure. She gave Blaine a dimpled smile that melted his heart. She looked like she should be on the cover of a magazine or in a movie.

"What would you all like? I'll start with the ladies."

Amber said, "I will take the summer crab cake salad, but no strawberries. I'm allergic. And I'll also have the piña colada. With two umbrellas."

"I will have the seafood boil and a Coke," Dawn said.

The guys ordered their expensive steak dinners and drinks too. Blaine watched the pretty waitress as she walked away. Dawn and Amber laughed out loud.

"You're mesmerized," Amber said. "I'm glad Regina isn't here because she would've punched that girl out."

"She would've," Dawn said.

"I didn't do anything. I just looked at her. God is the one who made her look like that. I think that she's a gift to the Body of Christ."

"What if she's not a Christian?" Akil asked.

"Then she's a gift to the body of Blaine. Or she could be."

Amber rolled her eyes. "He went from wisdom to hodom. That was quick."

"Well, we need to start one of those round-the-clock prayer wheels for him," Dawn said. "The church mothers love that kind of thing. Then maybe he could get delivered of his ho spirit."

"Or maybe he can go to the tarrying room and the mothers can have one of those cast-the-ho-spirit-out sessions. Remember they did that with that stripper who joined the church?" Akil said.

"That was crazy. That poor girl ran right back to the strip club! They scared her to death," Blaine said.

"Did you get her number before she left?" Amber asked.

"I'm shocked and appalled that you would even ask me that," Blaine said.

"Answer the question."

Blaine giggled. "Yeah, I got her number."

"You are a lost cause," Akil said.

"No, he's not. The blood still works," Dawn said. "God is still a miracle-working God."

Laughter filled their little corner of the restaurant as if Blaine's serious womanizing issues were something to be joked about. It was bad enough that Blaine wasn't sure if he'd be able to do it. He needed his closest friends to believe in him.

The waitress brought their food to the table and gave Blaine another dimpled smile. "Does everything look good?" she asked.

Everyone nodded and dug into their food. Dimples seemed satisfied with that response and went off to another table.

"You gonna get her number, Blainesky?" Amber asked.

Blaine scrunched his nose. When Amber said "number" and "Blainesky," it sounded more like "numma, Bainefy."

"Are you okay?" Blaine asked.

Dawn's eyes widened. "Oh snap, you're breaking out in hives."

Amber looked at Akil. "Aw, man! You got Benadryl?"

"Waitress!" Akil yelled.

The dimpled girl rushed back over to the table. By the time she got there, Amber's face was puffy and she was scratching her neck.

"What was in this salad?" Akil said. "Did you tell them no strawberries?"

"Oh yes. The salads are premade. They took the strawberries off. Was that not good enough?"

Amber shook her head. Akil growled. "She's allergic to the juice in the strawberries too."

"I'm so sorry."

Akil pulled Amber up from the table. "Come on. I've got Benadryl at the hotel."

"Do you need us to come too?" Dawn asked.

"No. Meet us back at the hotel later. Amber will be done for the rest of the night, though. That medicine is going to wipe her out."

Akil led Amber out of the restaurant while poor Dimples stood there with her eyes glistening. She was probably worried about her tip.

"Is she going to be okay?" she asked.

Dawn nodded. "Yes. I've seen her allergic reactions before. After she takes the medicine she's okay."

"I'm so sorry."

"It's not your fault," Blaine said. "You didn't prepare the food. It's okay, really."

"I'm going to take all of their food off your bill. Try to enjoy the rest of your dinner."

Dawn shook her head as the girl walked away. "It was absolutely her fault."

"No, it wasn't. She didn't make the salad."

"You're just excusing her because she's hot and you wanna hook up with her later."

Blaine laughed. "I don't want to hook up with her. She's cute, but she's not exactly my type."

Dawn rolled her eyes. "That girl is every guy's type."

"Nope. She's too skinny."

"Too skinny? Are you kidding me?" Dawn asked. "I wish I looked like her. Shoot, I've dieted trying to look like her. I can never seem to lose the weight, though."

"You are perfect, Dawn. You don't need to lose any weight."

Dawn gave Blaine an incredulous look. "Get the heck out of here, Blaine. I've been called pleasingly plump my entire life."

"Well, that's because those people have never seen you in a swimsuit."

Blaine gazed at Dawn for just a moment too long for her comfort, because she averted her eyes.

"I'm sorry," Blaine said. "I didn't mean to embarrass you. You just look really good. I didn't know."

241

"Thank you."

"I hope you don't mind my saying this, but your clothes do absolutely nothing for you. You need a whole new wardrobe."

"Rude! You are so rude!"

Blaine shrugged. "I'm just saying. You working with all that and nobody knows. Maybe that's what's taking Camden so long to seal the deal. Has he . . . has he seen you? I mean, has he seen you naked?"

"Blaine!"

" 'Cause if he had, I was just thinking y'all would already be walking down the aisle."

Dawn sighed. "Well, no. He hasn't seen me naked, but not because I haven't tried. I have. He says he wants to wait until we're married."

"That's honorable," Blaine said. "I guess."

"I know, I know. I should just be glad that I have a man of God who respects my virginity. But . . ."

"But what?"

"We've never even been hot and heavy. You know? We've been alone so many times, and we've never even gotten close. All my friends that are dating can hardly keep their boyfriends off them. But Camden never touches me. He gives me kisses so chaste it's like an uncle or somebody."

Blaine lifted his eyebrows and took a sip

of his drink. He didn't know what to say to this. The YouTube video played in his mind. If what Dawn was saying wasn't an exaggeration, then maybe there was truth to it.

"I don't know why I'm telling you this," Dawn said. "You don't understand."

"I do understand. You want to feel like a woman. You want to know that your man desires you, and with my brother you can't tell."

Dawn burst into tears and Blaine switched seats so that he was able to comfort her. He put one arm around her and squeezed.

"What if it's true, Blaine? What if it is? That woman. That Ivy? Why would she say those things? Why wouldn't she say that he wasn't gay? She wouldn't deny it. Maybe she knows something."

Blaine rubbed Dawn's back as she sobbed into his chest. He didn't know the words to make her feel confident. He wasn't confident himself.

"Blaine, am I really attractive to you? Did you mean that?" Dawn asked.

"Yes, of course, I meant it. I wouldn't lie about that."

Dawn slowly released one of her clenched fists and spread it across Blaine's chest. He groaned under her touch. She tilted her head up and planted soft kisses on his neck.

"Dawn, don't. . . ."

She shook her head. "Make me feel like a woman, Blaine. Please . . ."

Dawn kissed Blaine with a hunger he'd never encountered. It made him dizzy. Even though he knew it was wrong, he was responding to her touch. If she'd kissed his brother like that, Blaine didn't even believe the Holy Spirit could keep him from sinning.

That could only mean that Camden *was* gay.

If Blaine went there with Dawn, she would never be able to look Camden in the eyes again, which would be for the best. Dawn could move on with her life and Camden could be free to stay in whatever closet he chose. Royce London's or his own.

Blaine kissed Dawn on the forehead. "Don't worry, sweetie. I've got you."

CHAPTER 28

Camden still hadn't gotten the chance to confront Ivy about the interview. At the rehearsal, he knew that he was still too angry. The moment he'd seen her, he'd felt ready to explode. That was not where he wanted to be when he had the conversation.

But today was different. She had just done another song for her record in Royce's studio. It wasn't one of Camden's songs, so he wasn't present, but as soon as he heard her heels clicking on the marble floors in Royce's foyer, Camden rushed out of his bedroom.

"Hi, Camden," Ivy said.

"Ivy."

"How have you been? We haven't spoken since I . . . well, since I tried to kiss you."

Camden's nostrils flared. "Since you kissed me."

"Yes. I'm sorry I did that, Camden. I don't want you to hate me or not talk to me. I asked Royce what I should do because you just seem so very angry with me. You didn't say a word to me at the rehearsal. I've never made a man so angry with a kiss."

"You think that's the reason I'm not speaking to you? Because you *kissed* me?"

"If that's not it, then what? You said I disrespected you, and I-I'm sorry. If you only knew me and knew about my life, you wouldn't hate me so much."

Ivy took Camden's hand and pulled him inside his bedroom. He was momentarily disarmed by the tears freely flowing down her face, but he wasn't going to be fooled again.

"I don't hate you," Camden said, "and your life is really none of my business. I just want to know why you let that interviewer insinuate that I was gay."

Ivy looked genuinely surprised. "Is *that* what you're angry about? Oh my Lord. No one takes her seriously! She is the biggest joke in the gospel industry. Dr. Rae has accused just about every man in gospel and every megachurch pastor of being gay. She's obsessed. And the ridiculous thing about it is that she never loses any viewers or listeners to that little raggedy radio show she does."

"You didn't say that I wasn't gay," Camden said. "You could've said that."

"Camden, I don't know where you put your private parts. And to be honest, I don't care. I think you are a talented and anointed musician."

"But you felt confident enough to say something about Royce."

Ivy looked at the floor, and whispered, "I do know for a fact that Royce is not gay, Camden."

It took a moment for Ivy's words to sink in, but when they did his eyes widened. "You and Royce?"

"It was only once, before he got married, when I first moved here. He broke my heart when he got married. I was in love with him."

"Were you really attracted to me, then? Or were you just trying to make Royce jealous?"

Ivy sat at the edge of Camden's bed and slumped her shoulders. "No . . . I don't know. Maybe."

"What about your husband, Ivy? I like him. He seems like a good guy."

She nodded. "He is a good man, and he loves me. But I don't love him, Camden. He doesn't even know the real me. He thinks I'm just his beautiful church wife. He doesn't know who I really am. He doesn't satisfy me."

"Look, I'm not getting in that, Ivy. You and your husband need to go to counseling or something, but leave me out of it. I will pray for you all."

"I'm so sorry about what Dr. Rae said, Camden. Do you want me to try and fix it? I will," Ivy said.

Camden shook his head. "No. I don't. Don't worry about it. I know the truth, my woman knows the truth, and God knows."

"I guess I should go," Ivy said as she rose to her feet.

"You should. I wasn't kidding when I said I would pray for you and your husband. You should tell him how you feel, though. Don't let him be in the dark about it."

Ivy nodded. "I would hug you, but I don't know if that would be appropriate."

Camden smiled and held up his fist. "You can give me a fist bump."

"Really?" Ivy chuckled.

Camden wiggled his fist. "Don't leave me hanging."

Ivy lifted her arm and tapped Camden's fist with hers. "Can we still be friends?" she asked.

"As long as you keep your lips and your hugs to yourself," Camden said.

"You don't trust me?"

"I do not."

Ivy smiled sadly. "I deserve that, and I want you to know it hurt me so bad when you said I disrespected you. I didn't mean to do that to you."

"It's okay . . . really."

Ivy waved at Camden as he showed her out of his room. Royce's timing was perfect, because he happened to be walking down the hall as Camden opened the door.

"Oh!" Royce said.

Camden threw both hands in the air. "It's not what you think. We just had our come-to-Jesus moment about the whole Dr. Rae thing."

Royce nodded. "Not my business. I didn't see anything."

"Royce . . ." The longing in Ivy's voice was so real. Camden didn't know why he hadn't noticed it before.

Royce kept walking past Ivy and down the hall. "I hope you apologized, Ivy," Royce called from the other room.

Ivy's eyes watered again. "See you later, Camden."

"Okay."

Camden showed Ivy to the door and then went looking for Royce. He found him in the kitchen making a sandwich. From the smell of the bacon and the lettuce and tomato out on the counter, Camden assumed it was a BLT.

"That bacon smells good," Camden said.

"Applewood, man. Straight from the farm. From organically fed pigs. It's incredible."

Camden sat on one of the kitchen bar stools. "So, Ivy told me about y'all."

Royce chuckled. "I figured she would at some point. Ivy is so predictable."

"What happened? She said it was before you got married, so . . ."

"I didn't love her. She was my protégée, and I crossed the line, plain and simple. I wish I hadn't, because she fell in love."

"But you still deal with her? How's that work?"

"It's business. She's incredibly talented. But I made sure to never cross the line again. Don't let her cross the line with you."

"Oh, no. I won't. I'm good. I don't want to mess up what I have with Dawn."

Royce smiled. "Good, because between me and you, Ivy is crazy."

"Man . . ."

Camden felt bad for Ivy, so he didn't want to join in on Royce's bashing of her. As much as Camden wanted to stay angry at her, he pitied her. Whether she was crazy or not, she was clearly hurting.

"Did she apologize?"

"She did. I accepted it, and so I'm ready to move on and finish her record."

"Her stuff might be on hold because I think I'm ready to start with Spirited's record."

Royce assembled his sandwich and Camden waited for him to elaborate.

"So, God gave me this theme for the album. The theme is 'A move of God.' So many people go to church services, conferences, and everything else because they're trying to feel God move. We're going to give them that Holy Spirit experience with this music. They're going to feel His presence in their cars, showers, wherever they turn it on."

"I love it," Camden said. "I can't wait to get started on it."

"Get ready. You might want to bring your girlfriend in this weekend. They just finished up the show in Miami and killed it again."

"I think with the radio play that's just starting, the single will go to number one on the Billboard chart. What do you think?"

Royce nodded. "Yep. I agree. You know how gospel records take a minute to burn up the charts, but it'll stay on there forever."

"This is all a dream, man. It really is. We've worked so hard and now it's finally paying off."

"Everything in God's time, Camden."

Camden believed that God was opening these doors and finally giving the music a chance to be heard by the world.

"You know, Ivy was right about your voice, Camden. You should really be singing."

"I do. In the studio. I'm just not much of a performer. I just like singing in front of my piano or maybe at Bible study or something. I'm not an artist."

"Okay. Your choice. But if you change your mind, you know you can always sing with Spirited."

"If I decide to sing, I'll sing with my own group," Camden said with a chuckle.

"Oh, my bad!" Royce said. "You do have your *own* group."

"Yep."

"So let me run something by you. The record label wants to maybe add another female to So G.I.F.T.E.D. Maybe a soprano who can lead. Dawn is a great soprano on backgrounds, but she's not really a lead vocalist."

"Let's wait until they're done with this promo tour, and then we can discuss it. I'm open to it, but I don't want them to think I'm making the decision without their input."

"Oh, yeah, I forgot. You guys collaborate on everything."

Camden cracked up laughing while Royce devoured his sandwich. Royce ran his group with an iron fist. No one had a voice except him, but it worked for them. Spirited trusted Royce to make hits and to sell a lot of records, and at the end of the day that was what mattered for them. So G.I.F.T.E.D was family and they made decisions in that way. Maybe after they actually sold a substantial number of records, they would make decisions like Royce and his group.

Talking about them to Royce reminded Camden how much he missed his brothers ('cause he counted Akil as a brother too), sister, and his woman. Royce was right. It was time for a visit, but not in Dallas. He needed everyone to see him in his element in Atlanta. He wanted them to be proud. And maybe they'd go home and share the victory with Pastor Wilson. Perhaps he'd find a reason to be proud too.

CHAPTER 29

After the Miami trip, Blaine had avoided Dawn. Mostly because he wished that he could take what they did back. He'd taken Dawn's virginity, though, and that couldn't be restored. There was no turning back the hands of time on that, but he didn't have to let her think there would be something more than that one night.

And she *did* think there would be more. Dawn had blown up Blaine's cell phone with texts and calls for the two weeks they'd been back in town. He hadn't responded to any of them. It felt like the cold turkey approach was best. Since they were done touring and he was in Oklahoma City every Sunday, there would be space between them, and there would be time to get over him.

But now Amber was banging on his apartment door like the police, so Blaine guessed the cat was out the bag.

"Blaine, if you don't open up this door, I swear I'm going to kick it in!" Amber said.

Blaine considered his options. He could pretend that he wasn't home, but at least if he let them in, he could control the situation. It would be better to let Amber have a meltdown in his apartment than at church, because she wasn't beneath doing that.

Blaine sighed and got up to open the door. Before he could get there, Amber was banging again.

When he swung the door open, Amber dragged a crying Dawn into the apartment.

"Sit down!" Amber yelled at Dawn.

"Look. Don't come over here with all this ghetto hollering and screaming," Blaine said. "I don't want to hear it."

"Blaine, first of all, you do not want to say anything to me. You do not. I am five seconds away from committing capital murder when it comes to you. Like, for real."

"Ain't nobody scared of you."

"You ought to be. Shut up talking to me. Dawn . . . tell him."

"B-but I'm not sure. I'm not sure, Amber. Calm down."

Blaine got a sick feeling in the pit of his stomach. "Tell me what?"

"Tell. Him."

Dawn's hands shook frantically as she spoke. "I didn't get my period. It was supposed to come a couple days after we got back from Miami, and I didn't get it."

"It's been two weeks. Maybe it's just late."

"I hope that's what it is, but it's never late. I've never been late." Dawn sounded so stressed that he knew she wasn't making this up.

Blaine felt his knees buckle at the thought of Dawn being pregnant by him. He took the closest seat, a chair at his dining room table.

"Maybe your cycle is off because you had sex. That's probably what it is," Blaine said.

"You mean her cycle is off because your hoish self stole her virginity," Amber said.

Blaine held one hand up. "Hey! I didn't steal anything. She *gave* it to me. She begged me for it."

"And you just couldn't turn down a piece of tail? You disgust me."

"You just mad it was Dawn and not you," Blaine said.

Amber scoffed. "I suggest you get a full STD test when you do go to the doctor. Ain't no telling what this Petri dish is carrying. I'm surprised your vagina didn't start melting on contact."

"Amber, you are being very rude right

now," Blaine said. "We can talk about this if you want to, but you need to check your attitude. It's not helping anything."

Dawn seemed to calm a little bit, and look hopeful. That was not the effect Blaine was going for.

"Y-you haven't called me since we got back," Dawn said. "Do you hate me now?"

"Nah, I don't hate you. But in order for us to move forward, we can't acknowledge this. We need to act like it never happened."

"Well, since your swimmers decided to hit the mark, I don't think that's really possible," Amber said. "You need to man up, call your brother and confess. Then I don't know what you're gonna do after that. I guess you gonna be a pastor-slash-baby daddy."

Calling Camden was the last thing Blaine planned on doing.

"Camden doesn't need to know about this. It'll break his heart. If you are pregnant, Dawn, I'll help you do what you need to do about it, and then you and Camden can still get married and live happily ever after."

"B-but I thought you thought he was gay too," Dawn said. "Why would I still want to marry him?"

Amber exploded. She ran back and forth in front of Blaine screaming, "Oh my God!

Oh my God!"

"Girl, calm down!" Blaine said.

"You did not seriously try to act like your justification for sleeping with Camden's girl is that there is a gay rumor about him. You know good and well Camden isn't gay."

"Then why doesn't he want me?" Dawn asked. "I've been telling him for months that I'm ready, and he keeps talking about our wedding night, but then he never sets the date."

"I almost want to slap your stupid self too," Amber said. "How about the fact that Camden respects you? He loves you. He *cherishes* you. And you messed it up for no reason."

"It doesn't have to be messed up," Blaine reiterated. "Camden never has to know about this. Dawn, if you think he's gay then just move on quietly. He'll understand. Just leave me out of it."

"Leave you out of it?" Amber screamed. "You are the starter and finisher of this mess. You can't be left out of it, no matter how badly you want to be. You're in it."

"Okay, so what do you think I should be doing about it exactly?" Blaine asked.

The conversation had already wearied Blaine. He wanted to prepare for his weekend visits to Oklahoma City. Regina had prepared a list of questions he'd probably be asked by the potential church members. He wanted to memorize that.

"I think you should be comforting her, Blaine, since it was your errant man part that got her in this predicament. And I think you need to stand up and take responsibility for your baby."

"Whoa. Whoa! Whoa! You can chill with all that *your baby* stuff. We don't even know for sure if there even is a baby, and now you're giving me responsibility for it?"

"She took an early pregnancy test. It was positive," Amber said. "So there is a baby. You're just in denial about that."

"Look, you can just go visit Camden in Atlanta, seduce him and pass the baby off as his."

"What makes you think he'll want me this time, and not after all the other times I tried to give him some?" Dawn asked.

"All right, King David. You gonna put Camden on the front line of the next battle too?" Amber said, her tone angry and vile.

"She's not his wife yet. She's not even sure that he wants her," Blaine said.

This made Dawn cry harder. "I am so stupid," she wailed.

"Yes, you are," Amber said. "You two are just a bucket of dumb and dumber."

But then, as if Amber had a brief moment of empathy, she sat down next to Dawn and put her arm around her.

"Don't worry. Blaine is going to do the right thing."

As Blaine stared at Dawn in her broken state, he wanted to do the right thing. The only problem was, he wasn't quite sure what that was.

CHAPTER 30

Blaine wished he could be anywhere but in his father's study sharing the worst news ever. But he didn't think anyone could fix this mess except Pastor Wilson.

"So, son, how does it feel to have a number one record?" Pastor Wilson asked.

Blaine hadn't even had time to celebrate their number one. His life was too busy falling apart to care about So G.I.F.T.E.D. He'd gotten his brother's woman pregnant. It was the lowest thing he could've ever done. He wished he could take it back. He wished Dawn would get an abortion. He wished he had a time machine.

Anything but having this mess in his lap.

"The number one is great, Dad, but I need to talk to you about something."

Pastor Wilson seemed to sense that something was awry. "What's the matter, son? Regina giving you any trouble?"

Blaine bit his bottom lip and widened his

eyes. He'd forgotten about Regina. She was going to be an additional nightmare to contend with.

"No, it's not Regina."

"Then what is it? Don't keep me in suspense. I have a meeting with Delores and Stephen later."

Blaine gave his father an unblinking stare. His and Delores's meetings were an issue. Blaine had known about those meetings since he was a little boy. And since neither Delores nor First Lady Rita was going anywhere, apparently, they had a workable situation.

Blaine didn't have that with Regina. There would be nothing workable about him having a baby with Dawn. He couldn't even imagine telling her, much less her accepting it and moving on.

"Dad, Dawn is pregnant," Blaine blurted out.

"What? Well, I told Camden if he didn't put a ring on that girl's finger she was going to go out and find someone else. We'll have to replace her in the group, though. Can't have an unwed pregnant girl in a singing group."

Blaine shook his head. His father had gone straight into fixer mode without hearing the entire story.

"Dad . . ."

Pastor Wilson raised his eyebrows. "Wait. Was it Camden? Did Camden get her pregnant? Well, my Lord. I didn't think he'd do it. Might just be my son after all. Dawn is pretty and thick. I'm surprised he lasted this long. How far along is she?"

Blaine looked at the floor. He wished his father would stop cutting him off so he could just tell him.

"The baby isn't Camden's."

"What?"

Blaine cleared his throat. "The baby isn't Camden's. It's mine."

The pen that Pastor Wilson held in his hand clattered to the floor. His face looked frozen, the creases on the sides of his mouth downturned in horror. Like a mask intended to terrify someone.

"You slept with Camden's fiancée? What in the hell were you thinking?"

"I-I wasn't thinking at all. It just happened, really. Dawn and I heard those gay rumors about Camden and didn't know what to believe."

"What gay rumors?" Pastor Wilson asked as beads of sweat gathered on his forehead.

"A woman in Atlanta accused him of being gay because he wouldn't sleep with her."

"When was someone going to tell me

about this?" Pastor Wilson asked.

Blaine shrugged. "Not my business to tell. I'm trying to tell you mine."

"One of my sons is queer and the other one can't keep his hands to himself. Lord help me."

Blaine sat quietly, wondering what would come next. He could sometimes read his father and tell what he was thinking, but this time he drew a blank.

A single tear trickled down his father's face. "All I've ever done is groom the two of you for greatness. You've had nothing but the best, seen nothing but the best, lived the best. I can't believe this."

Blaine shifted in his seat. Pastor Wilson only seemed to remember the positive things about their upbringing. He obviously didn't remember his drinking or his womanizing.

"I tried to get her to have an abortion," Blaine said.

"And why would you do that?"

"I thought that's what you would want. I thought that would be best for the ministry."

"What would be best for the ministry," Pastor Wilson roared, "is for you to act like you got some damn sense!"

"Yes sir." Blaine felt himself reverting back to his childhood.

Pastor Wilson inhaled deeply and sighed. "You have to marry her. That's the only option to save the group and the Oklahoma City church."

"Marry her? *Marry her?* Everybody knows she's Camden's fiancée. That's going to look crazy."

"Ain't nobody buying no records from a gospel group with a baby's mama on soprano. Use your head, fool. You marry her now. Launch the ministry with her. Make a few more records and then quietly divorce once you're established."

"She's never going to go for that."

"Oh, my Lord. Do I have to spell out everything? You're not telling her about this. You're just going to present it to her as if you're going to do the right thing. She's a church girl to her heart. She won't turn you down."

"What about Camden?"

Pastor Wilson laughed. "*Now* you care about your brother's feelings? You wasn't saying what about Camden when you was going up in his woman."

Blaine felt his stomach drop. This was going to break Camden's heart, and there was no way around it. Not if they wanted to keep everything that they'd worked for. Not if So G.I.F.T.E.D was going to remain on top of the charts.

"I can't do this. Maybe I can talk Camden into marrying Dawn anyway," Blaine said in a panicked voice. "He would forgive her. I'd tell him it's all my fault. He could raise the child as his own. Knowing our genetics, it'd probably come out looking just like him."

"Pull yourself together and do what you gotta do," Pastor Wilson said. "And don't worry about Regina. I'll handle her."

Blaine closed his eyes. Regina. He didn't want to be with her anyway, but she seemed to be falling back in love with him.

"I'll talk to her," Blaine said. He wanted to see her face when she heard the news. Regina had been a sworn enemy before.

"You don't know Regina like I do. And you don't have the tools to make her keep the peace. I asked you to do one thing. Get Dawn to marry you. Go buy a ring, and take her to dinner. She will accept."

"I don't love Dawn," Blaine said in a quiet voice.

"So what? You're divorcing her anyway. Get out of my sight before you're proposing with a fat lip. I can't look at you anymore."

Blaine stood, trying to look unafraid, but desperately failing. His father's threats still struck fear into his heart even as a grown man.

"You're not hitting me, Dad. Just so you know. You aren't in your thirties anymore." Blaine's voice quivered a little bit as he said this, causing Pastor Wilson to laugh.

"You're right. I'm not going to hit you. You're a gospel celebrity now. Wouldn't want that in the headlines. Wouldn't want two sissy sons out there."

Blaine stormed out of his father's study and slammed the door. Usually, when they argued, First Lady Rita stood just outside waiting to comfort either of her sons. But not this time. She sat in her favorite chair next to the foyer, sipping a glass of tea.

"Mom . . . did you hear?" Blaine asked.

She nodded. "I can't believe I gave birth to you and rocked you to sleep. How did you turn out this way? Camden only ever had one girl, and you took her away."

Blaine shook his head. "You're wrong about Camden. He's had women. When we were in college he had his share, and he didn't care that Dawn was back home going to junior college and waiting on him."

"So that's why you felt it was okay to take that girl's virginity?"

"I'm sorry I did that."

She took another sip of her tea. "I want to see how you and your trifling father are going to swing this one."

"Don't you always say that God gets the glory out of everything?"

"Yes. He does. But that doesn't mean you won't be on your face begging for mercy somewhere. Don't mock God."

Blaine left the house with his mother's words echoing in his ears. Everything he did was a mockery. Standing in front of the people of God, singing worship music, and taking ministry classes like he could actually be somebody's pastor. It was all a farce.

But his father said that this could work. Marrying Dawn could fix it all. The group would remain intact and he would still be a pastor. And Camden would forgive him one day, as long as his precious music didn't suffer.

CHAPTER 31

Dawn stared down at the ring box in front of her and blinked several times. This was, of course, not the reaction Blaine was going for. He was expecting her to jump for joy and say yes. Blaine had resigned himself to his father's plan. He just needed Dawn to get on board too.

Dawn had seemed hesitant when Blaine had invited her to his apartment, but she did show up. That had to count for something. At least she was willing to hear him out.

"I don't think I want to marry you," Dawn said. "You don't love me."

"I could learn to love you. I know I'm not Camden, but you could learn to love me too."

Dawn looked confused. "But why? When I first told you about the baby — and there *is* a baby — you wanted me to get an abortion or try to trick Camden. Why do you now want to get married?"

"I'm going to tell you the truth, Dawn. My father told me that this would be the best plan for everyone. He thinks your being pregnant by me will destroy the group, and So G.I.F.T.E.D is part of the draw for the Oklahoma City church. I'm getting installed as pastor soon."

"So, I'm just supposed to go along with the program."

"Why wouldn't you? You'll be a first lady, and our child will be raised in the church. What's the problem?"

"I love Camden."

Blaine chuckled. "The man you think is gay."

"That was the devil whispering in my ear. I know that now. I want to try to see if I can salvage things with him."

Blaine threw his head back and laughed. "I'm sorry. I don't mean to laugh at you, but there is no way Camden is gonna be cool with his girlfriend getting pregnant by his brother."

"I thought about that. I'm not going to tell him the baby is yours. I'll tell him it's someone else's but that I don't want to reveal his identity."

Blaine paused for a moment. That plan could've actually worked. Maybe Dawn was more cunning than Blaine realized.

"Amber knows, so it'll never work. If you hadn't told her, I might have supported this plan. She will tell Camden."

"I didn't mean to tell her. I panicked when I saw the pregnancy test results. I didn't think about how she'd react."

"I honestly think you should just chalk things up with Camden. I know you love him, but some things you can't take back. He'll forgive us at some point."

"But you would be okay being married to me when you don't love me?"

Blaine kept the "quiet divorce" plan to himself. There was no need to talk about that now. And Blaine was sure they'd come to a consensus when they both realized they were unhappily married.

"Like I said, we can grow to love each other. My parents did it. My mother wasn't goo-goo ga-ga over my father when they met. But over the years she fell in love with him."

Dawn giggled. "Goo-goo ga-ga? Isn't that what babies say?"

"Huh?"

"Never mind. Go on."

"I think over the years we will find that we are a good fit. We both love Jesus and music, and we both love Camden."

"Do we really love Camden? I keep asking myself that. How could I have done this if I love him?" Dawn said.

"You weren't thinking, and neither was I. We let our flesh dictate our actions. Now we have to bear the consequences."

"There you go with that wisdom again. You are such a dichotomy, Blaine."

"What do you mean?"

"I mean you're a straight-up ho."

"Excuse me! That was very rude."

Dawn laughed. "Really, Blaine. Everybody knows that you are a non-apologetic skirt chaser. But then, God is tugging at your heartstrings. He wants to use you. You just have to conquer your flesh."

"That was encouraging. It sounded like wifely advice."

"I guess it did. Let me think about your proposal, Blaine. I'm not ready to say yes yet. I still want to see Camden. Maybe . . . maybe I'll still want to get that abortion. I don't know."

"Hold on to the ring. If you do decide to keep the baby, then we need to do the marriage thing. I'm not pressuring you either way."

"Thank you for letting this be my decision, and not yours or Pastor Wilson's."

"It's definitely not my father's choice."

Dawn smiled sadly as she put the ring in her purse. "It's not. But I know he put you up to this. It makes sense to keep the ministry above reproach, so I know it was his idea."

"That doesn't mean I don't agree with it."

Dawn rose to her feet. "Thanks again. I'm extremely tired and I need to lie down. I'm gonna go home and get some rest. Camden says that Royce wants to fly us all into Atlanta to celebrate the number one and to give us an announcement."

"Yeah, I got the message on my voice mail. Get some rest, and don't worry. It's all gonna work out."

Blaine walked Dawn to the door, but on second thought he decided to walk her all the way to her car. He wasn't sure if he was doing a better job convincing Dawn than he was himself. Deep down in his core, Blaine felt that everything wouldn't be all right. He remembered his mother's words about God getting the glory, and his begging for mercy. He hoped his mother was wrong and that he'd never have to do the latter.

CHAPTER 32

Blaine walked out of a meeting with his father at the church and ran into Regina in the hallway. She stopped and stared at him with an expression devoid of emotion. There was no anger, sadness, or even joy at seeing him, so Blaine assumed that she'd talked to his father.

"Regina . . ."

She held up one hand. "Don't fix your mouth to say my name. You are dead to me."

"Wow. Really? I thought it was just business anyway. I'm sure my father honored his contract with you."

"You know it was more than that. I can't believe I was stupid enough to let myself go there, though. That was my bad."

Blaine shook his head. "Whatever. I'm sorry it went down like this."

"You aren't sorry. You're never sorry. You don't have to be. Your father cleans up every one of your messes. You never have to worry

274

about remorse."

"Okay, you're being rude, so I'm about to keep it moving. You have a great day."

Blaine tried to pass Regina, but she stepped in his path. "Who was it?" she asked.

"I don't know what you're talking about."

"What ho is stealing my first lady position? Was it that trick in Houston?"

Blaine gently moved her to the side so he could continue down the hall. "There was no other woman. We just decided to go a different direction."

"You're a liar, Blaine. There's always someone else. There's always a woman."

"I wouldn't stress about it. You're still a part of the ministry. My dad seems to love you, so you'll always have a position."

"Your father does love me. That's more than I can say for your sorry self."

"I never claimed to love you. You and my father both said I needed you for this ministry. I disagree."

"You're going to pay for what you've done to me, Blaine. And all of the other women you've used and tossed to the side."

"I might have to pay for how I've treated some of them, but not you. You were bought and paid for. You don't love me, so don't act like you're heartbroken."

"There is something wrong with you. Like really," Regina hissed. "I think you're dead inside."

"We're kindred spirits, baby. If I'm going to hell, we're gonna be cell mates."

"I hate you."

"Aww, that's not very godly. Do you know Jesus as your personal savior?"

Regina gave Blaine a cold look before she walked away from him. He didn't care about her thinly veiled threats. His father had her on the payroll and in a position of power. That was all she wanted anyway. Love had nothing to do with her feelings for him . . . lust maybe, but not love.

CHAPTER 33

Camden hadn't realized how much he'd missed his friends until he and Royce were on their way to the airport to pick them up in Royce's Suburban. He was especially happy about seeing Dawn. He had a surprise for her that would change everything.

"There they are. Pull over!" Camden said.

Royce laughed. "Okay, calm down!"

Camden was out of the SUV before Royce came to a complete stop. Amber was the first one he reached, and she gave him a huge hug.

"Camdeezy! I missed you, man!"

Camden kissed her cheek. "I missed you too. I hate I wasn't out touring with y'all."

"You didn't miss much," Akil said as he gave Camden a fist bump. "Just crowds of adoring fans, five-star hotels, the beach, and sumptuous meals."

"Rub it in, why don't you!"

Dawn stood still, with a tiny smile on her

face. Camden rushed her and scooped her into his arms. She laughed as he spun her around.

"I missed you, babe," Camden whispered in her ear.

"I missed you too."

Camden released the embrace and looked at Dawn funny. "You okay? Why are your eyes puffy? It looks like you've been crying."

"Everything is okay now," Dawn replied. "I just missed you."

Blaine was last to greet Camden and he gave him a brotherly hug.

"Twin. Looks like you ain't been eating," Blaine said. "I thought they had some good soul food here in the A."

Royce said, "He's been working. No time to gain weight."

"Leave it to Camden to get here doing one project and then end up working on everybody's stuff," Amber said. "You go, boy!"

The guys packed everyone's bags in the car. Camden let Akil have the front seat so that he could snuggle up with Dawn in the back row. Her hair, her perfume, and even her flowered sundress all had a dizzying effect on him. He wanted to spend some time alone with her.

Camden was expecting her to be all over him too, but she wasn't. He hoped she wasn't still thinking about the gay accusations.

When they got back to Royce's mansion, his wife showed everyone to their rooms. The girls had one and the guys had another. After they all settled in, Royce invited everyone to the patio for lunch and to chill by the pool.

"I want to congratulate all of you on your number one. You couldn't have done any better on your debut," Royce said. "The record company is beyond pleased."

"They are? So does that mean we're going to get a million-dollar budget for our album?" Blaine asked.

Royce took a sip of his sweet tea before responding. Camden thought there was still a little tension between Blaine and Royce since the diva scene he pulled in Dallas, but Royce was being very kind to him.

"Not a million-dollar budget. That's unheard of in gospel. You've got to remember your genre. If you want million-dollar budgets, you should move over to R&B."

"You said you could see me doing that, right?"

"Not as a pastor, though, nitwit," Amber said. "You 'bout to sing bump-and-grind

279

music and then preach on Sunday? Whatever!"

"Maybe Regina will like it," Camden said.

When no one laughed at his joke but Akil, Camden *knew* something was going on.

"Where is Regina anyway?" Camden asked. "I thought she was shadowing you, Blaine."

Blaine shook his head. "Nah. She's working on some stuff with Dad, so she hasn't been with us at all."

Royce said, "You guys have gotten off topic already! We were talking about the record label and their plans for you."

"Sorry, Royce," Amber said. "This is what we do. We digress. Especially when you feed us yummy food. Compliments to whoever threw down on these fajitas."

Royce laughed. "That would be my wife Kita. You can tell her later how much you enjoyed them."

"So, the record label wants to make a slight change to the group," Camden said. "They would like for us to add a member."

"We've been singing together forever. I don't know why we need someone else," Blaine said. "We're fine the way we are."

Royce said, "They want the group to be able to sing a diverse selection of music, and they don't feel you have a soprano solo-ist."

"I sing soprano," Dawn said.

"And you do a wonderful job, babe," Camden said. "They are looking for some-one to do what Amber and Blaine do, though. On the soprano notes."

Dawn frowned and looked so upset that Camden almost wished they hadn't told her.

"No one is being replaced," Royce said. "But what if one of you get sick? There's not enough depth here. I would really like to add an alto too, who can back Amber up, but we'll start with the soprano."

"They have a really fun way that they want to make it happen. They want to do an open audition here in Atlanta and film it like a little reality show for the Gospel Music Network. Royce will host it, and we'll be featured. It's great publicity and it'll be a good look for us," Camden said.

Amber pushed away her plate of fajitas. "Oh, I'm about to be on TV? Let me fall back on this yumminess so I can look completely snatched in my wardrobe. My husband might see me on TV."

"Royce, she's always waiting for her husband to find her," Akil explained.

"Yes. He will find me and not the other way around. But I do not have a problem with presenting my best self for all potential boos."

"Amber is going to be funny on reality TV," Royce said. "She might end up upstaging everyone and getting her own show."

"That's what's up! I'm glad Royce recognizes greatness when he sees it," Amber said.

"Speaking of which," Royce said, "I have someone picked out for the group already. We'll do the reality show. It's great promotion for the group, but the girl has been selected."

Blaine cracked up. "So it's rigged?"

"It's not like it's a competition with rules and contracts," Camden explained. "We're just doing an open call. What y'all think?"

"When are we doing this?" Blaine asked.

"This week, while you all are here," Royce said.

"It sounds like fun," Akil said. "I'm down."

"Me too," Amber said. "Do you have your keyboard somewhere, Cam? I want to let you hear something I've been working on."

Camden stood up. "Come on, y'all can come to the studio."

Amber shook her head. "No, I don't want everybody to hear it yet! You know I'm shy about my songs."

"Okay. Come on, Ambreezy."

Camden showed Amber to the studio. He started turning on equipment and pointed to a place for Amber to sit. Instead of sitting, Amber closed the door and stood beside it.

"Everything okay?" Camden asked.

"That's what I want to ask you. Is everything all right with you?"

"Yeah, why do you ask?"

Amber sighed. "You know I saw the YouTube video."

"What did you think about it? Did you believe it too?"

"Too? Who believed it?"

Camden shrugged. "Dawn asked me about it, and now she's acting funny."

Amber puffed her cheeks and blew the air out slowly, as if she had something on her mind.

"Cam, I want to tell you something, but I'm . . . well, I'm caught in between you and my girl."

"Spill it, Amber."

"How do you think things are between you and Dawn, I mean outside of the YouTube thing?"

Camden sat down and tapped a few keys on the keyboard. "Well, I admit that we had a few issues about my leaving, but I think we're okay. I-I was actually planning to propose while y'all were here."

Amber's lips formed a little "O." "You were? That's so romantic, Camden."

"Well, now you've got me questioning my decision. What's up?"

Amber balled her hands into fists and then released them. She bit her lip and sighed again. All nervous gestures.

"I trust that if there was anything that could hurt me, you would say it, right?"

"Oh, don't do that, Cam. Don't do the guilt trip thing. Please."

"You're the one who dragged me down here. Just tell me what's on your mind."

"Let me just say that if I was you I would hold off on the proposal."

"Why?"

Amber shook her head. "Camden, I can't give you the details, so can you please just trust what I'm saying?"

"So you know something that if I knew it I wouldn't want to marry Dawn."

Amber lifted an eyebrow. "Maybe."

"Why are you just now telling me? Why didn't you call? Why wait until we're all here together?"

"I have been struggling with saying anything, Camden. Like I said, I love both of y'all. I wish I didn't know anything."

"So that's it?" Camden asked.

"Yeah. Maybe she'll tell you the rest. Give her the opportunity to share what's on her heart."

Camden knew Amber almost as well as he knew Dawn. She would never betray Dawn or tell her secrets. For her to open her mouth at all, this information must be so devastating that she would be harming him by *not* saying anything.

"Thank you, Amber. I know how hard this must be for you. Thanks for the heads up."

"Love you, Cam! I want you to have the best."

She threw her arms around his neck and squeezed. He hugged her back.

"Love you too, Amber."

"Are you going to go to Blaine's church? I mean are you gonna be a member?"

Camden chuckled. "I don't know. I just can't . . . I know too much about him. I don't know how to ignore all the stuff I know."

"I guess it's a good thing he's going to be in Oklahoma City. No one really knows his dirt there."

"Are you going there?"

Amber shrugged. "Not sure. Like we know some stuff about your dad and we serve under him. So, is it any different? Akil wants me to go. Maybe I'll move out here to Atlanta with you."

"Are you serious about that?"

"Maybe. We write together. We sing together. And there are a lot of opportunities for me here. Like I could be in gospel stage plays or something. Maybe Tyler Perry will hire me."

"You want Royce to get you an audition with him?"

"Royce got it like that?"

"Yeah, he does. This dude is amazing."

"Wow. I'm impressed with his little self. You think he'd let me live here too?"

"Um . . ."

"I'm just playing, boy. I wouldn't want to move in this man's house."

"Oh. I just thought of something. I'm only here temporarily. I do plan to come back home, you know."

Amber looked at the floor. "Something tells me, God might have you here a little bit longer than you think."

"What is God whispering in *your* ear?"

Amber just smiled and sat down at the keyboard. She started playing her song and singing along with the music. Camden couldn't focus on the melody or lyrics. He could only think of Amber's ambiguous warning.

The only one who could answer his questions and calm his fears was Dawn. He was going to follow Amber's advice and let her speak her heart.

CHAPTER 34

"The seafood here is wonderful," Camden said to Dawn. "Order whatever you want, though. Don't worry about the cost."

Camden had decided to take Dawn to one of his favorite restaurants since he got to Atlanta — Ray's on the River. He loved the food and the view. It was a little pricey, but since he'd decided to go forward with his marriage proposal, he figured he should pick somewhere nice.

It wasn't that Camden didn't believe or trust Amber. He just trusted God more. He prayed about what to do with Dawn, and he felt peace in his spirit about proposing. He definitely didn't feel as if the Lord was telling him not to marry Dawn.

"Why would I worry about the cost?" Dawn asked. "I assume you can afford this place if you brought me here, right?"

Dawn looked beautiful. Her hair was swept into a twist on the back of her head.

She wore a small amount of makeup, but the pink-tinted lip gloss made her full lips look plump and juicy. Camden tried to forget Amber's warnings so he could enjoy himself, but he couldn't.

"So, tell me about the tour. What was it like being onstage? Did you enjoy it?"

Dawn nodded. "It was almost like being at church. Amber and Blaine worked the crowds, and me and Akil sang the harmonies. It's just different people in the audience."

"Are you feeling okay about us adding another soprano to the group?" Camden asked.

"I wish you would've warned me about that. You knew ahead of time, right? I was kind of embarrassed."

"Why were you embarrassed? It wasn't personal."

Dawn shook her head. "It's like no one realizes what it's like to sing with all these phenomenal singers and just be the backup person. I already know I don't sing like Blaine and Amber."

"I never knew you felt like that."

"Now you do."

The waitress walked up to their table. "Would you like to try our house Pinot Grigio? It's the special wine of the evening."

"You want wine?" Camden asked. "I can get the whole bottle."

Dawn shook her head. "No. No wine. I'll have a lemonade, please."

"No wine? What's up with that?" Camden asked as the waitress left to put in their drink orders.

"I'm just not in the mood. That's all."

"Oh."

"Camden, can I ask you a question? This has been bugging the heck out of me ever since I watched that video."

Camden rolled his eyes. "Really? You still on that?"

"What made that interviewer even ask that in the first place? What did she see to make her think that about you?"

"I don't know. I never met the woman. I think she's just used to stirring up gossip."

"And the woman you wrote songs for couldn't be sure if you were straight?"

"No, she couldn't. We've never been together. So how could she be sure?"

Dawn sipped her water. "Okay, that's all I want to ask about that, I guess."

"What? Do you want me to take you to the car and take your virginity in the backseat? Is that what you want? Will that prove anything to you?"

"No. It wouldn't prove anything, and I

290

wouldn't want you to do that. I just don't know about us. It's been such a long time. We've been together forever."

"And you love me, right?" Camden asked.

"I do, but I don't know if I'm in love with you anymore. I keep asking myself that question. If I'm in love with you. And I can never give myself a definitive response."

"So what do you think we should do about this?"

"I think God's already done it."

Now Camden was confused. "What do you mean?"

"Well, He gave you an opportunity far away from me, and it's allowed me to gain some clarity about who I am and what I want."

"What is it that you want?"

"I want a man who is proud of me. Proud enough to tell everyone that he wants to spend the rest of his life with me."

"And you don't think I feel that way?"

"I think you used to. I don't know how you feel now."

Camden touched the bulge in his pocket that contained the ring, but he didn't reach in and pull it out. He used to be one hundred percent sure she'd say yes when he proposed, but this Dawn was different. Even her face was different and more mature. Her acne was gone and there were little worry lines at the corners of her eyes and mouth.

"I feel the same way about you, Dawn. Maybe you feel differently about me. It's okay to admit that if it's true. I'd rather know the truth than continue to live a lie."

"The truth is . . . I met someone."

Camden swallowed hard. Amber had tried to tell him her secret, but couldn't betray her girl. Dawn had chosen to come clean.

"You say you met someone like it was an accident or something. Did you not try to meet him?"

"I didn't plan it."

"Who is he? Did you sleep with him?"

Dawn shook her head. "Not answering those questions. I just want you to tell me that it won't affect So G.I.F.T.E.D. It's our time now. I can tell by the reactions we get when we get onstage."

"The music is the music. Our relationship has no impact on that."

"Good. Because I wouldn't want to harm everyone else because you and I aren't together anymore."

It took everything in Camden not to explode with anger. Amber knew that Dawn was cheating on him with some other dude. She'd warned him.

The waitress came back to the table and

asked, "Are you ready to order your dinner yet?"

"We're not staying," Camden said. "Please bring the check for the beverages."

The waitress nodded and walked away.

"So we're not eating now? That's immature."

Camden stroked the ring again, and felt his nostrils flare. "If you want, I can take you by the McDonald's drive-thru on the way back to Royce's house. I know you don't think I'm spending hundreds of dollars on you. That's boyfriend stuff. You have to call your other dude for that."

"Okay, I deserved that. I did."

"You deserved more than that, but I'm trying to be more like Jesus. I'm extending you grace and mercy."

"You're angry. I'm surprised about that. I never expected you to be angry when I told you. You hardly show any emotion regarding me, but you're angry now."

Camden was furious, but not for the reason she thought. He could've forgiven her for going on a date with someone else, maybe even sleeping with that person. He was the only man she'd ever dated, so her being unsure and testing the waters wasn't unforgivable.

What enraged Camden was her reason for

finding someone else. Deep down, she believed the insinuation that he was gay. After being with him for a decade, she believed the words of a person he'd never even met.

But now they were both free. Camden to pursue his musical dreams and Dawn to find her husband and start having children. Camden hoped that one day Dawn regretted her choice, but he'd never regret chasing destiny.

CHAPTER 35

Ivy and her husband had graciously allowed Camden and the rest of the group to use their church for the open call. Camden was absolutely not in the mood for frivolities, but he had a smile on his face nonetheless. Dawn was quiet, but this was not out of character for her. On the surface it seemed as if all was well.

Amber linked arms with Camden as the camera crew set up the social hall for the event. Dawn, Akil, and Blaine were sitting in the makeup chairs getting prepped for their time on camera.

"She told you," Amber said.

Camden nodded. "I almost gave her a ring. It was in my pocket the whole time."

"Seriously? You didn't believe me?"

"I didn't want to believe you. I knew that we had issues, but I thought it was just because I'd taken too long to propose. How could she believe that I'm gay?"

Amber shook her head. "I don't think she believes that. I think that's the excuse she's giving herself."

"Well, either way, it's over."

"Ugh. How is this going to affect the group, though? I don't like drama."

"There won't be any. By the time we're all together again at home, I'll be over it. I'll probably have a new girlfriend. You know anybody you can hook me up with? The chicks here in Atlanta might not be trying to holla with the rumors and all."

"Oh, gay dudes get women all the time," Amber said.

Camden tugged playfully at Amber's puffy hair. She slapped his hand away.

"This hair is a masterpiece, honey. Each strand is laid with love and perfection in mind."

Camden shook his head and laughed. "Well, the bigger the hair, the less attention given to the ripened produce."

"You just reminded me, I need to sprinkle some glitter on these babies."

Camden laughed at Amber as she commandeered a container of glitter off the makeup table and liberally spread it over her cleavage.

"Are you Camden Wilson?"

Camden turned to see who was asking,

and he immediately recognized her from her publicity photos. Kenya Summers was much prettier in person, though. Her honey-brown skin seemed to glow, and her almond-shaped eyes were surrounded by some of the thickest lashes Camden had ever seen.

"I am. You're Kenya Summers, right? Royce speaks very highly of you, and your demo was incredible. I'm pleased to meet you."

"This isn't the first time we're meeting, Camden. You don't remember."

Camden shrugged. "I'm sorry! I'm sure I would recall meeting you."

"My dad was over the Texas Gospel Alliance for many years. I was in the youth choir with y'all."

"Oh, Deacon Summers! I just don't remember him having a beautiful daughter."

Kenya blushed and looked at the floor. "He didn't. Not back then, anyway. He had an ugly duckling daughter."

"Now she's a swan."

Kenya smiled at Camden. "I don't feel like that every day. Today, I do. After the makeup crew went to town on my face."

"Come meet the rest of the group. Royce told them about you, but you might as well meet them in person."

Camden brought Kenya over to the makeup area. Blaine immediately perked up, as he did whenever an attractive woman was in his presence. Some things never changed. Dawn stared her up and down with a look of pure contempt.

"Hey, y'all, this is Kenya Summers, the soprano we told y'all about."

Blaine said, "Go ahead and hit a note."

"Right now?" Kenya asked.

"Yep. I hope you aren't shy," Blaine said. "You can't be shy singing with us."

Kenya laughed. "Honey, I am *not* shy."

"Then go ahead and belt something out."

Kenya opened her mouth and sang a classic, "I Surrender All." Her talent was undeniable. Amber shook her head and made the face all the church mothers made when someone really *sang* a song. Dawn had tears in her eyes, and Akil clapped his hands together. Blaine's expression was the most priceless of all. He looked absolutely smitten.

"All right then," Amber said. "Welcome to the group, honey. We'll take all of that with a side of macaroni and cheese."

Kenya ran over to Amber and hugged her, which started a chain reaction of hugging. Even Dawn, who was giving her the mean face in the beginning, gave her a squeeze.

"So, how are you going to practice with us?" Dawn asked. "Do you live here?"

Kenya shook her head. "No, I live in Fort Worth."

"You can't possibly be from the DFW," Blaine said. "I know I would've laid eyes on you before."

"I am in Atlanta a lot, but Fort Worth is my home."

"Y'all remember the Texas Gospel Alliance Youth Choir? She was in it with us. Her daddy directed it."

Akil tilted his head to one side. "I remember you! You lost a lot of weight. She led us on 'I Love the Lord.' "

"That's right! See, Camden, I told you I was there."

Camden's jaw dropped. He did remember the girl who led that song because he, Blaine, and Amber had made some pretty mean comments about her. They'd called her the teenage Nell Carter. And Akil's comment was an understatement. She hadn't just lost some weight. She'd lost about two people. Two large people.

"Well, God surely transformed you!" Blaine said as he lifted his hands to heaven and muttered in some fake tongues.

"You are *silly*!" Kenya said. "But I did work really hard to lose the weight. I run marathons now."

"You do?" Dawn asked. "I just started doing 5K races. I want to work my way up to a full marathon."

"We should train together, then! I find it's great for my voice too, because the way your lungs have to work to run a marathon definitely gives you more breath to hit those notes," Kenya said.

"Well, y'all don't have to worry about me running any marathons," Amber said, "because I've got way too much jiggleation going on. I will stand at the finish line with bottles of water, though."

Kenya laughed some more. "Jiggleation?"

"Amber has a whole separate language dedicated to her boobs," Akil said. "They're her prized possessions."

Amber squeezed her breasts and smiled. "Love thyself! And stop being a hater."

"See, women can get away with this type of thing," Blaine said. "If I went around squeezing my favorite body part all day, then everyone would just think I'm some type of freak."

Amber and Dawn gave Blaine straight-faced blank stares.

"You are some type of freak," Dawn said.

"Yeah, but you like it, though."

Amber rolled her eyes at them and looked

back at Kenya. "Welcome to the group, Kenya. We'll act all surprised when you sing today on camera. But you betta bring it."

"And you know I will! I've got to go and line up with the rest of the girls auditioning. Talk to y'all later!"

When she was gone, Camden asked, "So what do y'all think?"

"She's all right," Dawn said.

"Don't hate, Dawn," Camden said. "Her voice is incredible."

Dawn got up from the makeup chair and stormed away from the group. Amber usually followed Dawn when she was having a moment, but not this time. She busied herself with reapplying glitter that had rubbed off during Kenya's impromptu hugging session.

"What's going on with y'all?" Blaine asked. "She's been tripping all day."

"She has? Well, Dawn broke up with me, so I don't know why she's tripping. I just agreed to what she wanted."

"She broke up with you?" Akil asked. "That's crazy. Y'all supposed to get married."

"Did she say why?" Blaine asked.

Amber glanced up from her cleavage and raised an eyebrow at Camden.

"She's met someone else, apparently. It

only took a couple months of me being in Atlanta to decide that she needed to get with someone else."

"How does this affect the group, though?" Akil said. "I don't want us to fall apart."

"Who's falling apart?" Camden said. "I've still got a long road ahead of me on Royce's project, so Blaine and Amber are really going to be at the forefront of the group. I mean, I write the songs. I don't have to do that from Dallas."

"You staying here, bro?" Blaine asked.

"The only things anchoring me to Dallas were Graceway and Dawn. I'm banned from the church and dumped by the girl. Makes sense to me."

"What if Dawn changes her mind?" Akil asked. "You guys have been together a gazillion years. One argument doesn't have to mean it's over. Amber, say something!"

Amber looked up slowly and swallowed. "I support Camden's decision. Maybe it's time for a change."

Blaine got up from his makeup chair. "As long as we keep it all about the ministry, we can all succeed. I'm trying to live like Royce. That man is like a gospel emperor or something."

"I'm trying to get there too," Camden said. "But people hearing the message is enough for me."

"Yeah, well, we want them to hear it and pay for it. Our video from Miami has over two hundred thousand hits on YouTube, but according to our sales, we haven't even hit fifty thousand on that single," Blaine said.

"Royce said those numbers are great for gospel. Almost unheard of."

"Still, cheap church folk can go up to the hundred-dollar offering line, buy two-hundred-dollar tickets to a pastor's gala, and go to the soul food brunch on Sunday, but they can't pay one dollar to download our song?" Blaine said.

"People think gospel music should be free," Dawn said. "They have no guilt about watching us over and over again on YouTube without buying anything."

"Maybe that's what your first sermon should be about," Akil said, "bootlegging Christians."

Blaine cracked up laughing. "Dad would fall out on the floor and need to be resuscitated."

"And Delores would run her Spanx-wearing behind over and give him mouth-to-mouth," Amber said with a chuckle. "Do y'all know she had the audacity to tell me my skirt was too tight a couple weeks ago?"

"It was too tight," Akil said. "I thought

you were about to explode like one of those cans of biscuits."

"Lifetime hater award goes to Akil!" Amber said.

Camden laughed and enjoyed the banter and jokes that had been the trademark of their friendship for years. No matter what he told everyone else, he hadn't been sure that So G.I.F.T.E.D would survive his and Dawn's breakup. But it was clear that everyone wanted to press forward.

It was ministry over everything. Ministry came before love, broken hearts, and egos. Camden said a short prayer and gave thanks to God for everything — even the pain. It was going to push him closer to his goal.

Camden also opened his heart to forgiveness. He forgave Dawn for not believing in his manhood; for her doubt. He prayed that she would be happy in spite of it all. He almost finished his prayer, but then thought of one other thing.

Camden prayed that he would be mature enough to be happy for Dawn — once his love, now his sister in Christ.

CHAPTER 36

It was the week after they had returned from Atlanta, and Blaine had called a group meeting and rehearsal at his apartment. So G.I.F.T.E.D was going to sing at the Oklahoma City church the coming Sunday. It was a celebration service leading up to his installation on the first Sunday of September.

Blaine had invited Dawn to come over a couple hours early. He was concerned that there were still loose strings with them. Dawn had obviously decided to break things off with Camden, but she hadn't given him an answer on what she wanted to do regarding the baby, or marriage. Pastor Wilson wanted an answer soon.

Dawn walked into Blaine's apartment looking completely different. She'd cut her hair very short. It wasn't unbecoming, but it wasn't particularly flattering to Dawn's chubby face.

"You cut your hair," Blaine said as Dawn sat down.

"Yeah. I want to go natural. Amber's been trying to get me to do it for years, but I haven't had the nerve. It's time for a change."

"So we're going to have two Afro chicks in So G.I.F.T.E.D?"

"Looks like it. You got one glamour girl, though. Kenya's got that long blow-in-the-wind hair."

Blaine could tell there was a bit of jealousy in Dawn's voice concerning Kenya. It was to be expected. Kenya came in singing her part, and singing her under the table.

"So, you want to talk about what went down with you and Camden in Atlanta?" Blaine asked, cutting to the chase.

"No. Not particularly. I broke it off with him."

"So, you decided not to try and seduce him and all that? Does that mean you've accepted my proposal?"

"No. It doesn't mean that. It means that I know it would never work trying to trick Camden, and that I didn't want to do it anyway. I was stupid to believe Camden might be gay. I let the devil get all up in my head."

Blaine didn't know how to respond. It

didn't seem right to press the marriage issue when she obviously was still in emotional turmoil regarding what had happened between her and Camden. Unfortunately, Blaine needed an answer. It couldn't wait.

"Pastor Wilson wanted . . ."

"He wanted what? To know if I'm gonna go along with y'all scheme to save the Oklahoma City church? I don't give a damn about that right now. I'm up here trying to figure out if I'm keeping this baby."

Blaine felt hopeful again. If Dawn got rid of the baby, all of this could go away. He wouldn't have to marry Dawn or Regina, and he'd be free to find the queen of his new congregation.

"I didn't know that was still on the table. You seemed very much against it at first."

"I am *still* very much against it, Blaine. I just keep thinking how everyone is going to be so disappointed in me. My family, *your* family. Your mother. My God. She loves me, and now she's going to hate me for hurting her son."

Blaine silently agreed with that sentiment. His mother would probably never embrace Dawn as a daughter after what she'd done to Camden. He wasn't even sure his mother wouldn't disown him.

"And having an abortion would resolve all

that? Do you think you'd go back to Camden?"

Dawn shook her head. "Too many people already know. Do you actually think Amber would never tell Camden about us? She already threatened to tell him if I didn't break up with him."

"She did? Wow. I thought she was your best friend."

"She is, but she said that she couldn't let us do this to Camden. He's her *other* best friend."

"Do what to Camden? Everybody acts like he's a saint or something. He had plenty of chicks while we were in college. Did he tell you that? While you were home with your legs snapped shut, he was getting it in. Camden is not a saint."

"He cheated on me in college?"

Blaine laughed. "No one even knew he had a girlfriend. Y'all gave it a good run, and now it's over. I mean, if you keep the baby, we can do what we do, but if you don't want to keep it, I'll back you up. Whatever you need from me, I'll help you."

"Thank you, Blaine. I just . . . I need to think about it some more. I wish I could pray about it. But I can't ask God what He thinks about me ending the life of this child. I already know what He thinks."

Blaine didn't give his opinion. He didn't want her to think he was a horrible, ungodly person. He knew what his father would do. Pastor Wilson would see that she was weak regarding the abortion, and he'd apply just the right amount of pressure. He'd add in the guilt factor about how Camden would be devastated and how her mother would be embarrassed at her loose daughter.

But Blaine wasn't his father. Not yet.

"Do you want something to eat? Are you thirsty?" Blaine asked, wanting to give her something else to think about for a minute.

"I would love some juice. I haven't really been able to keep much of anything down."

Blaine went to look in his refrigerator. "I've got orange juice and apple. Which one?"

"Apple."

Blaine watched Dawn quickly drink the juice like she'd been lost in the desert and that was her first glass of water after being rescued.

"You want more?" he asked when she handed him back the glass.

"Yes, please. And a sandwich. Do you have lunch meat?"

Blaine laughed. "Why don't you come in here and look for yourself. This is a bachelor's pad."

Dawn walked into the kitchen and rifled through the refrigerator. After a moment, she pulled out a box.

"Wow," she said.

"Wow what? Does the lunch meat have mold on it?"

She shook her head. Blaine walked over to take the box from her hand. As soon as he saw what it was, he knew why she said "Wow." It was a box of chocolates that had been left behind by Regina. There was an explicit note on the box telling him where she was keeping a particular piece of chocolate warm.

Blaine snatched off the note and balled it up. "Sorry."

Dawn just shook her head. "No. I'm sorry. I need to apologize to myself. I know who you are. Why would I let myself get knocked up by the manwhore of the year?"

"Well, I'm putting that behind me," Blaine said. "I can't keep that up and be a pastor. I'm not stupid. I was just a young man, doing what young men do."

"And I'm supposed to think I can satisfy you. I don't know anything. I wouldn't know how to melt some chocolate with my body. You're used to *those* women."

"You were fine, Dawn. I didn't have any complaints."

"Yeah, sure."

"If we end up getting married, I'll teach you everything you need to know. You don't have to worry about that."

Dawn nodded. "But you'd rather I have the abortion and make this whole situation disappear."

"I would rather you make the decision you can live with. But if you were still on the fence about keeping the baby, why did you break up with Camden? You could've still made things work."

Blaine closed the refrigerator and reached into the cabinet. He pulled out a box of graham crackers and handed it to Dawn. She took it and sat down.

"I broke up with him because I didn't think I deserved him after what I'd done with you. But now you're telling me he was unfaithful in college. Maybe I should've just stayed with him. We'd be even."

Not quite even, Blaine thought. Camden hadn't slept with one of Dawn's sisters. The girls at college didn't have anything to do with Dawn, and Camden sure hadn't gotten anyone pregnant. But Blaine kept his thoughts to himself.

There was a knock on the door, so Dawn took her graham crackers and sat back down on the couch.

Blaine opened the door and invited Kenya inside. She was wearing a cute powder blue halter and shorts set that flattered her figure. Her long brown hair was pulled away from her face, but hung straight down her back. There was no mistaking it, Kenya was fine. And there was absolutely no hint that she used to be over three hundred pounds. Blaine expected there to be a stretch mark or a pocket of skin or something, but her body had been completely transformed. It was miraculous, and Blaine definitely appreciated the view.

"I hope I'm not too early. I wasn't quite sure where you lived and I wanted to make sure I wasn't late."

"You're fine. Want something to drink? Juice? Tea?"

"Tea would be fantastic."

Kenya sat down on the couch next to Dawn. "Hey, Dawn, how are you? I love your haircut. It's stunning on you."

"Thank you," Dawn replied with a dry yet polite tone.

"So is everyone else going to be here soon?" Kenya asked.

"Yeah, Amber and Akil will probably be here in a few minutes," Blaine said. "Amber is always on time."

"Okay good. The reality show taping was

wild, right? So many girls showed up."

"And so many of them sounded a hot mess," Blaine said.

Kenya laughed. "I know, right? I don't know what possessed some of them to come. Maybe they heard that they would be on TV. Some people will do anything to get on TV."

"Or maybe they'd been told by family and friends that they could sing, and they believed it," Dawn said. "I could tell that most of them sang in the choir at the churches. Maybe they just didn't know."

Kenya scrunched her nose with skepticism. "Really, Dawn? Some of those girls weren't even fit to sing in the choir."

"Well, I don't go around judging someone who wants to give their gift to the Lord. The Bible says to make a joyful noise unto the Lord. How do you know that He wasn't pleased?"

"I-I don't," Kenya said.

"Well, then maybe you should think before you say such bad things about people."

Dawn got up from her seat and disappeared into Blaine's bathroom. Kenya looked sad, but there was nothing he could do to make Dawn like someone who could possibly take her spot in the group.

"She doesn't like me," Kenya said.

"Give her some time. She sings soprano too, so you know . . ."

Kenya nodded slowly. "That's what it is. Okay. I was thinking maybe my breath was funky or something. I heard she and Camden were dating. Was he the one who made the decision to add me to the group? Maybe that has something to do with it too."

"Oh, well, yeah, she and Camden broke up while we were in Atlanta, so she might just be in a general grumpy mood for a while."

Blaine had also heard that pregnant women could be pretty evil, but he didn't add that part of the explanation.

"What? Camden is single now? Mmm . . . I have had a crush on him from afar for years."

Blaine laughed. "Well, I suggest that you keep that tidbit of information a secret for now. This definitely wouldn't be the time to pursue that."

"I wouldn't pursue it anyway. Men chase me, not the other way around."

Blaine laughed. "I bet they do. You never sit home on a Saturday night, do you?"

"I do, but only because I'm picky. I'm only going out with a man who's worthy of me. My dad always told me that I'm royalty, so I act accordingly."

Blaine was shocked to hear those words come out of a woman's mouth. She sounded like a female version of himself.

"You keep thinking like that, a king will find you. Like minds think the same."

"Huh? Do you mean great minds think alike?"

Blaine shrugged as there was a knock on the door, signaling Amber and Akil's arrival. Amber walked in and went straight to the couch and plopped down.

"It feels like the seventh level of Hades out there," Amber said. "You need to install some air-conditioning from your parking lot all the way up the path to your door. This heat don't make no sense."

"Yeah, I hope I don't smell like recess," Akil said as he took a seat in the armchair opposite the couch where Amber and Kenya were sitting.

"If you do smell like recess, I'm gonna need you to remove your funky self from my furniture," Blaine said.

"Naw. I'm joking. I'm good. Where's Dawn? I saw her car outside."

As if on cue, Dawn came from the back of the apartment. She waved at Amber and Akil and took a seat at the table.

"Now that we're all here, we can get started," Blaine said. "We're singing in

Oklahoma City this Sunday. I think we should just do a praise and worship medley. Of course they want to hear 'Born to Worship.' "

"I did a new arrangement of it that really highlights Kenya's range," Amber said.

"Thank you for doing that. I was content to sing in the background for a while until I got up to speed."

Amber waved her hand dismissively. "Honey, please! That voice was not made for the background. You gave me all types of Holy Ghost fever when you sang for us in Atlanta. That instrument needs to be on the front line. We got you."

"Thank y'all for embracing me," Kenya said. "I was telling Blaine earlier that I've admired you all from afar for many years. Every time I would see y'all singing at a youth conference or something, I wanted to be a part. This is a dream come true for me."

Amber hugged Kenya. "Well, aren't you the sweetest?" Amber said.

Dawn said nothing. She nibbled another graham cracker without the slightest acknowledgment of Kenya's gushy sentiments. Dawn obviously had not a care to give about a beautiful newcomer.

"We are happy to have you," Blaine said.

"You've definitely added to our depth. Not taking anything away from Dawn, who has held down the soprano for years, but you are a godsend."

Blaine pulled out his keyboard and played the opening to "Born to Worship."

"Go ahead and teach us your new arrangement," Blaine said to Amber.

Amber took the floor and started teaching the parts without missing a beat. The group would absolutely survive this change and come out stronger, of this Blaine was sure. But he wasn't sure what would come of his and Dawn's situation, or if So G.I.F.T.E.D could survive that part too. The amount of fallout was up to Dawn. Blaine caught himself praying that she made the right decision.

He had no idea if God was listening.

CHAPTER 37

Blaine sat in Pastor Wilson's study at Graceway Dallas, and briefed his father on the flow of service for the coming Sunday, including the addition of Kenya to the group. Blaine took out his phone and showed his father a picture of Kenya, a selfie she'd taken with Blaine at his apartment after practice.

"This is Deacon Summers's daughter. The one that used to be hefty. She's sure looking good now," Pastor Wilson said.

"She is. And she sings like an angel too."

"She should be a welcome addition to the group. Especially since you all may have to get rid of Dawn."

Blaine frowned. "What do you mean? No one's replacing Dawn."

"Do you think she's going to be able to tour the country singing with a baby on her hip?"

"Lots of women do it, Dad. They hire

nannies. Plus, I'm not even sure she's planning on keeping the baby. She hasn't told me her decision."

"You proposed to her? You got her a ring?"

Blaine nodded. "I did everything you told me to do. She wouldn't budge. She was confused about what she wanted to do. For a minute she was thinking of trying to seduce Camden and make him think the baby was his. Then she scrapped that idea totally. Dawn doesn't know what she wants to do."

"So you *tell* her what she wants to do. Don't leave it up to her. She's not thinking clearly. Pregnancy hormones got her all twisted up. Your mother said Camden called her and told her about Dawn breaking things off with him."

"Was he okay?" Blaine asked.

Pastor Wilson shrugged. "Your mother seemed happy to hear that. Dawn is nothing but a little slut to her now, so she doesn't want her anywhere near Camden."

"She doesn't care if Dawn is with me, though?"

"Well, Dawn is carrying her first grandchild. That counts for something. But your mother will probably never forgive her for hurting Camden. Especially once he finds out that you're the father."

"I know. I'm more concerned about him forgiving me."

"He will. Your brother expects you to be a whore, but not his woman. I tell you this: He'll forgive you before he forgives Dawn."

"I was thinking that I want him as the Minister of Music in Oklahoma City."

Pastor Wilson shook his head. "I already said no to that idea. Why are we still talking about it?"

"Because, I disagree with you, Dad. Camden did nothing wrong by going to Atlanta. In fact, his going to Atlanta has made the group stronger and in turn will make my ministry stronger. I want my brother here."

Pastor Wilson laughed. "Then you better hope Dawn decides to abort your child, because *your brother* won't be in any pulpit with you if he finds that out."

"Of course. I was talking about if I didn't have to marry Dawn."

"She's going to start showing soon. We want to get you two married before everyone starts counting backward from her delivery date, if that's the path we have to take."

"Well, then you talk to Dawn. I can't make her budge."

"Get her on the phone right now."

Blaine dialed Dawn's phone number and after three rings she picked up. Blaine put

320

her on speakerphone.

"Dawn, you're on speaker. My dad wanted to talk to you."

"Hello," Dawn said.

"Dawn, I need you to get down to the church as soon as possible. We need to have a discussion."

"A discussion about what?" Dawn asked.

"Your future, my son's future, and my grandchild's future."

Dawn did not reply right away. Then after a long silence she said, "Why do *you* need to be a part of the discussion?"

Pastor Wilson's nostrils flared with anger. Blaine closed his eyes and shook his head. She'd unleashed the monster.

"You think you're calling the shots, don't you, you little whore? Get down to this church right now. I will not allow you or anyone else to destroy what I've taken years to build. You're going to do what the hell I say, or you might just find yourself on the outside looking in. I can marry Blaine off to Regina today, and then you'll just look like a pastor's mistress. Is that what you want? Or do you want to be the first lady of this church?"

"If I wasn't worried about my soul's salvation, I would've already terminated this pregnancy," Dawn said. "I don't want any part of what you're doing."

Pastor Wilson laughed directly into the speaker. "Do you think you can judge me? You led one of my sons by the nose for a decade and then slept with his brother. You are the lowest of low. You are not fit to judge me. Either get down to this church on your own, or I will send someone to fetch you."

Blaine could hear Dawn sniffle over the phone. His father had been exceptionally harsh, but maybe that was what needed to happen. Dawn for some reason was acting like she held all the cards. She carried the baby in her womb and her decision would impact everyone, but she refused to make that decision, leaving everyone in limbo.

"I'll be there in twenty minutes."

Blaine disconnected the phone, and Pastor Wilson sat back in his seat.

"We will have a decision today," Pastor Wilson said.

Blaine believed it.

CHAPTER 38

Blaine was in panic mode. Dawn had surprised both him and Pastor Wilson by not showing up at the church for his mandatory meeting. When he sent Stephen to Dawn and Amber's apartment to bring her to the church, she was gone.

The next day, it was Saturday and they were supposed to be on their way to Oklahoma City. Blaine paced his apartment living room, sick with worry. He had no idea what Dawn was planning to do. She could ruin him. She could ruin everything.

Blaine called Amber's phone.

"What, Blaine?"

"Have you heard from her yet?"

"I got a text saying that you and your father tried to threaten her and that she was going away for a minute."

Blaine sighed. "I didn't threaten her. You know I wouldn't do that. It was my father. He threatened her."

"I mean, both of y'all really need to stop for real. How you gonna act like she's the villain in all this? You're the bigger villain in my opinion."

"How you figure?"

"Because you know you seduced her, Blaine. You and your dad are acting like two demons right now."

"I keep telling you it's not me! I am supporting whatever decision Dawn makes, but we just don't have time for her to hold out if she's gonna keep the baby. If she chooses that we need to get married now, or the group, the church, everything is destroyed."

"Well, I guess y'all just gonna have to keep wondering, because I don't think she's coming out to play anytime soon."

Blaine disconnected his phone and threw it across the room. He wished he'd never laid a hand on Dawn. Or on Regina, or on any of the women who were now insisting on making his life a living hell.

Blaine went and retrieved his phone and scrolled through his text messages, looking for any notification from Dawn. There were none. But there was a text from Kenya.

What time are you picking me up?

Blaine had forgotten that he'd promised her a ride to Oklahoma City along with the rest of So G.I.F.T.E.D. She didn't deserve to be a part of the drama, but she had joined right in the middle of chaos.

He texted back. *We'll be there at 4.*

It was noon, and he had only a few hours to find Dawn and make her come with him to the church service. If not there would be hell to pay, and Blaine didn't want to be on the receiving end of Pastor Wilson's fury.

CHAPTER 39

"What do you mean she's not with you?" Pastor Wilson roared in his hotel suite. The guests on either side probably thought there was a war breaking out.

"Calm down, B. C.," First Lady Rita said. "You're making a scene. You don't like making scenes."

Pastor Wilson cut his eyes at his wife and then turned his attention to Blaine. "Are you telling me that you have no idea where this ho is? When I find her, I'm gonna choke the hell out of her myself."

"Has anyone called her family? Her mother? Her grandmother?" Delores asked.

Blaine wished that Delores would shut up. The very fact that she was in his parents' hotel suite for this meeting seemed to infuriate his mother, and with good reason. Her opinion was not needed, nor was it requested.

"Her family has been reaching out to *us,*"

Pastor Wilson said. "They think Camden has done something to her. They didn't even know that she'd broken up with him."

"What did you tell them?" Blaine asked.

"I told them that we would get in touch with them as soon as we heard from her, and I asked them to do the same. Then I prayed with her mama on the phone. She was a blubbering fool too, crying and carrying on. I wanted to tell her how much of a grown woman her daughter was."

"I'm glad you didn't," First Lady Rita said. "That wouldn't have helped anything."

"No, but it would've made me feel better. Do you need her to sing in the morning?"

Blaine shook his head. "No. Kenya can sing her part on all the songs."

"Perfect. Then stop reaching out to Dawn. Stop calling and texting her. I think she just likes the attention she's getting. She's got everyone in limbo. It's like negotiating with a terrorist."

"Who is possibly going to be the mother of your grandchild and your future daughter-in-law," First Lady said. "Don't decide that you hate her too much."

"You all keep acting like she's a victim. That girl ain't a victim. She thought Camden might be gay and got scared she might never be a part of this family. Then what

327

did she do? She laid up with this dummy and got herself some insurance. Dawn just might be smarter than everyone in this room."

Blaine shook his head. His father always gave everyone the worst of intentions. He knew that Dawn didn't have any of those thoughts in her head when they slept together. She was broken and afraid, and vulnerable. Amber was right. He was the villain, and not Dawn.

"I agree with Dad. We should just give her some space. She'll come around when she's ready and then we can figure out what comes next."

"What if she's big and pregnant when she comes out of hiding?" Delores asked.

"She knows what's at stake. She'll know what she'll have to answer to if she does that. What we'll have to answer to. So if she stays in hiding until then, we'll have to deal with those consequences too."

Pastor Wilson smirked at Blaine. "Well, listen at you. Calm in the face of adversity. You just might be learning something after all. You didn't handle that Regina situation well, but you're doing better with this one."

"What happened with Regina anyway?" First Lady Rita asked. "She also resigned as my assistant."

"She's going to do what she always wanted to do," Pastor Wilson said. "I gave her some seed money and a staff and she's starting her own church in Fort Worth. Not an extension of Graceway, but under our covering."

Blaine burst into laughter. "Regina as a pastor? She's the most evil and vindictive person I know."

"And that doesn't disqualify her," Pastor Wilson said. "We are called in spite of our shortcomings. Noah was a drunk, Moses was a stutterer, and David was like you — a womanizer to his core. That didn't stop God from calling him. He qualifies the ones he chooses."

Blaine listened to his father's words. He'd heard them before — always when he was trying to justify some shortcoming he had or some struggle he was facing (almost always a woman).

Blaine wondered if God would qualify him for this ministry. He could read the Bible and interpret it like any other Bible scholar. He'd done it his entire life. But would God qualify him to lead His people in spite of his flaws?

Even though Blaine knew all of his father's shortcomings, he also knew that Pastor Wilson had helped lots of people. There were people who attributed all of their success in life to his father. Pastor Wilson was guilty of much, but as long as his church was unaware, they continued to worship God and get their breakthroughs.

"Well, we can't worry about Dawn right now. As long as we have tomorrow's service covered, I'm content to handle her later," Pastor Wilson said.

Pastor Wilson's tone was menacing, which didn't bode well for Dawn. Blaine hoped that she gathered her wits sooner rather than later, because he didn't want to know what might happen if she made his father wait too much longer. Pastor Wilson didn't play when it came to *his* church.

CHAPTER 40

Camden watched the streaming service from Graceway Oklahoma City. Nothing had changed about his father and his uncanny power to mesmerize the people of God. In just four weeks, he had gone from one hundred members to six thousand, people abandoning their storefront and childhood churches all over the city to join up with Graceway for the "supernatural transference of wealth."

Camden had watched every service and witnessed the testimonies of the new members who claimed to have had breakthroughs in their finances, health, marriages, and child rearing after sowing a sacrificial offering. Camden prayed for them all, including Pastor Wilson.

He watched Blaine lead So G.I.F.T.E.D in singing his song. The new arrangement was almost perfect, and Kenya's voice sounded beautiful blending with Amber's.

But Dawn was missing. Camden wondered where she was. He hoped she hadn't let her jealousy about Kenya's vocals cause her to doubt herself. Dawn was a strong vocalist, and she was one of the founding members. It wouldn't be the same without her. The sound would be different.

Blaine led the church in the prayer for this week's offering — another sacrificial one. But in this prayer, Blaine promised emotional healing to the broken. He called down to the altar everyone who was suffering with depression or a downtrodden spirit. He said that God had spoken to him during the song, and that God had said it was time for the chains to be broken.

Blaine then sang a remix of Camden's upbeat praise song. He turned "I Am Free" into a battle cry, and the wounded broken souls came from all over the auditorium seeking a touch from Blaine and a touch from God.

Camden was surprised at how easily Blaine had morphed into a carbon copy of their father. He might even be better than Pastor Wilson in his ability to be the Pied Piper to the lost. He'd be a megachurch millionaire pastor soon. Pastor Wilson's vision for him would come to pass.

Camden paused the Internet video when

his cell phone rang. He hesitated before answering. It was Dawn. He didn't want to talk to her, but he was curious about why she wasn't at church.

"Hello."

"Hi, Camden. It's me, Dawn."

"I was just watching the recording of your church service this morning. Why weren't you there?"

"I'm at my cousin's house in Texarkana."

"What in the world are you doing out there?"

"I needed to get away from everything. The group, the church, and your father."

Camden was confused. "My father. Why do you need to get away from my father?"

Maybe someone had told Pastor Wilson about Dawn breaking up with him, but why would he feel the need to say anything to Dawn about that? He'd banned Camden from the ministry, so he couldn't have cared about who he was dating.

Dawn let out a heavy and burdened sigh. "Camden, there is more to what I told you when I was in Atlanta."

"Oh."

"And you're gonna hate me for this, but I have to tell you. I can't continue to live this with you not knowing the truth."

"Okay, now you're scaring me. What did

you do?"

"The guy . . . the guy that I was talking about was Blaine. And we slept together."

Camden took the phone away from his face and looked at it. Then he shook his head and looked at the ceiling. He had to be dreaming. There was no way that what Dawn had just said could be happening in real life.

"You slept with Blaine. Did he . . . did he force you?"

"No. It was consensual. I can tell you the reasons, but they'll just sound like excuses, and I don't have an excuse."

"Humor me. Tell me the reasons anyway. I have to understand why my girlfriend of ten years would decide to have sex with my twin brother."

"Camden, you're yelling."

Camden chuckled. "Am I? You think?"

"It happened in Miami. I was feeling some kind of way about the gay accusation, and you were acting distant."

"Oh no. You're not going to blame me. I've never been distant. I've been working, I've been in another state, but I have not been distant. You, however, have been needy and selfish. You didn't want me to come here and go after my dream so you punished me by having sex with my twin."

334

"It wasn't like that. I wasn't trying to punish you."

"Good, because you've punished yourself. Have fun with Blaine. I hope you don't catch any diseases, 'cause he gets around."

"Camden, I'm pregnant. Your father wants me to marry Blaine, and I don't know what to do."

"Do you love him?"

"I care about him. We've been friends forever."

"Ask yourself if you want to be married to someone you don't love," Camden said. "It doesn't matter to me. Have a great life."

Dawn burst into tears. "Camden, please don't hate me. Please. I love you more than anybody on this earth. I know I've done wrong, but please don't hate me."

"What do you want me to do, Dawn? I can't wrap my mind around this. Do you know I was planning to propose to you in Atlanta? You were sitting up there pregnant with my twin brother's child and I was about to give you a ring."

Dawn sobbed and choked over the phone. She begged and pleaded for his forgiveness, but Camden felt nothing. Not even pity.

"What if I got rid of the baby?" Dawn asked. "Do you think we could get past this?"

"Are you *crazy*? If I was you, I wouldn't add one sin on top of another. What did that baby do to deserve that? All things work together for the good, Dawn. If you love the Lord, and repent, He'll forgive you."

"What about you, though, Camden?"

"Don't break my heart and ask me to be like God."

Camden disconnected the call and sobbed. He hadn't cried when Dawn broke up with him. Maybe, deep down, he thought they were just having a rough patch and eventually they'd get back together.

But there was no coming back from this. Nothing that could make him want to be with Dawn ever again.

Even though he wanted nothing more to do with his brother or Dawn, Camden wanted them to see him one last time. He wanted them both to see the pain they'd caused him. They would know and have to live with their damage.

Camden looked at the clock on his phone. Nine o'clock P.M. He dialed Amber's phone number. She answered on the fourth ring.

"Cambreezy, this nap that I was just taking . . . my God. It was straight from the throne of grace. What's up, though?"

"Amber, I want to ask you out on a date."

"What in tarnation? Stop playing, man."

"No. I'm serious. I need a date. To Blaine and Dawn's wedding."

■ ■ ■ ■

PART II

■ ■ ■ ■

CHAPTER 41

"B.J.! Leave your brother alone! He's trying to have his nap!" Dawn hissed at the rambunctious five-year-old throwing toys into the crib where one of her six-month-old twins was sleeping.

As soon as B. J. woke Jacob, the other twin Jayla would wake and they would both be screaming at the top of their lungs, destroying any hope Dawn had of a moment of peace and quiet.

"I wanna pway wif him," Blaine Junior protested as Dawn picked him up like a football and tucked him under her arm.

Once they were outside the babies' nursery, Dawn closed the door and put B. J. down. He had tears in his eyes. He loved his younger siblings even though they were brand new, and if he could, he'd spend all day running back and forth picking up the toys and pacifiers they hurled across the room.

"So, how would you like a snack? You can eat some Goldfish and have a juice box. By the time you're all done and your cartoon is over, the babies will be awake."

B. J. gave his mother a smile that was the spitting image of his uncle Camden's. His smooth brown skin was just as dark as Camden's and his black wavy hair lay down just the same. Dawn felt sorry for the girls who would be in his path one day. But she planned to raise him to respect women, a lesson that his father could never teach.

Dawn led her handsome son into the sprawling kitchen and sat him at the table. Every room in the ten thousand square foot house was sprawling, and Dawn took pride in it. Her home was one of the few things she could take joy in.

Blaine walked through the house, talking on his cell phone, with Akil at his heels.

"I don't care what it costs, I want a new audiovisual system in the sanctuary. What we have now looks amateurish on the broadcast. We are an international ministry, we need to look like one."

Blaine disconnected the phone and looked at Akil. "Can you make sure they do what I asked on that? I don't see why this is so hard. I'm the one signing the checks, right?"

"Yeah, man."

"Did you close on that condo you wanted?" Blaine asked.

"Yep. I have got all my furniture ordered already. It should be totally done by the time we go on tour."

"Good."

B. J. squirmed in his chair. "Daddy! Daddy!"

Blaine picked his son up and spun him in the air. B. J.'s giggles filled the room. Dawn sat their son's snacks down on the table and started preparing Blaine's lunch.

"What are you doing?" Blaine asked Dawn.

"Making you a sandwich."

"I don't want a sandwich. Why don't you ask me what I want to eat before you start making it?"

"What do you want to eat, Blaine?"

"Nothing. I'm good. Akil and I just had steaks."

Dawn made her lips into a line and tossed the sandwich fixings in the trash.

"You didn't have to waste that food. You could've put it away for another time," Blaine said. "You can't expect God to continue to bless us if you're going to be wasteful."

Dawn walked out of the kitchen and toward her office. She didn't want to hear

343

any more of Blaine's criticism today. Maybe he and Akil would leave again and she could have that peace and quiet she was trying to find.

"You left your son," Blaine called after her. "I've got business to attend to, I know you don't think I'm watching him now."

Dawn turned on one heel and walked back into the kitchen. She scooped up B. J. along with his snacks. Then she took her son into the children's playroom and closed the door.

She slid down the wall and sat on the floor in the corner of the room and watched her son play.

"Sing to me, Mommy."

"I don't feel like singing, baby."

"Pwease . . ."

Dawn cleared her throat and sang "Jesus Loves Me" to her son. He clapped and danced in a little circle. How could he not enjoy music? He was the product of musical parents. He carried the names of both his father and his musical uncle. Blaine Camden Wilson III, like his grandfather.

Dawn could hear Blaine and Akil's voices outside the playroom. She wished they would leave.

They were planning another tour for So G.I.F.T.E.D. Another tour that she wouldn't be a part of. When Camden and Royce added Kenya to the group, they'd said it wasn't to replace her. It wasn't the truth. As soon as B. J. was born she was told that they didn't need her services anymore. They'd even added another female soprano to solidify her exit from the group.

Dawn was a first lady, a mother to beautiful children, and a wife.

"Dawn, come out here for a second," Blaine called.

Dawn slowly got up from the floor and went to see what Blaine wanted.

"Akil and I are going to San Antonio tomorrow to scout out locations for our conference. We'll be back Sunday morning in time for service."

Dawn knew that trip would include Blaine hooking up with some woman he'd met years ago or maybe even someone new. He never touched her anymore. Over the course of their five-year marriage, Dawn could count on her hands the number of times they'd had sex.

"You should get your hair done. Have a spa day or something. You look horrible."

Dawn wanted to spit at him, but she just nodded. She did look horrible — haggard was a better description. She'd gained weight. That thick hourglass physique she'd had when Blaine had first taken her was replaced by rolls of fat, and stretch marks. Her breasts hung low, heavy with milk for the twins.

"Amber said she was going to drop by and check on you later," Akil said. "She wants to know if you want Chinese food."

Blaine laughed. "Only if she's bringing a Chinese salad."

"Tell her I said yes. She knows what I like," Dawn said, ignoring Blaine's unfunny joke.

Dawn waited for a moment to see if Blaine wanted to say anything else. When he went back to checking the emails on his cell phone, she assumed he was done. She opened the playroom door and caught B. J. just as he was about to pour his juice box on the floor. She took it from him. "No. Don't do that, baby. You're making a mess."

"The babies awake?"

"Not yet. Let's watch a movie."

He shook his head. "Wanna go wif Daddy."

"Auntie Amber is coming over. You can play with her."

B. J. grinned big. He loved Amber. Sometimes Dawn thought her son loved Amber more than he loved her. But then, Amber spoiled him rotten.

Dawn felt herself relax when Blaine and Akil finally left. But her relaxation was only brief, because Jacob had already started his slow whimpering. In a few minutes he would be at full blast and Jayla would be next. Then she'd have to hold them both in her lap and nurse them at once. It was the only way they liked to nurse. One on each breast. Until they sucked her dry.

Tears trickled down Dawn's face. B. J. quickly wiped them away.

"No crying, Mommy. No."

Dawn forced herself to smile and then rose to her feet. She took B. J.'s hand and led him to the nursery. Her babies were crying. They needed her.

She needed them too. They were the only things keeping her alive.

CHAPTER 42

Camden listened to the new artist Ivy had brought to his studio. Angelique had an incredible voice, but very little vocal training. Ivy wanted to make her a teen gospel sensation, if there even was such a thing.

"What do you think?" Ivy asked. "Can you and Amber work with her?"

"Amber can definitely work with her, but I'm not sure how the record label can market her."

Angelique said, "I don't need marketing. I'm an evangelist. The Lord is gonna open every door I need opened."

Camden tilted his head to one side and nodded. "Okay, Evangelist. Well, the record label will still want a marketing plan, even if they don't need one."

Amber burst into the recording studio. "Ooh, I'm sorry I'm late, y'all. My flight just got in a couple hours ago, and you know I had to get something to eat."

"Your greedy self still smells like Pappadeaux. Did you bring me some?" Camden said.

"What you're smelling is my to-go box, and I could be convinced to share with you. Sing something for me, baby. I hear you got a voice like an angel."

"I do. That's why my mama named me Angelique. She said my first cry sounded like a song."

"No one can say you're not confident."

Angelique belted out a song for Amber, and Amber gave her a round of applause.

"Yes, she'll be great. We can work with her."

"Camden says they won't be able to market me," Angelique said.

"He did? Since when did you start caring about record label stuff? We're here for the music all day every day. And you, girlfriend, can blow, you hear me?"

"That's all I needed to hear," Ivy said. "We'll call you and set up a development schedule."

"Okay, girl," Amber said.

"Are you going to be in town on Sunday? We'd love to have you sing with the praise team," Ivy said.

"I think I will be here. I'll come on up to the pulpit when I get to service."

Ivy hugged Amber. " 'Kay. Love you lots."

"Love you too."

Ivy and Angelique left the studio and Amber plopped down in one of the soft leather chairs. Camden dug into Amber's leftover food without heating it up.

"How's everything in Dallas?" Camden asked. "Your mom all right?"

"You know she doesn't take her blood pressure medicine like she's supposed to, so I had to get in her behind about that. But other than that she's okay."

"What about Akil?"

"You know he's living the life being Blaine's henchman. Blaine just bought him a new condo."

Camden rolled his eyes. "Yeah, okay. You were in OKC too?"

Amber nodded. "You know I had to see about Dawn."

"Oh."

Camden waited for Amber to elaborate, because she always did. She insisted on keeping him up to date with every birthday, holiday, and milestone in Dawn and Blaine's life. He wished she wouldn't. It didn't make him feel any closer to forgiving them. Five years hadn't dulled the sting of their betrayal.

"So when are you going to give up that

apartment in Dallas and move here full-time?"

She smiled. "Why would I do that? I have lots of boos in Dallas."

"You've got lots of boos in Atlanta too."

"You're right."

"It's easier for our consulting and artist preparation business if you're here in Atlanta full-time."

"I'll take that under advisement. Are you going to ask about your nephews and niece?"

"Sure. How are the children who are my blood relatives that I don't know?"

"Well, B. J. looks more and more like you every day. He looks like you're his daddy, to be honest."

"But I'm not, though."

"I know, but I just wish you could see him. It's been five years. The babies are beautiful. The twins have pretty hazel eyes and curly hair like Blaine. It's time for us to come back together. We used to all be family. I can't take this."

"You're around them all the time. It's never going to be the same again."

"But you say you're over Dawn."

"Been over Dawn."

"So why can't you forgive?"

Camden stared at the ceiling and groaned.

He was so tired of having this conversation with Amber.

"Why can't they apologize?" Camden asked. "No one has once opened their mouth to say we're sorry for hurting you."

"Dawn apologized."

"Barely. She justified her actions. There was no justification for what she did."

Amber stroked Camden's smooth hair and shook her head. "Cam, the forgiveness is for you, not for them. Let it go. You haven't fallen in love, your music isn't the same."

"The music is fine."

"Well, sure. Technically it's fine, but you haven't written anything close to 'Born to Worship' since all of this happened. Something is broken inside you. Forgiving them lets your healing begin."

"I hear what you're saying, Amber, and I know what you say is true. It's just very hard to practice that when someone ripped your heart out. It's dang near impossible."

"Come home with me the next time. Come visit. Your mother wants to see you."

"She is welcome to visit here. I even offered to fly her in."

"She's refusing because she wants you to come home. Please, Camden. Come home with me. If it is too much for you, we can always leave."

"If I do it just once, will you leave me alone?"

Amber said, "Maybe. Maybe I'll leave you alone. I can't promise you that."

Camden would do this for Amber, and because he missed his mother terribly. But he had absolutely no interest in Blaine, Dawn, or their children. He also didn't care about putting So G.I.F.T.E.D back together again in the way that it was. There was a time and season for everything, and Camden's season for dealing with Blaine was long past. This was Camden's season for moving on.

CHAPTER 43

Kenya stretched across the hotel room bed in the red lingerie that Blaine bought her to celebrate their first anniversary. She was trying to get Blaine's attention, but he was busy reading his emails and responding to them.

"Come on to bed, babe. We don't have much time," Kenya said.

"We've got all the time we want, sweetie."

"But we have to leave tomorrow morning to get back to church."

Blaine set his phone down and came to bed. He untied his robe and slid under the sheets naked.

"Come over here, girl. You got me ready now."

Kenya crawled over to Blaine and purred. "You know what gets me ready?"

"What, baby?"

"When you tell me you love me and that you're going to leave Dawn."

Blaine said, "Do we have to talk about that right now? You know how I feel about you. I've known you'd be mine from the very first time I saw you."

"So what took you so long to come after me?"

"Don't you remember that Dawn was pregnant when we met? You were worth the wait, though."

"I was. Does anyone know about me?"

"Does anyone know? What do you mean? Why would I tell anyone about you?" Blaine asked. "I'm a pastor. I can't go around broadcasting that I've got a woman on the side."

"Not even Akil?"

Blaine was pretty sure Akil knew exactly what was going on between him and Kenya. It was his job to know. But they'd never had a conversation about it, and Blaine had never admitted it. Akil simply looked the other way and made sure no one else found out about his indiscretions.

"Why does someone need to know other than us, sweetie? We're the only ones that need to know."

"If you'd told someone else, then I'd believe what you tell me about us being together someday."

"Do you think I'd lie to you, make you

355

angry and destroy So G.I.F.T.E.D? We just had another number one record. I mean it when I say we're going to be together."

"When?"

"My youngest children are six months old. I don't want to split up with Dawn while she has babies to care for. That would be cruel, and I can't have my congregation thinking I'm cruel. It's better if she leaves me anyway."

"Please. Why would she do that? She's living in a mansion. She's the first lady. She's not gonna leave."

"She knows she'll always be well taken care of as long as she has my children. But she's not very happy right now. She might just get fed up."

Kenya kicked her feet out in front of her and pouted. "I don't like the odds of that. I want something more definite."

"I'm sorry, baby. It's the best I can do right now. But it doesn't change how much I love you."

Blaine wasn't lying when he said he loved Kenya. She was everything he wished Dawn was. He'd fallen in love with her soon after she'd joined the group, although she ignored his flirting due to his being married to Dawn. The more his church grew, the more Kenya received his advances. He'd bought her cars, and a house, and would give her more if Dawn would just leave.

It seemed no matter how badly he treated Dawn, she wouldn't budge. She just took it all like a dog took kicks from its master. He couldn't divorce her, not if he didn't want his church to go bananas, but she seemed to have no intention of leaving.

"I love you too, Blaine. I love you so much," Kenya said. "I just hope you don't take too long to make me your wife."

Blaine knew who he needed to talk to about this. The one man he knew who'd had a mistress for his entire life and had managed to keep everyone in line. Pastor Wilson. He'd know exactly what to do.

CHAPTER 44

".Bring my handsome grandson over here!" Pastor Wilson said as B. J. ran across his study and scrambled into his lap.

Blaine was always amazed to see how his father doted on his grandson. He couldn't ever remember him being so hands on when he and Camden were little. He didn't deal with them at all until they were almost teenagers. He acted like young children were women's work.

"Grandpoppy, I can count to one hundred! You wanna hear me?"

"I do, but I think your daddy wants to talk to me first. Want to go and see Grandma? Somebody told me that she was making cookies!"

"Cookies!"

B. J. scrambled out of Pastor Wilson's lap and Stephen led him out of the study.

"Sit down, son. To what do I owe this visit? Where are Dawn and the babies?"

Blaine sat down in front of his father's desk. "Dawn's at home. I wanted to come and talk to you by myself. I need your advice about something."

"Is it the ministry? I watched your broadcast last Sunday. Son, you just may be a better preacher than me."

"What did you say?"

Pastor Wilson laughed. "There's no way I'm ever repeating that. It was a one and done."

Blaine laughed with his father, although he wasn't in a joking mood.

"Dad, remember what you told me to do when I married Dawn? You told me to divorce her quietly after a few years."

Pastor Wilson sat up in his chair. "Things bad between the two of you?"

"I just don't want to be with her. I love someone else."

"Your mistress, Kenya. You've fallen in love with the sidepiece. You know that's against the rules."

"What rules? I can't control what my heart does, or Dawn's either. She's never loved me like she loved Camden. I feel like we're both miserable."

"Well, a divorce is out of the question right now. Your ministry is exploding and a divorce would halt your forward progress."

Blaine sighed. "But what about Kenya? She'll leave me if I don't get a divorce soon. I don't know what I'd do without her."

Pastor Wilson shook his head. "More powerful men have been destroyed by what's between a woman's legs than anything else."

"Kenya doesn't want to destroy me."

"Look, you need to teach Kenya her place. She can accept the fact that she's not your wife, or she can move on. But she can't move into the top spot, not now. The group almost didn't recover from your marriage to Dawn. It definitely wouldn't weather your divorce from her."

There had been an uproar when Dawn and Blaine had gotten married. Camden never responded in the media, but the gay rumors rose again. The only thing that had quieted the rumors was the birth of their first child. It gave people something else to talk about.

"I guess you're right."

"Does Dawn complain about the time you spend with Kenya?"

Blaine shook his head. "I only spend time with Kenya when I'm away on travel for ministry. Dawn doesn't know about her."

"Well, you think she doesn't. She may not know it's Kenya specifically, but she knows it's someone. They always know."

"Does Mom know?"

Pastor Wilson sighed. "She knows and she tolerates it. She's never accepted it, but I don't flaunt it in her face."

"So, you're saying if I am stern with Kenya about her place, she'll accept it?"

Pastor Wilson said, "Don't be stern with her. Reiterate her position, and give her a gift while you do it. The mistress *does* have some leverage when the wife doesn't know she exists. My mistress has no leverage when it comes to my wife. That's the best way."

"You think I should tell Dawn?"

"No. Absolutely not, but if she happened to find out and stayed anyway, you'd have the best of both worlds."

"Thank you, Dad! I know exactly what I need to do now."

Blaine stepped around the desk to hug his father. He felt tremendously close to him now.

"You're welcome, son. Now, go bring me my grandson so I can hear him count to one hundred."

Blaine went into the kitchen to find his mother and B. J. She had indeed baked cookies, just like she used to do when he and Camden were little.

"Hi, Mom."

"He looks just like Camden," First Lady Rita said, ignoring her son's greeting.

"He does."

"It's too bad he's never seen him."

"That's his choice," Blaine said. "No one is keeping him away from my children."

"Did you ever think that it's too painful to be around you, Dawn, and your family?"

"Maybe it is."

"So you should extend an apology, and an invitation," First Lady Rita said.

"Camden knows that I love him, and the only reason why this thing happened with Dawn is because *she* thought he was gay and pushed up on me."

"You're never accountable, are you? It's always someone else's fault, but never yours."

"I wonder if you would be this hard on Camden if it was the other way around."

"Of course I would, but Camden isn't the type of man who would do that to his brother. You are your father's child through and through."

"I take that as a compliment," Blaine said. "My father is one of the most anointed preachers in the country."

"And he's the biggest whore. No matter what your father tells you, God doesn't look away from his adultery. He won't look away from yours either."

"You would curse me, Mom? I'm your son."

She shook her head. "This isn't me cursing you. This is a law of the universe. Whatever a man is sowing, this he will also reap."

"Tell me this. What did your precious son Camden do to reap everything that's befallen him? Sometimes things just happen, and we pick up the pieces and we move on."

"I don't know. Maybe he's like Job. The devil just wants to attack him because he's righteous."

Blaine's anger level rose, and his skin turned red with fury. "Camden is not Job! He was selfish! He dated Dawn for ten years and then left to chase music! He's no saint, and he ain't righteous. But he can do no wrong in your eyes."

Blaine lifted B. J. into his arms and walked back toward his father's study. That was a sanctuary for him, but his mother was on the constant attack.

"You *fix this*!" First Lady Rita shouted at Blaine's back. "You broke this family. *You* go and get *my son*!"

Blaine shuddered with anger but maintained his composure. He'd given his mother a daughter-in-law and grandchildren. He'd maintained a successful church, but still it wasn't enough — *he* wasn't enough. He wasn't Camden. Sweet, gentle, kind, self-serving, and ambitious Camden.

Blaine gave up on trying to please his mother. As long as Pastor Wilson smiled on him, he was satisfied.

CHAPTER 45

Camden had practiced his approach over and over again, but he was still concerned he'd be a failure. As he listened to Amber tell him an animated story at dinner, all he could think of was how beautiful she was, had always been. Her copper brown skin seemed to glow from within — it was her internal joy. The thing that attracted him to her most.

"And that child hit that high note! She hit it like it stole her last chicken nugget. She went all upside that note's head. And after that I told her, 'Don't tell me you don't have range, baby.' "

Camden laughed. "You bring the best out of so many singers. That is a gift, you know. I can hear when something is right, but you inspire them to be great."

"I do? Well, I just love good singing, Cam. It makes my soul smile. Can a soul smile?"

"Yours can. Yours does every day."

"Did you think over what I said about visiting home?" Amber asked. "Your father asked me to sing at his anniversary dinner next month."

"Yes, this marks forty years in ministry for him. Forty years of being a pastor. Forty years of hoing around on my mother, and almost six years of disowning his son. A milestone."

"He didn't disown you, Camden. He felt like you abandoned Graceway for your music."

"Don't defend him."

"I'm not! He's definitely wrong for that, and that stuff with Delores is beyond shameful. But your daddy has done some good too. He's done a lot of good."

Camden shook his head. "Do his good deeds cancel out his evil?"

"No, but the blood of Jesus does. He can repent just like anybody else."

"In order to repent, you have to acknowledge wrongdoing. My father thinks he's above God's laws. My father thinks that he defines what is holy and righteous."

"Okay, Camden." Amber took a bite of her salad and shook her head.

"Why'd you bring them up? We were having a good time."

"Because I want you to get past this,

Camden. It's eating you up inside and you don't even know it."

Camden softened. "If you really want me to go to Dallas with you, I will. But I'm not staying under his roof."

"You can't stay under *my* roof," Amber said with a giggle. "So, I guess you'll be getting a hotel room."

"Why would I want to stay under your roof anyway?" Camden asked.

Amber bit her bottom lip and grinned. "Camdeezy, I see the way you look at me. When you gonna man up and ask me out on a date?"

Camden threw his head back and laughed. The speech was gone out the window now. Amber had kicked the door in, so he might as well walk through.

"Will you be my date at my father's anniversary celebration?"

"I'd be honored. But before we start this thing, I want you to know that I'm celibate."

"Okay, I am too."

Amber gave him a blank stare. "No. I'm for *real* celibate. Not that, celibate-till-I-get-some-celibate. The next person I'm giving it up to is my husband."

"Was this required information before the first date?"

She laughed. "Yes. Y'all Wilson men are

quite randy. I need you to know what you ain't gone get."

"I got you. Oh, before you manhandled me into asking you out on a date, I kind of had a speech planned."

"A speech?" Amber asked. "What kind of speech?"

Camden cleared his throat. "Amber, you have always been there for me. You've been my best friend, you've prayed for me, and I wouldn't be where I am today had it not been for you constantly being in my corner. I love you so much."

Amber's eyes filled with tears. "I love you too, Cam."

"These last five years, working with you, I've just come to see a whole new side of you. You're sexy —"

"I've always been sexy."

Camden laughed. "Stop interrupting."

"Okay."

"You're sexy, funny, can cook your butt off, and you're fine. You are everything I want and need in a woman."

"Aw shoot! Did I say I was celibate? Lord help."

Camden cracked up laughing. "I can't get through this if you keep making me laugh."

"Sorry."

Camden reached in his pocket and took

out a box. He placed it in front of Amber.

"We haven't even gone out on a date yet, Camdeezy. Isn't this putting the cart before the horse?"

"Open it!"

Amber opened the box and removed a beautiful charm bracelet that had several charms attached.

"Oh, it's beautiful! Put it on me!"

Amber thrust her wrist out and Camden put the bracelet on.

Camden said, "The music note charm is pretty obvious, and the cross is because you love God with every part of your being. The flip-flop is because you love the beach."

"And the heart key is 'cause you love me," Amber said.

"I do. But the heart key is because you have my heart. It's yours. I've known it for a long time, but I didn't know if you'd want me."

"What? Boy, stop."

"No, I always thought you had a crush on Blaine all those years. I actually thought y'all would end up together."

"Don't get me wrong, Blaine was good-looking and a serious flirt. But I like my men tall, dark, and brooding."

Camden laughed. "Well, that's me. Especially the brooding part."

"I can't wait to show up in Dallas with you on my arm! Chocolate arm candy. Yes, sir!"

"Do you think everyone will be surprised?"

"Not at all," Amber said with a giggle. "I think they'll say, 'It's about time.' "

CHAPTER 46

Blaine inhaled deeply and exhaled slowly. Kenya had just prepared him a wonderful dinner — lasagna, one of his favorite meals. The best part about her cooking for him was that she liked to do it in lingerie and heels. She was a fantasy come to life.

But Blaine was nervous. He was about to do what his father told him to do, inform Kenya of her place. He couldn't lose her. Wouldn't lose her. But she had to be patient.

Kenya carried the tray of lasagna to the table in her sheer teddy, and Blaine's mouth watered. Her body was perfection. She worked out every day, so there wasn't an ounce of fat on her. She sat down at the table and smiled.

"You hungry, babe?" she asked.

He was hungry. In more ways than one. But he had to stay focused. He couldn't let her distract him with sex. Not tonight.

"You know I love your lasagna, babe."

"You could have it all the time, and every other thing you love."

Blaine was silent while she put food onto both of their plates. She poured wine into their glasses, and Blaine took a sip.

"We need to talk," Blaine said.

"That sounds official. Are we about to finally make things official?"

Blaine shook his head. "Kenya, you know I love you, right?"

"Yes, I know you love me. I love you too."

"If things were different, I'd ask you to marry me today."

Kenya frowned. "I already don't like where this is going."

"Well, you asked me about when I was going to divorce my wife."

"And?"

"My father thinks it wouldn't be good for the ministry for me to divorce my wife with two small babies."

"So you're not going to leave her. You've been lying to me this entire time."

"I haven't been lying. Don't you like all of the expensive gifts I can buy you? Your cars, jewelry, shopping sprees?"

Kenya perked up a little. "Yes. I do."

"Well, the ministry is what pays for all of that. I could never afford to keep you this well taken care of if it wasn't for my church.

So we have to protect that."

"But don't you still . . . don't you still sleep with Dawn? I don't want to share my man."

"I hardly even touch her."

This was the truth. Kenya wasn't sharing Blaine sexually. The sight of Dawn naked disgusted him, so she absolutely did not have to worry about that.

"Will you ever leave her?"

Blaine nodded slowly, even though he was unsure of this. "When the time is right, babe. I have to do it when the time is right."

"I'm not going to be your mistress forever."

Blaine pulled her into an embrace and buried his face in her hair. He loved the way she smelled. He loved the way she made him feel. He loved who he was when he was around her. He loved everything about her.

If only he'd disobeyed his father long ago and never married Dawn to begin with. Maybe he would've been in a position to marry his queen when she finally came along. But now, no matter how he looked at it, he was stuck with a woman who was beneath him.

Camden should be the one dealing with her overeating and stretch marks. He deserved more. He was Pastor Blaine Wilson of Graceway Oklahoma City. His destiny had led him to greatness. Why would God give him so much and then punish him to be stuck with someone like Dawn?

CHAPTER 47

Dawn heard the doorbell ring as she nursed the twins and looked up at the clock. Who could be visiting at noon? The only girl-friend she had was Amber, and she was in Atlanta. Blaine was in Dallas working on ministry strategy with Pastor Wilson, or at least that was where he said he was. She'd stopped trying to check up on him years ago, as long as he left her alone.

Perhaps it was a package being delivered. Blaine had most of his items delivered to the church, but sometimes she ordered things in the mail. Had she ordered anything lately?

Since the doorbell continued to ring, Dawn took the babies off her breasts and put them in their cribs. She straightened her gray sweatsuit and went downstairs with B. J. at her heels.

She looked through the peephole and was surprised to see that it was Kenya. Dawn opened the door slowly with her eyes wide.

"Hi, Dawn!" Kenya said with a bubbly tone.

"Um . . . hello."

"Well, are you going to invite me in?"

Dawn looked over her shoulder. "Sure, but are you here for Blaine? He and Akil are in Dallas right now."

"I'm here to see you!"

"What? Why do you want to see me?"

"I can't drop by and visit my first lady? I thought we were friends."

Dawn's first instinct was to not trust Kenya. Why should she? Kenya was the one who'd stolen her spot in So G.I.F.T.E.D. She'd come with her songbird trills and runs and had gotten Dawn unceremoniously removed from the group.

But it was lonely as first lady of a megachurch. No one just dropped by to say hello. That wasn't official protocol. Many of the women didn't think she was good enough for Blaine and were vying to be her replacement, so they couldn't be trusted. And the older women judged her home. It was either too untidy or too extravagant. She was never enough for them.

So even though Kenya wasn't exactly a friend, a visit from her wasn't totally unwelcome.

"Well, sure you can come on in. I was just about to make myself and B. J. some lunch. We can share."

Kenya gave her a bright smile and stepped inside. "You've got some new furniture."

"Yes, we did a little remodeling. Blaine picked out all the original furniture. I wanted to give the house more of a feminine touch."

"Well, it looks really good. You did a good job."

Kenya followed Dawn into the kitchen, and Dawn took out some chicken salad that she'd made the day before, croissants, and fruit.

"Would you like herbal tea?" Dawn asked.

Kenya nodded. "Yes, please."

As Dawn moved around the kitchen she found that she enjoyed this little bit of excitement. Her chicken salad was really tasty, and she loved for people to try her food.

"I have chicken salad and fruit. Oh, and I made a cream cheese pound cake the other day. Would you like some of that too?"

"Yes to the chicken salad and fruit. No thank you on the pound cake. I don't really eat sweets. They wreck my figure."

Dawn looked down at her rolls. "Well, they wreck mine too, but that doesn't seem to stop me."

"You've had babies, girl! And you have a man already. It's okay to let yourself go a little bit. I'm still single. I have to find myself a man before I start eating pound cake."

"You shouldn't have a problem finding a man. I don't believe that."

"There is a limited pool of *good* men. Trust, by the time we hit thirty, most of the good ones have already been snapped up. You know anyone you can introduce me to?"

She thought about it for a moment. "What about Akil?"

Kenya burst into laughter. "Those guys are like my brothers! Plus, Akil is a player extraordinaire. I don't think I'd be able to trust him, knowing half the things I know."

"He did used to get around back in the day."

"Back in the day? He still gets around. Pray for his salvation."

The topic of conversation made Dawn uncomfortable. She remembered, all too vividly, that Akil was always Blaine's partner in crime. If Akil was still hoing, she wondered if Blaine was too. Deep down she *knew* Blaine was cheating. How could he not be? He wasn't touching her, so she knew he was touching someone.

"Maybe the guys know someone to hook you up with. There are quite a few single brothers in the congregation, but I don't know them well enough to offer a recommendation."

"I will ask them at our next rehearsal, because a sista is pretty desperate. Do you know I set up an online dating account?"

Dawn's eyes widened. "On the Internet? Did you see anyone with potential?"

"A few, but the competition online is just as stiff as at a church or anywhere else."

Dawn sat a plate in front of Kenya at the breakfast bar and another in front of B. J. at the kitchen table. Then she prepared the cups of tea, slid them across the bar, and took a seat with her plate next to Kenya.

"You're so lucky to have Blaine," Kenya said. "How did you land him anyway?"

Dawn laughed. "You may not be able to tell now, but I once had a very nice shape. He saw me in a bathing suit and the rest was history."

Kenya joined in on the laughter. "Girl, all you need is to work out a little. You could get your shape back."

"I know. I just don't have any motivation."

"Aren't you motivated to keep your husband?"

Dawn couldn't tell Kenya the truth, but

some days she wished Blaine would leave. A woman like Kenya would never understand that. She saw Blaine as a prize. Dawn knew the truth.

"Sure I am. But these children have me worn out."

"Why don't you have a nanny?"

"A nanny? I don't have a job, so I didn't think I really needed one."

"You're rich. Rich women have nannies whether they have jobs or not."

"I don't know what I'd do all day if I had a nanny. The children take up my whole day."

Kenya laughed. "You could go with me to the gym. We could get our hair and nails done. We could go shopping."

"We? We could do these things."

"If you want to. Remember, I used to be over three hundred pounds, Dawn. I know what it's like to work hard and get the results. Let me help you."

"I'll ask Blaine about it and see what he says."

"Don't ask him. Just do it. Ask forgiveness and not permission."

Dawn laughed out loud. "Did you plan all this out before you got here?"

"Well . . . to be honest, I saw you at service last Sunday, and you looked so depressed. Something in my spirit told me you needed a friend."

Dawn smiled. She wanted to jump up and hug Kenya, but she restrained herself. She had been extremely depressed at church last week. She was on the verge of tears the entire service. Before service started, Blaine told her that she looked like Sofia from *The Color Purple* in her dress. He thought of the meanest things to say to her.

"Amber is my friend, but she spends most of her time in Atlanta. So I wouldn't mind hanging out with you."

"Good! All of my friends are back home in Fort Worth. I would love to have a girlfriend in Oklahoma City."

"That's great."

"We'll start by finding you a nanny tomorrow. Then we'll start going to the gym next week. You ready?"

Dawn nodded eagerly. It was the most excitement she'd had since she'd married Blaine. It had been a long time since Dawn felt like she had something to look forward to. And she didn't care what Blaine had to say about it. She wasn't asking for permission *or* forgiveness.

CHAPTER 48

Camden called his mother for their weekly chat. Even though he hadn't been back home since he'd left to work for Royce years ago, he still made sure to talk to his favorite person once sometimes twice a week.

"Hello, my son," First Lady Rita said.

"Hi, Mom."

"How are you? I saw that there were tornadoes touching down right outside of Atlanta."

Camden had seen the damage done from the tornado, and it was pretty surprising that no one had gotten hurt.

"It was about an hour away from me, so I'm fine, but thank you for asking."

"Thank you for asking! I'm your mother. I'm always going to inquire about your well-being. Speaking of which, have you found a girlfriend yet? I want more grandchildren."

Camden started laughing. It was usually less than thirty seconds into the call before his mother started badgering him about his love life, but this time he had great news to share, so he didn't mind.

"Well, since you asked, Amber and I recently started dating."

His mother squealed through the phone. "Hallelujah! I just love her!"

"I know you do, Mom."

"You know, I always hoped that you'd choose Amber over Dawn. Even when you were teenagers."

"You did *not*! You thought that Amber was a hot tail. That's what you always said."

"She was fast! But she was spirited. I always loved that about her. She says what's on her mind and she doesn't try to please anyone but God."

"Well, I love all that about her too."

First Lady Rita cleared her throat. "I hope you don't take too long getting this one to the altar. She's no spring chicken. Don't want to start too late on those grandbabies."

"I hear you."

"It's not like you have to get to know one another. You've known each other your entire lives."

Camden should've known that his mother would go from zero to sixty in five seconds. This was the woman who took Dawn to bridal shows before she even had a proposal.

"Do you think she'll tell Dawn the two of you are dating?" First Lady Rita asked.

Camden had considered that. Even though he hadn't spoken a word to Dawn since that day at the church when she married Blaine, Amber had remained close to her. She was the godmother to all their children and spent birthdays at their house.

"I think she will, but maybe not right away."

"That child is gonna be devastated if you and Amber end up married."

"Why?" Camden scoffed. "She has who she wanted."

"Now you know good and well that shotgun wedding isn't what she wanted. That's what your father wanted."

"Well, she went along with it. You know, I really don't want to talk about that. I was just sharing my good news. I don't really care about Dawn or Blaine."

"Okay, honey."

"I have some more good news for you," Camden said.

"You do? Well, what is it?"

"I'm coming to Dad's anniversary celebration. Amber asked me to accompany her."

First Lady Rita must've dropped the phone, because all Camden heard was scuffling, shouting, and yelling. Camden laughed and waited for his mother to come back on the phone.

"God is good! I'm going to see my baby! Are you going to play too?"

Camden said, "Well, no. I wasn't invited to do that. But I will be in attendance."

"Wonderful. That's just wonderful."

"Mom, do me a favor, and don't tell Dad, okay. If he said he didn't want me there . . ."

"He wouldn't say that," First Lady Rita said. "But I'll respect your wishes and not tell him."

"Thank you."

Camden was unsure about attending his father's anniversary celebration, but he had promised Amber, so he would definitely attend. But if Camden got wind of his father saying he didn't want him there, Camden *was* sure that he'd probably never lay eyes on him again.

CHAPTER 49

Blaine stared in disbelief at the middle-aged woman who was in his home, feeding his son lunch. He had just returned from a trip to Dallas to find a stranger in his home. Well, perhaps not a stranger. The woman was vaguely familiar, but he didn't know her name.

"Are you a friend of Dawn's?" Blaine asked suspiciously.

"Hello, Pastor Wilson," the woman said. "I'm Sister Vera Jennings. I'm one of the ushers at Graceway, and your wife hired me to be your nanny."

"Sister Jennings. Well, carry on, then. Is my wife home?"

Blaine tried to hold his anger in check in front of Sister Jennings. He didn't want any of his members to see him explode the way he was going to do when he got his hands on Dawn. He would just wait a week or so and relieve Sister Jennings of her duties.

But first, he had to deal with Dawn. Who did she think she was hiring someone to come into their home? Those types of decisions needed to go through him. And what in the world did she need a nanny for anyway? She didn't have a job, nor did she have any hobbies.

"First Lady Wilson isn't in. She went to the gym. She says she had a spinning class."

Dawn was exercising? Well, maybe he wouldn't be too hasty with his anger. Lord knew she needed to get rid of some of that jelly she was carrying around. Maybe she'd be in a better mood if she was exercising on a regular basis.

"How long ago did she leave?"

"She's been gone for a couple hours. She should be back soon."

"Thank you."

Blaine went into his study to work on his remarks for his father's anniversary celebration. It was taking place in under a month, and Blaine was the keynote speaker. There was so much he wanted to say about his father; they had grown very close since Blaine had followed in his footsteps. He was happy that he made his father proud, even though his mother felt differently.

For a brief moment, Blaine considered inviting Camden to the event. There were celebrities and preachers coming from all over the country. It would be one of the most well-attended gospel events of the year. Since Camden was a revered gospel artist, some would probably find it strange if Camden wasn't in attendance at his own father's anniversary party.

Blaine decided that he would invite Camden. The worst that he could say was no, and he just might say yes. If he could convince Camden to come home for a visit, maybe, for once, their mother would be happy with something Blaine did.

Blaine dialed Camden's cell phone number. The phone rang three times before going over to voice mail. Blaine didn't leave a message. He'd call him later.

Blaine opened his laptop and started typing notes for his speech. He concentrated for a few minutes, but then he heard voices. It was Dawn . . . and was that? No. It couldn't be.

He rushed out of his office and into the kitchen where the voices were coming from. He felt his stomach drop when his eyes confirmed what his ears had just heard. Standing in the kitchen with Blaine's wife was his mistress.

"Dawn, where have you been?" Blaine asked.

Dawn walked over and kissed him on the cheek. While Dawn's back was to Kenya, Kenya lifted an eyebrow at Blaine and grinned. He didn't know what kind of game Kenya was playing, but she needed to stop immediately.

"Glad to have you back home, honey," Dawn said.

Blaine gave Dawn a strange look. *Honey?* She didn't call Blaine any pet names. Never had. She was probably trying to keep up appearances for Kenya.

"I missed you and the kids, babe. Imagine how surprised I was when I got home and you weren't here. We have a nanny now?"

Dawn smiled. "Yes! It was all Kenya's idea. She dropped by one day last week and challenged me to get my butt off the couch. She even helped me pick the nanny."

"She did? How good of her!"

"I saw my first lady looking down and out, and I wanted to offer my assistance. I hope you don't mind, Blaine."

"I don't mind at all. I've been wanting Dawn to get to know more of the women in the church. You two have singing in common, so . . ."

"Singing isn't the only thing we have in common," Kenya said.

Blaine narrowed his eyes at Kenya and

tilted his head to one side. He knew this woman wasn't crazy. He thought she wasn't.

"Weight loss," Dawn said. "She lost a lot of weight before, so she's passionate about losing it and keeping it off."

"Oh, you have that in common?" Blaine said with a chuckle. "I'm happy to hear that."

Dawn's expression darkened. "Yes, Blaine. I would like to lose weight."

"That makes two of us. I would like you to lose weight too."

"You know, Blaine," Kenya said, "you could stand to lose a few pounds yourself. Your gut is expanding. You look about four months pregnant. Maybe you should come to Zumba class with us."

Dawn covered her mouth, but some of her giggles escaped anyway. Blaine couldn't wait to get Kenya alone. He had some real choice words for her. This had crossed the line.

"I'm a man. A gut on a man is sexy. Y'all the ones that need to keep it tight," Blaine said.

"Six-pack abdominals on a man are sexy. Don't you agree, Dawn?"

"Uh . . ."

"Yeah, she knows better," Blaine said. "Do you need to see about the babies? When is the last time you nursed them?"

Dawn frowned. "The babies are fine. I pumped milk for the nanny to give them."

"Well, good then," Blaine said. "I'll leave you ladies to your girl talk. I've got work to do."

Blaine stormed out of the room, angrier than he could ever remember being in his life. Why would Kenya try to help Dawn lose weight and become more attractive? It didn't make any sense. He didn't know what Kenya's plan was, but it couldn't be good.

In fact, Kenya's presence in his home felt like a threat. If she thought she was going to force his hand about divorcing Dawn or if she thought he'd let her do anything to harm his ministry, she had another think coming. Graceway Oklahoma City was *his* church, and no mistress was going to be its downfall.

CHAPTER 50

Dawn looked down at the scale and grinned. She'd lost eight pounds in a week. One week of eating the diet that Kenya put together for her and one week of going to Kenya's personal trainer, and she was down eight pounds. *This* was motivation.

"When do you plan on firing that nanny?" Blaine asked from their bedroom.

Blaine's voice annoyed Dawn. Why did he keep harassing her about the nanny? The children were fine, Sister Jennings was great, and she was staying. That was the end of it.

Dawn stepped out of the master bathroom. "I can't take the children to the gym with me."

"Well, then I guess you're just going to have to use that fitness room that we have in the house. Maybe you can pull out some of those DVDs that you ordered from those late-night infomercials."

How could Dawn explain to Blaine that it

wasn't just the exercising that was motivating her, it was the fellowship and the getting out of the house? She'd never given friendship with Kenya a chance in the past, but now that she'd gotten to know her, she realized she was a great person.

"I enjoy spending the time with Kenya," Dawn said. "I needed to get out outdoors again. I feel better than I have in a long time."

"At the expense of our children. I don't want them being raised by a nanny. I want their mother making them cookies and putting bandages on their cuts and scrapes. My mother didn't have a nanny, and she worked at the church, so you definitely don't need one."

"I'm not your mother," Dawn protested.

"You got that right. My mother would never leave us hungry or with a babysitter while she went to the gym. And still she managed to stay looking good for my father."

"That didn't stop him from cheating on her, though," Dawn said.

Blaine jumped up from the bed and stood in front of Dawn, towered over her. "Don't say anything negative about my father. At least he was around. You don't even know yours."

"We slinging insults about our parents now?" Dawn asked. "Is that what we're doing?"

"What is this about, anyway? You never cared how you looked before. You got a man on the side?"

Dawn laughed. "A man on the side. You're hilarious. I barely have a husband, but now you're accusing me of a man on the side?"

"I was just wondering. I mean, you cheated on my brother with me. My mama always said, 'The way you got her is the way you're gonna lose her.' But then again, my mama doesn't like you all that much."

"I don't care what your mother thinks of me."

"Okay. You know what? Keep the nanny. I don't care. But if anything happens to my children, you're going to regret it."

Dawn walked past Blaine and sat down on the bed. "Do you realize how many times a week you threaten me? Most of our conversations end with you threatening me or you calling me fat."

"What are you trying to say?"

She shrugged. "Nothing. I'm just noticing it. You don't like me very much, do you?"

"You're the mother of my children and the first lady of my church."

"That doesn't really answer the question,

does it?"

Blaine finished tying his tie and grabbed his suit jacket off the hanger in the closet. "I don't have to answer your questions. Have fun with your new friend."

Dawn didn't reply. She watched her husband leave the room. She exhaled as the door closed, as if a weight was lifted from her.

Dawn didn't want to admit it, but she thought that maybe she hated Blaine.

Her cell phone buzzed with a text. She smiled as she read it. *You ready to feel the burn, homegirl?*

It was Kenya. And yes, she *was* ready to feel the burn.

Dawn texted back, *Are you here?*

In ten minutes.

Dawn finished putting on her workout clothes and went downstairs to give her final instructions to Sister Jennings. She was feeding each of the twins baby cereal prepared with breast milk. They'd be fine until she got back.

Blaine was ridiculous. The children loved Sister Jennings, and she loved them back. They couldn't have asked for a better nanny, and Dawn couldn't have asked for a better workout partner.

Dawn opened the door for Kenya when

she rang the doorbell. Kenya had her thick black hair pulled into a ponytail on top of her head. Dawn couldn't wait until she could wear the same kind of workout clothes that Kenya wore. She had on a sports bra and a pair of spandex boy shorts that stopped right beneath her buttocks. That was it. Dawn still had to cover her body with long sweats.

"Good morning," Dawn said.

"Good morning, girl. You know, I was thinking about you all the way over here."

"You were? What were you thinking about?"

"I was thinking that you need to rejoin So G.I.F.T.E.D. You were one of the first people in the group. It doesn't feel right that you're not in it anymore."

Dawn searched Kenya's face for any signs of insincerity. When she saw none, she replied, "I don't think that's for me anymore."

"Why not? Your voice is still as strong as ever. We were just singing in the car the other day."

Dawn wanted to tell her that she didn't want to spend more time with Blaine than she had to. She didn't want to be in So G.I.F.T.E.D anymore because it would require her to sing onstage with and travel with Blaine. She enjoyed when he left home for days at a time. She wished he would do it more often.

"I like singing at home to my children. I'm good," Dawn said.

"Well, anytime you want to, let me know. We'll double-team Blaine and Akil."

Dawn laughed. "Why are you doing all this? Helping me work out, encouraging me to sing. Am I your pet project or something?"

"No. You're my first lady. I'm here to serve in whatever capacity you'll have me."

"Right now, a friend is good enough."

"Okay, well you got me. Let's go burn off this fat."

Dawn laughed. "Girl, you don't have any fat."

"I know," Kenya said. "I'm talking about yours."

Both women laughed as they walked to the car. Before Dawn got in on the passenger side, she said, "You know, I don't think Blaine wants us to be friends. Maybe he thinks I'll ask to be back in the group."

"Well, nobody cares what Blaine likes. This has nothing to do with him. He's got armor bearers, deacons, ministers, and friends. He's never alone. Why should you be?"

CHAPTER 51

Blaine sat in the dark inside Kenya's condo, waiting for her to come home. He'd had the key since he bought the place for her, but he'd never used it. Had never needed to, because he was never there without Kenya being at his side.

But he was waiting to confront her about her friendship with Dawn. He couldn't figure out what she was trying to do, but no matter what it was she was about to cease and desist. She'd forgotten her place again. A sidepiece was not allowed to approach the wife for any reason whatsoever. It was just a courtesy to all parties.

Kenya wasn't being courteous at all by coming into his home to spend time with Dawn. In fact, she was being very rude.

What Kenya was doing smelled like desperation, and Blaine didn't understand that. It was obvious that he loved her and not Dawn. Kenya was spoiled with homes, cars, and anything she could ever want. All she was lacking was his last name.

Finally the front door opened, signaling Kenya's return. Blaine slowly rose from the couch so that he would be standing when she turned the lights on.

Kenya turned the lights on and screamed when she saw Blaine standing in the middle of her living room.

"Oh my God. You scared the crap out of me. What are you doing here? It's a weeknight. Don't you have a family to be getting home to?"

"I don't know what you're doing, Kenya, but you need to stay away from Dawn."

"What? Why? I feel like we never really got to know each other since you had her kicked out of the group. We could've been friends."

"I didn't have her kicked out. That was Camden. Royce suggested it, and he didn't try to stop it."

"Well, that's not what she thinks happened. I like her version better."

"If you try to tell her about us, I'll deny it. It won't get you what you want."

Kenya laughed. "You don't even know what I want."

"I do. You want me. You want to be the first lady of my church."

Kenya stepped in close and stroked Blaine's chest. "I want to be your wife. She's in the way."

Blaine removed her hand. "I told you that I would handle it, in time. Stop being so impatient."

"That's the thing, though. I don't have very much time. I only have nine months."

Blaine shook his head and sat down, his legs suddenly feeling weak. "You're not pregnant. Don't tell me that you're pregnant."

Blaine's clothing felt too tight. He felt sweat gather under his collar. He was not going to be forced into a marriage again.

Kenya burst into laughter. "You should see yourself, Blaine. Oh my God. You look like a doctor just said you have one week to live."

"You're not pregnant?" Blaine asked.

"No, dummy. I wouldn't get pregnant by a married man. I'm not that stupid. But I do want to have your baby."

A huge flood of relief rushed over Blaine. He almost never wanted to have sex with Kenya again. Almost.

"Don't ever do that again, Kenya. That wasn't funny."

"I'm sorry. It was funny to me."

"Let's see how funny it is when I repossess all this stuff I've given you."

"Really, Blaine? I earned all of this. Don't play with me."

"You're the one playing games."

Kenya said, "Well, I actually like Dawn. She's fun. We've been having a good time together. She's sweet and she's a great cook."

"Joke time is over. If you don't stay away from Dawn, I'm cutting you off."

"Cut me off, and I'll tell her all about us."

Blaine shook his head. "Dawn knows I'm not faithful to her. Go ahead and tell her. I'm calling your bluff. You're not going to blackmail me."

And Blaine meant that. He'd rather deal with the aftermath of Dawn learning about Kenya than with bowing down to Kenya's demands. Blaine believed that this was what his father would do. He would never let his mistress control the situation.

"So that's it?" Kenya said.

"I'm done. I've said everything I need to say. If you love me like you say you do, you'll leave Dawn out of this, and we can go on."

"I do love you, Blaine."

She wrapped her arms around Blaine's neck and squeezed. Blaine wondered if his father would tell him to cut Kenya off after her stunt with Dawn. If Blaine didn't love her so much, he probably would.

Chapter 52

"I think our personal trainer has a crush on you," Kenya said as she and Dawn had mimosas at their favorite after-workout café.

Dawn spat orange juice and champagne across the table from the force of her laughter. "Girl, stop," she said. "I am always tore up from the floor up when he sees me. Sweaty, stanky, and with fat rolls plopping out of these spandex pants."

"I see the way he looks at you when you're not looking," Kenya said. "I mean, I know you're not interested. I just thought you should know."

Dawn narrowed her eyes with disbelief. "You are silly. I think the last time a man looked at me and wanted me was that weekend in Miami when I got with Blaine."

Kenya shook her head. "Are you serious? I see men checking you out at church all the time. Why would you think that no one wants you?"

Dawn had a husband who let her know every chance he got that *he* didn't want her and that he didn't think she was attractive. Maybe that was why she didn't notice all these men Kenya noticed. Dawn chuckled. Maybe Kenya was delusional.

"Honey, I don't think about that at all," Dawn said. "I'm married with three kids. Who cares if someone wants me?"

"I guess you're right, but I love when guys look at me. It makes all of this hard work worth it."

"Maybe when I get like you, I'll feel the same way."

Kenya said, "I remember when I first met you. I thought you were fly. You must've had that special something extra."

"Something extra?"

"Well, I heard that you are the only woman that had both Wilson boys in love with her."

Dawn took another sip of her drink to try to calm her nerves. No one had talked about Camden to her in years. It was like that chapter of her life had never happened. These five years with Blaine had erased her decade with Camden.

"I don't know if Camden was ever in love with me."

"But you loved him?"

Dawn nodded. "I did. He was my first love. We dated for ten years."

"Well, you were right to move on," Kenya said. "I love Camden to pieces, but ten years and no ring? He was tripping."

Dawn didn't really feel comfortable rehashing this stuff with Kenya. She wanted to change the subject.

"Yep, but that was a long time ago."

"It was, and you've been blessed with something better. I'm like you. If something isn't right, I move on. Men think that they're calling the shots, but we are. We can go without them far longer than they can go without us."

"That's the truth," Dawn said.

"I have deal breakers in my relationships," Kenya said. "If a guy cheats on me, hits me, or doesn't want to go to work, he's got to go."

Dawn thought about this. She didn't know what her deal breakers were. She was sure Blaine cheated on her. He'd hit her more than one time. But he did take good care of her.

"Those are good ones," Dawn said. "No man will mistreat you."

Kenya reached across the table and squeezed Dawn's hand. "No one should mistreat you either, honey."

"What do you mean?" Dawn asked as she snatched her arm away.

"I hear how Blaine talks to you. I go on the road with him. I know what he does."

"What do you mean?"

"Blaine is not a good man. You deserve better."

Dawn took in every word that Kenya said. She asked herself if she wanted proof or if she could just believe Kenya at her word. Amber had dropped hints over the years, but gave nothing solid.

"I'm not you, Kenya. I don't know that I have deal breakers."

"You should," Kenya said. "You don't deserve to be treated badly."

Dawn shook her head sadly. Kenya just didn't understand. Dawn had done the unforgivable to Camden. She wasn't even sure if God had forgiven her, much less Camden. Dawn admired the women who were able to say what they wouldn't take from their men. She wished she could have deal breakers too. But what Kenya didn't know was that Dawn felt like she was in reaping season. She'd sown horrible seeds with Blaine, and her unhappiness was reaping.

Dawn prayed that if she endured the pain,

then maybe God would have mercy on her soul.

CHAPTER 53

Camden and Amber sat in the airport waiting in vain for the departure screen to show that their flight had been rescheduled. Stormy weather across Oklahoma and Texas had them grounded in Atlanta two days before Pastor Wilson's anniversary dinner.

"Maybe, it wasn't meant for me to be there," Camden said as he slid down farther into his seat.

"Of course you're meant to be there. It's just a little weather. It'll pass."

An elderly man sitting next to them said, "They say they're expecting these storms to last for the entire weekend. Said something about a super tornado outbreak in Tornado Alley."

Camden had been monitoring those same weather reports, and was genuinely concerned that he wouldn't be able to get home. He was anxious to see his mother, and even though he wouldn't admit it, he wanted to see his two nephews and niece — especially B. J., who looked so much like his uncle.

Amber made a phone call. "Yes, girl. We're at the airport, but ain't no telling what time we're getting out of here. How is the weather? . . . That bad, huh? Well, you know Dallas. It'll be sunny again in five minutes. Even if we don't make it in today, we'll get there in plenty of time for the celebration. . . . Mmm-hmm. . . . Y'all driving in tomorrow? . . . Okay. See you in Dallas. Love you."

Camden looked at Amber and waited for an explanation.

"Who was that?" Camden asked.

"Oh. That was Dawn."

"You kept saying *we*. Did you tell her I was coming?"

Amber nodded. "Yes, but she promised not to tell Blaine or your daddy. She's happy you're coming."

"Did you also tell her about us?"

"No. Not yet. I . . . I don't know how she's going to react. I don't know if she'll be as thrilled as we are about our relationship."

Camden laughed. "Nah. She's not gonna be thrilled at all. My mother mentioned that she's paying for choosing Blaine. I know it's wrong, but I don't feel sorry for her."

"I do," Amber said. "Blaine is a monster. He teases her about her weight, and he cheats on her. Akil always knows what he's up to. I have to catch him in the act."

Camden frowned at the mention of Akil. He was another friend who'd chosen Blaine. He and Akil spoke so infrequently that Camden couldn't still count him as a close friend. But Amber delivered Camden's songs to the group. They didn't need much contact.

"Akil has always been ride or die for Blaine. His wingman for life. I don't expect him to give you any details on Blaine's shenanigans."

"I know. I just don't want you to be mean to Dawn when you see her. She's going through enough as it is."

"Not thinking about being mean to her. I just don't plan on interacting with her."

"Okay, Camden."

Camden groaned when the departures screen changed and added another two hours to the departure time for their flight.

"At least it's not canceled," Amber said.

"Not yet."

"Don't be so positive," Amber said.

Camden chuckled. "I can't help it. I just have this feeling that something horrible is going to happen when I see my dad. Like he's going to say something crazy to me, or I'm gonna end up punching Blaine in the face. I owe him that at least."

"Five years of pent-up aggression. Not good."

"Exactly. Blaine actually called me a couple weeks ago. I didn't answer."

"Why didn't you? Maybe he was calling to invite you to the anniversary celebration."

Camden scoffed. "The fact that I need an official invitation is annoying. He needs to call and apologize to me."

"You still need an apology after all this time?"

"Yes, I do."

"What if you never get it? You just gonna stay angry?"

Camden sighed. "I don't know. I guess one day it won't bother me anymore. It's not today."

"Lord, Jesus. I need to pray."

"You do that, please. I don't know how to pray about it. I stopped trying."

Amber reached out her hand. "Give me your hand, Camden."

"What? You're about to pray right here?"

She nodded. "Yes. You need deliverance. We're about to pray it up."

Camden was surprised by her boldness, but he offered his hand. She prayed, "Dear

Heavenly Father, I am coming to You right now asking healing for Camden. Lord, allow him to be released from his brother's transgressions. Allow him to be freed from the unforgiveness he has in his heart. Lord, touch him in a mighty way. Let him know that his anointing is being blocked by the bitterness in his heart. Let him know joy again. Let him live the lyrics he's written. Oh, Lord, once Camden wrote, 'I am free.' Let him walk in it. You gave him the lyrics 'born to worship.' Let him remember his birthright. God, we know that Blaine, Dawn, and his father have broken his heart in pieces. Lord, be the glue. Put him back together. In the matchless name of Jesus we pray."

The words of Amber's prayer shocked Camden. Every word she said was true. He didn't flow in his gift like he once had. There was a blockage in his spirit when it came to the music, but Camden thought he just needed to buckle down and spend more time with God. It wasn't fair that someone else's sin was impacting his anointing.

"Thank you," Camden said.

"I've been praying that prayer for you for the past two years, Camden. I've been praying for God to be the glue, but I think my prayers aren't enough. We need to touch and agree on this. Don't you believe the songs you write?"

"I do."

"Well, you wrote that song for Ivy. Your lyrics said it all. All you need is two or three, and God will come in. Pray with me. Invite him in, Cambreezy."

"Cambreezy," Camden said with a smile. "You haven't called me that in a long time."

"You haven't been *him* in a long time. I want you back. I want the whole Camden, not the fractured one. He's the one I love."

"You don't love the broken me?"

"Yeah, I do. But I'm not sure if the broken Camden can love me back. Not the way I need."

Amber hugged him and whispered more prayers in his ear. He let her words penetrate his spirit and deal with him on his bitterness. He couldn't promise that he would let it go this weekend, but he could promise to try.

Chapter 54

After arriving in Dallas, Blaine dropped Dawn and the kids off with his mother and took Pastor Wilson to a pre-anniversary dinner at Buttons. It was one of his dad's favorite restaurants, and on Friday nights the women came out in droves. Pastor Wilson could enjoy his smothered pork chops and Blaine could enjoy the view.

"This rain is really coming down," Pastor Wilson said as they were seated at their table. "I hope it doesn't delay some of my guests from getting here."

"I had Akil check on flights coming out of Atlanta. Most have been canceled until morning. We've got a few artists coming out of there, but they should be able to make it in time for the dinner."

"Storms clearing by the morning?"

Akil nodded. "Yes, that's what the weather report said."

"Good, good. We can't have it raining on

the red carpet. You know how many hair weaves and wigs are going to be on that red carpet?"

Blaine laughed. "Yes, I do. That would be a catastrophe."

"A hairtastrophe!" Pastor Wilson said, laughing at his own joke. "I'm a preacher. I can make up words if I want to."

"I do it all the time. I must get that from you," Blaine said with a laugh.

A cute waitress came to the table. "Hi, Pastor Wilson," she said. "Would you like your usual to drink?"

He nodded. "Thank you, baby."

"And what about you, Pastor Junior?" the waitress said with a smile.

Blaine smiled back. "I'll have a glass of Pinot Noir. I'm in the mood for some red wine tonight."

"Okay. Bourbon for the pastor, Pinot Noir for the son. I'll be back right away."

Blaine and Pastor Wilson watched the girl in her extremely short and tight spandex skirt as she put their order in at the bar.

Pastor Wilson laughed. "I am too old for all that. She'd probably put me in cardiac arrest."

"Speak for yourself, old man. She's just about my speed."

"No, son. Not her. She's the type to get

attached. She'll cause problems for Dawn. You don't want that."

Blaine's expression changed. His father's advice reminded him of Kenya. She was still spending time with Dawn, even after their conversation. After his threats. He told her that he was calling her bluff, but apparently she was calling his.

"I've already got one that's attached. I can't afford to have two."

Pastor Wilson said, "You haven't handled Kenya yet?"

"She's been spending time with Dawn. Started taking her to the gym and out to eat. I came home and she was in the house."

Pastor Wilson frowned. "That ho done lost her damn mind. They don't make 'em like Delores anymore. No loyalty at all."

"None! After all I've done for her."

"Son, you've got no choice. Tell Dawn about her. Come clean and beg forgiveness."

Blaine's eyes widened. "What? You want me to tell her?"

"Yes. That ho plans on outing you. It'll be better if it comes from you. Wait until you get back home, though. I don't want you ruining my anniversary celebration."

Blaine shook his head and laughed. "Okay, Dad."

The waitress came back to the table and sat their drinks down. "I know what Pastor wants for dinner. Smothered pork chops, right?"

Pastor Wilson nodded.

"What about you?" she asked Blaine.

"Chicken and waffles. And bring each of us an order of the fried green tomatoes as an appetizer."

"I'll put that order in for you."

As soon as the waitress walked away, the restaurant manager walked out into the center of the restaurant.

"Good evening, guests. I've just received word that there is a rain-wrapped tornado on the ground and it is coming in our direction. It's not safe for you to leave, so we ask that everyone please shelter in place. Please, move quickly and get under your tables facing the wall and cover your heads from debris! This is not a drill."

Blaine jumped up and moved the table out of the way. The tornado sirens roared outside as he helped his father to the floor. Pastor Wilson prayed out loud as everyone in the restaurant panicked.

On the floor next to Blaine and Pastor Wilson was a young woman who looked terrified. She looked over at Pastor Wilson and said, "We're okay, right? The man of God is in the building."

Pastor Wilson smiled. "God's got us, daughter. Just make sure you cover your head."

Someone screamed as the wind whipped outside. Blaine thought of his wife and his children and hoped they were safe. It sounded like a train was right outside the restaurant.

Suddenly, the roof was torn off the restaurant. Furniture and people were tossed through the air. It seemed that the tornado was directly on top of them.

Frightened for his life, Blaine screamed out, "Lord forgive me!"

No sooner had the words come out of his mouth than an airborne car landed directly on top of Blaine. He cried out as a searing pain ripped through his body. Then everything went black.

CHAPTER 55

Camden rushed through the hospital hallway, searching for his mother. He and Amber had come directly from the airport, having gotten word of the accident from his mother while they were still in Atlanta. His mother had no details at the time, only that he needed to get to the hospital as soon as possible.

As soon as First Lady Rita saw Camden, she broke down in tears. He sat down next to her and enfolded her in his arms. Amber sat down on the other side of her and patted Rita's back.

"Mom, what happened?"

"T-they were at dinner. At Buttons, and a tornado touched down and blew the restaurant away. There's nothing left."

"Dad and Blaine were there? What about Dawn and the kids?"

"They're fine. The babies are at the house, and Dawn is sedated. They had to put her under."

"Is Blaine . . . ?"

Rita shook her head. "No, thank God he's still alive. But he's paralyzed from the waist down. They had to pull him from underneath a car."

"Oh my God!" Amber said.

First Lady Rita sobbed into Camden's chest. He rocked her back and forth.

"What about Dad?" Camden asked, not sure if he wanted to know the answer.

"They found his body several hundred yards away from the restaurant. He . . . he didn't make it, Camden. He's gone."

"Dad is dead?"

Camden was in shock. He wanted to comfort his mother, but he couldn't form words. Pastor Wilson was dead. He hadn't spoken to his father in over five years, and now he would never see him again.

Amber switched sides and sat down next to Camden. He was shaking. He didn't realize it until Amber grabbed his hands.

"Jesus, Jesus, Jesus," Amber chanted quietly. "Oh, sweet Jesus."

A doctor appeared in front of them, Camden had no idea where he'd come from.

"Are you Blaine Wilson's mother?" the doctor asked. "His wife is unable to make a decision on his behalf, and we need consent."

"Consent to do what?" First Lady Rita asked.

"Blaine's right leg was severely crushed by the car, and we're unable to repair it properly. We must, however, have consent to amputate."

"Oh, dear God!" First Lady Rita cried. "What now, Lord?"

First Lady Rita went into hysterics. She slid out of her chair onto the floor. Camden barely touched her fingers as she went down because he was completely useless as well.

Amber rushed to Lady Rita and then looked up at Camden. "You have to decide. He's immediate family, Doctor. This man is Blaine's brother."

"You're Camden?" the doctor asked.

Camden nodded.

"Please, there isn't much time. They'd like to remove the leg while they're in surgery trying to repair his spinal cord injury. If they wait, the leg may become infected."

"There's no chance of saving it?" Camden asked.

"In all my years of orthopedic medicine, I have never seen a leg this badly mangled. Some sections of bone were completely ground into a powder."

Camden prayed for strength. He could fall apart later, but now he had to be strong for his mother and for Dawn.

"Do it. Do whatever you need to do to get him well," Camden said.

The doctor nodded and rushed back to the operating room. Camden shook his head and let a few tears fall. Amber tended to his mother. She pulled her up into the seat and fanned her.

Akil hurried down the hallway with a cup of coffee in his hands. He tried to hand the cup to First Lady Rita, but Amber took it from him when she was unresponsive.

"I'm so glad y'all are here," Akil said. "This is too much."

Akil hugged Amber and Camden. He lingered with Camden, gave him an I-haven't-seen-you-in-five-years hug.

"I've missed you, bro," Akil said.

"Missed you too," Camden replied.

If tragedy hadn't struck, Camden was sure his reply would've been different. But the reasons they hadn't spoken seemed so trivial now. Every moment seemed precious.

"People are gathered at the church for the anniversary celebration," Akil said. "It was too late to turn them away. What should we do? Should we make an announcement?"

Amber looked at Camden. "That's up to you."

"Yes. I think you should have Stephen make an announcement, if he can."

"Man, he's catatonic," Akil said. "He blames himself. He said he should've been with Pastor Wilson. He thinks he failed somehow."

"So Assistant Pastor Brennan then. He needs to get ready anyway, since he's probably gonna end up being the pastor."

"B. C. wouldn't want that," First Lady said. "He'd want you or Blaine to take over."

Camden shook his head. "In the interim, let the assistant pastor do his job. We can decide on everything else later."

Camden didn't care what anybody said, he wasn't taking over that church. His father's shoes were ones he never wanted to fill.

"Akil! Tell me something! What is going on?" Kenya ran down the hospital hallway with a frantic expression on her face. "Is he okay?"

"Are you talking about Blaine?" Amber said. "He's in surgery now. His *wife* is resting two doors down."

Kenya glared at Amber. "I was talking to Akil. Is he going to be okay? What is his prognosis?"

"Last I heard, he was paralyzed from the waist down. . . ."

"And now they're amputating his leg," Amber said.

Kenya's legs buckled and she stumbled into the wall, which gave her support. "Amputation?"

"You've got your update," Amber said. "You should probably leave the hospital before his wife wakes up."

"I'm Dawn's friend. She'll want me here," Kenya said.

"Not when I tell her you're screwing her husband. You need to go," Amber said.

"I'm not leaving this hospital until I know Blaine is going to be okay."

"Learn the rules," Amber said. "Sideline hos don't make bedside hospital vigils."

Kenya lunged toward Amber, and Akil held her back.

"Honey, you do not want to go there. I will drag you in this hospital. Blaine is my brother and Dawn is my sister. You are messing with my family."

"Blaine is *my* family too," Kenya said.

"Fly away, bird, before you get them wings clipped!" Amber rose to her feet and slipped out of her shoes.

"Come on, Kenya," Akil said. "Let's leave. I'll keep you updated on Blaine. I promise.

Now isn't the time for this."

Camden looked over at Amber for an explanation.

She shook her head. "He's been messing with her for over a year now. They thought I didn't know, but I saw him creeping up out of her hotel room once when we did a show."

"Was he going to leave Dawn for her?" Camden asked.

"Probably not," Lady Rita said. "He is your father's son. I guarantee he wasn't going anywhere."

First Lady Rita stopped crying for a moment and took the cup of coffee from Amber. "I need to take a walk and clear my mind. I'll be back," she said.

"You want Amber to come with you?" Camden asked.

"I'm fine. I want some time to myself. Thank you, though, honey."

Camden felt as if someone had dropped an anvil in his lap and then pushed him overboard. His father's death and his brother's critical injury were too heavy a burden; too insurmountable a mountain. He had no idea how he was going to make it to the other side of this.

Amber moved over one seat and placed her hand inside Camden's. "I'm here for you, honey. If you don't want to say another word or make another decision, you don't have to. I've got you."

It felt good to know that Amber had his back. More than anything, he now knew that she would be the perfect wife for him. He would marry her as soon as this drama passed.

Even though Amber had his back, Camden knew that he would have to stand up and lead his family. Ready or not, he was the man of the family in this crisis. He couldn't let his mother down. But he needed every bit of Amber's help . . . and God's.

CHAPTER 56

Camden sat next to Blaine's bed in the intensive care unit. He had not yet awoken from surgery, and Camden wanted to be there when he did. Dawn was still sedated, and Lady Rita couldn't bear to see her son lifeless in the hospital bed. Camden was the only one who had the courage to break the news to Blaine about his condition and about their father's death.

Finally, Blaine began to stir. His upper body, at least. His lower body was deathly still — the paralysis still in effect.

Blaine opened his eyes, and looked around the room in a panic. "Where am I?"

"You're in the hospital, Blaine. It's me, Camden."

"C-Camden? Wait . . . where's Dad?"

"You and Dad got caught in a tornado at Buttons. Do you remember?"

Blaine blinked rapidly. "Yes. Yes. The entire roof was torn off the building, and a car . . ."

Blaine looked down at his legs and screamed. "I can't feel my legs! Camden, I can't feel my legs."

Camden pulled in a deep breath and then exhaled. "The car that fell on you crushed your legs and injured your spinal column. The doctors believe they have repaired the damage to your spine, so you should be able to feel again soon. But they couldn't save one of your legs."

Blaine broke down and sobbed like a baby. Pity filled Camden's heart. No matter what they'd been through, this was his twin. He hurt for his brother. He hurt *with* his brother.

"They took one of my legs? Oh my God. Where's Dad? Was he hurt too?"

Camden nodded. "Dad didn't make it. The tornado hurled him far from the building. Just about every bone in his body was broken in his fall."

Blaine stared at Camden in utter disbelief. "No. That can't be true. You're lying. You're lying! Get out of here! You're still angry at Dad. You just wishing he died! It wasn't him! Dad can't be dead!"

Blaine made such a commotion that the nurses rushed into the room and gave him drugs to sedate him. Camden sighed. He knew Blaine would take the news harder than anyone, and the worst part was yet to come.

Camden stepped out of Blaine's hospital room and into the hallway. He sent up a quick prayer and tried to feel a little peace.

"Hello, Camden."

Camden looked up and saw Dawn standing in front of him. Five years had changed her immensely. Her Afro was pulled away from her face, and she was at least thirty pounds overweight. But that wasn't the biggest change Camden saw. There was no joy in her eyes. Dawn had always been the one to look on the bright side, but now there was only sadness.

"Dawn."

"It's funny how it happened, huh? A tornado levels an entire building and only two people are hurt. Your father and Blaine. And then the tornado dissipated. That's crazy, right? It's like God sent His finger down from heaven and struck them both."

"Is that what you believe?"

She nodded. "Your father was the devil himself, and Blaine is his spawn. I don't know why God didn't take him too."

"Dawn, you don't mean that. That's just the shock talking."

"I mean it. Yes I do. Amber told me

Blaine's mistress was up here, acting a damn fool. I thought she was trying to be my friend, warning me about Blaine's cheating, when *she* was the one sleeping with him."

"Wow. I don't know what to say to that."

"You don't have to say anything, Camden. You're probably happy all this has happened to me. I don't blame you."

Camden shook his head. "I wouldn't wish this on anyone, Dawn. I would never wish this on you."

"Well, thank you, for being here and handling this. You can tell your brother when he wakes up that I'm leaving him. I'm not nursing him back to health. I don't have it in me. I might wind up killing him."

"So no in sickness and in health?"

Dawn laughed. "Are you kidding? Tell him to have one of his mistresses wipe his behind and teach him how to walk again. I'm filing for divorce."

"Maybe you should wait before you make that decision. You might change your mind after the dust settles. Think about your children."

"I am thinking about my children. I don't want Blaine raising my sons." Dawn took a few steps and closed the distance between her and Camden.

"You know I never stopped loving you,"

she said. "Maybe that's why it's so easy for me to leave Blaine."

"Well . . ."

"I know that you're with Amber now. I'm not trying to get back with you or anything like that."

"Good."

Dawn looked at the ground and then back up at Camden. "You and Amber deserve to be happy. If anybody should be happy, it should be you two."

"Thanks. I want you to go and get some rest, though, Dawn. Don't make any decisions until after my dad's funeral. Promise me that."

"I should stay by Blaine's side during all that, huh? Good-bye, Camden. I'll take what you said under advisement. Come by your mom's house and meet the children. The oldest looks just like you."

"That's what everybody tells me."

Dawn walked away from Camden looking like she was carrying the same heavy burden that Camden had. His father was gone, and if Dawn's theory was correct, it was by the hand of God. Camden didn't know if he believed that, but he did know that their family needed the power of God if they would ever heal. Camden knew they couldn't do it on their own.

CHAPTER 57

Pastor Wilson's homegoing service was a star-studded fiasco.

Camden felt so much relief when Regina, Stephen, and Delores took over the planning of all the events. It was like a church conference, with just as many attendees and just as many guest speakers. Camden was overwhelmed with the logistics of it all.

At least Camden didn't have to worry about his mother. Amber shadowed Lady Rita day and night and anticipated her needs before she even spoke them. But after her first emotional breakdown at the hospital, Lady Rita had been extremely strong concerning the death of her husband. What caused her to have a setback was when anyone asked about Blaine.

Since Blaine was still in critical condition, he wasn't going to be able to attend the homegoing service. Someone had suggested that they postpone until Blaine was out of the hospital, but the doctors couldn't even estimate when he would be released or even well enough to leave his hospital bed. The tissue surrounding his injured spinal column had to heal, and the swelling had to go down before he would have any feeling in his lower extremities, and that was when the true rehabilitation would begin. Talk of a prosthetic leg and learning to walk again left Blaine depressed, so Camden stopped trying to talk to him about it.

Camden had arrived at the church with his mother, Amber, Dawn, and the children in a stretch limousine, specially ordered by Stephen.

They filed into the sanctuary through a sea of well-wishers. So many people had loved Pastor Wilson, and Camden could feel that love in the air. These people didn't really know the man he was. They only knew the man he portrayed to them. Camden wondered how they'd feel if they knew the truth.

When they got to the seats reserved for them, Delores came up to Camden and whispered in his ear. "Are you going to speak? We have you in the program, but you don't have to if you aren't up to it."

"I'm going to do it. I prayed about it, and I'll do it."

"Okay. I'll let Pastor Brennan know."

Just as she was about to walk away, Camden grabbed Delores's hand. This time he whispered to her. "Are you okay?"

Delores gave Camden a tiny, sad smile as she shook her head. "No. I'm not," she whispered back.

Delores glanced at Lady Rita before she fled to some place behind the scenes, where she always stayed. No matter how much Delores had loved his father, Camden was glad that she always respected his mother. No one could ever accuse her of not knowing her place.

Camden sat down next to his mother and put his arm around her. He could see his father's body in the casket, but couldn't go up and look at it. Amber and Dawn walked up to the casket hand in hand, paid their respects, and came back to their seats.

"Mom, do you want to go up?" Camden whispered.

"I can't. I just can't do it."

Camden nodded. "It's okay. Neither can I."

The service started soon after the family arrived. There was standing room only in the huge sanctuary, built to hold five thousand attendees. Camden saw friends and congregation members crying and dabbing their eyes with tissues.

The service went by in a blur. Amber sang a lovely rendition of one of his father's favorite songs, "Precious Lord, Take My Hand," and the choir did a full medley of Pastor Wilson's other favorites. Minister after minister got up to give words about how his father had impacted their lives and their ministries.

Finally, it was Camden's turn. He slowly rose from his seat when he heard his name called, and he paused in front of his father's casket before he ascended into the pulpit. Suddenly, he was flooded with regret for not coming home sooner. His grief almost overwhelmed him, but he continued on up to the podium.

Camden cleared his throat and looked out over the audience. He took a deep breath and began.

"If you knew my father, B. C. Wilson, then you would know that he would be very impressed with this turnout at his celebration of life. He was a man who loved being loved, and he gave it back to so many of you sitting in attendance. My father counseled some of you, bailed some of you out of jail, paid some of your mortgages, and put groceries on your tables. He did this without any fanfare, and sometimes without thanks. He believed that God had blessed him with so much only to be a blessing to others."

Camden paused for a moment to let his words sink in. He had chosen to stay on the positive side of Pastor Wilson's character. No need to disparage him in front of those who loved him most. Maybe he was already paying for his misdeeds in the afterlife; perhaps he'd been forgiven. Camden didn't know.

"He was a man who believed in honor, a man with a heart for ministry and with a passion for this church. You never knew his struggles because he didn't want anything to detract from the message. He wouldn't want you mourning him now — well, not for too long, anyway. He'd want you to continue his work. He'd want you to help with the tornado relief efforts in our neighborhoods that were damaged by the storms that took his life. He'd hope that his life wasn't in vain. He'd want someone to accept Christ as their personal savior before they leave this sanctuary. My father didn't know he was about to draw his last breath when he sat down with my brother for one of his favorite meals. He would tell me and Blaine to always be ready. That was the way he lived his life. Ready for whatever challenge he might face. I challenge you to be ready as well. On behalf of my family, we ask for your prayers for my brother Blaine, who is still hospitalized. Thank you for your support."

Camden was glad that Stephen had jumped up from his seat as he finished speaking, because Camden wasn't sure he'd be able to make it back to his seat. He felt like he was falling apart. He'd held it together long enough to do the speech, and now he was spent. Stephen and Pastor Brennan helped him back to his seat.

Lady Rita took Camden's hand when he sat down. She whispered, "Your father would've been proud of you."

Camden nodded and stared straight ahead. If only he could've been proud during his lifetime. Camden had lived honorably, was marrying a woman he loved, and had chased and caught his dreams. But it had never been good enough for him.

Camden moved silently through the rest of the day. He held his mother's hand as they closed the casket on his father. He shed a few tears at the burial and made sure that his mother was okay. He received guests at his parents' home.

When everyone was gone, Camden sat in his father's study. In his father's honor, he poured himself a glass of bourbon and sat down at the desk. He imagined his father's laugh, his baritone voice when he was giving a lecture. It was as if he could feel his father's presence in the room.

Camden scanned the room and looked at the awards and plaques on the walls. His father's many accolades. Then a smile spread onto Camden's face as he looked down at the framed photographs on his father's desk. There was a picture of Pastor Wilson and Camden taken at his college graduation. Pastor Wilson had the proudest smile on his face. As a matter of fact, Camden and Pastor Wilson had identical smiles in the picture.

Seeing this photo placed where his father could see it every day made Camden's heart swell. Maybe Blaine was his favorite son, but Pastor Wilson had a place in his heart for Camden as well. In that moment, Camden vowed to lead their family to a place of healing and victory. After all, grace and power was the Wilson brand.

EPILOGUE

Camden straightened his bow tie and stroked his goatee. He couldn't be more ready to marry the love of his life. Amber. *His* Amber.

He was anxious to get the day over with, especially since they'd honored Amber's vow of celibacy. He was beyond ready to get to that part of the evening. He and Amber probably wouldn't even make it through twenty minutes at the reception before they dipped out.

Dawn poked her head into the groom's preparation area and delivered B. J., Camden's mini-me, who was all set to be the ring bearer.

"Is Blaine here?" Camden asked her.

Dawn shrugged. "I'm not sure. You know it's not my job to keep up with him these days. You should ask Akil."

"Okay."

"I gotta go put on my bridesmaid dress.

See you shortly."

Although it felt strange having Dawn as the matron of honor at their ceremony, Amber had insisted on it.

Camden had asked Blaine and Akil to be groomsmen, but Blaine had only half committed. He'd gone as far as getting fitted for the tuxedo, but he complained about going down the aisle in a wheelchair. Plus, Dawn still had nothing to do with him, so he wasn't thrilled about being paired up with her.

Camden almost wished they'd just gone away and gotten married on an island somewhere.

Lady Rita walked into the room with a big smile on her face. "My God. You look just like your father on our wedding day. He was a handsome man, but I think you might be just a tad bit more handsome!"

"That's because I've got your genes mixed in."

"Yes, baby. I am the icing on the cake."

"You are. Do you think Blaine is gonna do it?"

"He is so stubborn, and he doesn't want to do it if it doesn't come easily. Just like he could get Dawn back if he really tried."

Camden laughed. "I don't know, Mom. I think you're reaching on that one. You want them back together, but you might be the only one."

Dawn wasn't playing when she left Blaine. She filed for divorce the day after their father was buried. Then she proceeded to take half of Blaine's assets. She was a millionaire bachelorette and completely content with her status.

"Well, as long as she takes care of my grandbabies, that's all I could hope for. I just hate to see him battle this alone."

"He's not alone. Me, Akil, and Amber have been there for him."

They had all helped Blaine during his rehabilitation, even though his mistress Kenya had moved to Atlanta and started working on her solo project. Camden guessed she was cutting her losses, and since only their inner circle knew about her affair with Blaine, she was still viewed as a gospel songbird. She just better hope that Blaine never got well enough to want revenge or that Dawn would never serve it up either.

Blaine's progress had been slow and steady, and in the year since the tornado, he had done things the doctors said he'd never do again. But he hadn't walked with his prosthetic yet, even with the extensive physical therapy.

Camden looked at the clock and raised

his eyebrows. The ceremony was supposed to start in thirty minutes, and he still hadn't seen Blaine.

Then, just when he was about to start making phone calls, B. J. ran out of the room shouting, "Daddy!" Blaine had arrived.

Blaine rolled into the room in his motorized wheelchair with B. J. sitting in his lap. "Hey, Camden. You ready to get your ball and chain?"

Camden laughed. "Yep. I sure am."

"Okay. Well, you can't say I didn't try to talk you out of it."

"Yes, you did."

Blaine smiled. "But in all seriousness, I wish y'all the best. I love y'all."

"Love you too, man."

Blaine set B. J. on the floor. "B. J., go find your grandma. I need to talk to Uncle Camden for a minute."

When the little boy ran out of the room, Blaine motioned for Camden to close the door.

"What's up? Is everything okay?" Camden asked.

Blaine nodded. "Cam. I want you to know how much I appreciate you and how much you've blessed me over this past year. I have done so much to hurt you, and I never even apologized for it, but you were still here for me when I didn't even deserve it."

"We're brothers."

"We are. But you could've given me the cold shoulder for what I did to you. I am so sorry for what happened with Dawn. If there's one thing I could take back, it would be that night."

"It all worked out, right? God had a different plan. I forgive you."

"Thank you, Camden. God bless you."

Camden leaned over to hug Blaine, and they embraced for a long moment.

"So are you going to do it? It's okay to use your wheelchair going down the aisle. Everyone's just happy you're still here."

"Yeah, I'm gonna do it."

There was a knock on the door. It was the wedding planner coming to rush Camden to the altar. It was time.

Blaine slapped him on the back. "Go get your woman!"

Camden rushed down the aisle and stood proudly waiting for the ceremony to start. Two other groomsmen and bridesmaids made their way down the aisle to a beautiful medley of songs composed by Camden.

Camden knew he was supposed to be quiet, but he leapt for joy and shouted when he saw Blaine using a walker to proceed down the aisle. Dawn walked patiently beside him with her bouquet as he slowly took each step. Camden could see the struggle and effort on Blaine's face, but he smiled the entire way. At the front of the church, Dawn led Blaine to a seat in the front row, because he was exhausted. She then went and took her place with the other bridesmaids.

Then, at the back of the church, Amber emerged, holding her father's arm with one hand and a microphone with the other. Camden heard the introduction to "At Last" by Etta James and grinned from ear to ear. Amber serenaded him as she came down the aisle.

When she got to the last line, "And you are mine . . . at last," Amber was standing in front of Camden at the altar.

One year ago, Camden thought that with all the pain he felt over the loss of his father he'd never feel joy again, but now his heart was about to explode with it. He and Amber were proof that ashes could be traded for beauty and sorrow for laughter.

As tattered and broken as their family was, the Wilsons were surviving the storm. And as Camden glanced at his once-arrogant brother who had today asked him for for-giveness, Camden knew God wasn't finished with them yet. There was more story to be told, more chapters to unfold.

God was writing His own ever after.

A READING GROUP GUIDE:
THE FAVORITE SON

TIFFANY L. WARREN

ABOUT THIS GUIDE
The following questions are intended to
enhance your group's reading of THE
FAVORITE SON.

DISCUSSION QUESTIONS

1. Pastor B. C. Wilson always tells Blaine and Camden that Graceway Church is their legacy, and has no problem inserting his sons into ministry positions — ready or not. How do you feel about this? Should pastors be able to do this? Why or why not?

2. Is Blaine's womanizing behavior typical of a pastor's son? Do you believe that he can truly impact people's lives in ministry with his own personal demons front and center?

3. Was Dawn stupid for dating Camden for more than ten years? Should she have given him an ultimatum sooner?

4. Did Camden's close relationship with his mother affect his relationship with his father? By the same token, does Blaine's closeness to his father alienate his mother?

5. First Lady Wilson turns a blind eye to Pastor Wilson's indiscretions, but Dawn is unable to do the same. Were women of yesteryear more willing to accept the "other woman"?

6. When Blaine and Pastor Wilson encounter their final unfortunate event, did you feel as if it was a judgment from God?

7. What characters would you like to see in a subsequent story?

ABOUT THE AUTHOR

Tiffany L. Warren is an author, playwright, songwriter, mother and wife. Her debut novel, *What a Sista Should Do,* was released in June of 2005. Her second book, *Farther than I Meant to Go, Longer than I Meant to Stay,* was a national bestseller. She is also the author of *The Bishop's Daughter* and *In The Midst of It All.* In 2006, Tiffany and her husband, Brent, founded Warren Productions and released gospel musicals, *What a Sista Should Do* and *The Replacement Wife.* Tiffany is the visionary behind the Faith and Fiction Retreat. Tiffany resides in northern Texas with her husband, Brent, and their five children. Visit her online at www.TiffanyLWarren.com.